CRESCENT MOON

LORI HANDELAND decided she wanted to be a writer when she was ten years old and was struck with the sudden that she might read all the books in the world and be with nothing interesting to do. Detours into waitressing, ing, business management and motherhood pushed her of writing back a few years, but she eventually sold rst novel in 1993. Since then her books have spanned ontemporary, historical and paranormal genres. She is ent of many industry awards, including the PRISM for Paranormal Romance. Lori lives in Wisconsin with sband, two sons and a yellow labrador named Elwood. an be reached through her website:
lorihandeland.com

PRAISE FOR LORI HANDELAND'S
NIGHTCREATURE NOVELS

deland has the potential to become as big as, if not ger than, Christine Feehan and Maggie Shayne'
Publishers Weekly

on to your seats! Handeland delivers a kick-butt ne ready to take on the world of the paranormal. *Moon* is an awesome launch to what promises to be a funny, sexy, and scary series'
Romantic Times

and has more than proved herself a worthy author ncreasingly popular world of paranormal romance vith these slick and highly engrossing tales'
Road to Romance

Also by Lori Handeland

Blue Moon
Hunter's Moon
Dark Moon

CRESCENT MOON

LORI HANDELAND

PAN BOOKS

First published 2006 by St Martin's Press, New York

First published in Great Britain in paperback 2008 by Pan Books
an imprint of Pan Macmillan Ltd
Pan Macmillan, 20 New Wharf Road, London N1 9RR
Basingstoke and Oxford
Associated companies throughout the world
www.panmacmillan.com

ISBN 978-0-330-45133-8

Printed and bound in Great Britain by
Mackays of Chatham plc, Chatham, Kent

Visit **www.panmacmillan.com** to read more about all our books
and to buy them. You will also find features, author interviews and
news of any author events, and you can sign up for e-newsletters
so that you're always first to hear about our new releases.

For my agent, Irene Goodman:
Just for being Irene

Dear Reader,

Crescent Moon takes place in New Orleans and was written before the tragedy of Hurricane Katrina. Although the French Quarter appears to have sustained much less damage than the rest of the city, there may be places in the book that are no longer the same. I hope that *Crescent Moon* captures the wonder that was, is, and will be New Orleans again.

Lori Handeland

CRESCENT MOON

I

A life spent fulfilling a vow to a dead man is really no life at all, but I'd loved Simon Malone, and I'd promised.

I'm a zoologist by trade, a cryptozoologist by choice. If I'd followed my training, I'd be holed up in a zoo or worse, studying giraffes and pygmy goats.

Instead, I trace rumors of mythical animals and try to prove they exist. A frustrating exercise. There's a reason no one's captured a Bigfoot. They don't want to be found, and they're a lot better at hiding than anyone on earth is at seeking. Or at least that's my theory, and I'm sticking to it.

Most cryptozoologists attempt to find undiscovered species or evolutionary wonders—real animals, nothing paranormal about them—but not me. Nope. I'd made that vow.

Foolish, but when a woman loves a man the way that I loved Simon, she does foolish things, especially when he's dying in her arms.

So I follow every legend, every folk tale, every scrap of information, trying to uncover something mythical and prove it real. Though I've never believed in magic, my husband did, and the only thing I've ever believed in was him.

I was having very little luck with my quest until the night the phone rang at 3:00 A.M. Insomnia and a very empty checking account made me answer it despite the hour.

"Hello?"

"Dr. Malone?" The voice was male, a bit shaky, old or perhaps ill.

"Not yet."

I needed to find a cryptid—translation: unknown animal—prove its existence, write a thesis. Then I could attach those lovely letters—Ph.D.—at the end of my name. But since the whole vow incident, I'd been too busy chasing lake monsters and Sasquatch clones to spend time finding a new breed of anything.

"Is this Diana Malone?"

"Yes. Who's this?"

"Frank Tallient."

The name sounded familiar, but I couldn't figure out why. "Have we met?"

"No. I got your number from Rick Canfield."

Swell. The last guy who'd said those immortal words, "You're fired."

Rick was a lawyer who'd gone on a fishing trip with a bunch of other lawyers near Lake of the Woods, Minnesota. In the middle of the night he'd seen something in the lake. Something slick and black and very, very big.

Being a lawyer, he was smart enough to know he shouldn't tell the others he'd lost his mind. Not yet.

Instead, he'd gone home, searched the Internet, and

made some phone calls, trying to find someone to help him discover if what he'd seen had been real or imagined. He'd found me.

"Rick thought you'd be free to help me," Tallient continued.

I was free all right. Unemployed. Again. A common occurrence in my life. I was very good at looking for things, not so good at actually finding them. However, I was one of the few cryptozoologists willing to travel on a whim for cash.

I wasn't associated with a university—not anymore. Not since Simon had gone over the edge, tarnishing both his reputation and my own.

I depended on the kindness of strangers—hell, let's be honest and just call them strange—to fund my expeditions. Until tonight, I'd been fresh out of both.

"Since you didn't locate Nessie—" Tallient began.

"Nessie's the Loch Ness Monster. I was searching for Woody."

Which was the name Rick had bestowed on the thing. People have no originality when naming lake beasts, always opting for some variation of the body of water they supposedly resided in.

Typically, the moment I'd arrived at Lake of the Woods with my cameras and recorders whatever Rick might have seen had gone *poof*. If it had ever been there in the first place.

In my expert opinion, an obscenely large muskie was responsible for the tales, not a supernatural lake monster, but I hadn't been able to prove that, either.

"I have a job for you," Tallient continued.

"I'm listening."

I had no choice. Though my parents were incredibly wealthy, they thought I was nuts and had stopped speaking to me the instant I married Simon.

After all, what could a handsome, brilliant, up-and-coming zoologist from Liverpool see in a not-very-pretty, far too sturdy grad student unless it was her parents' millions? He already had a green card. That Simon had told them exactly what they could do with their money had only made me love him more.

In truth, I fit into Simon's world better than I'd ever fit in my own. I stood five-foot-ten in my bare feet; on a good day I weighed a hundred and seventy. I liked the out-of-doors—didn't mind dirt or sun, wind or rain. I'd joined the Girl Scouts just so I could camp. I'd done pretty much anything and everything I could think of to emphasize my differences from the never-too-rich, never-too-thin lifestyle of my mother.

"Can you access the Internet?" Tallient asked.

"Hold on." I tapped my laptop, which sprang from asleep to awake much quicker than I ever did. "OK."

Tallient recited a www-dot address. An instant later, a newspaper article spilled across my screen.

" 'Man Found Dead in a Swamp,' " I read. "Not unusual."

Swamps were notorious dumping grounds for bodies. If the muck didn't take them, the alligators would.

"Keep going."

"Throat torn. Feral dogs. Huh." I accessed the next page. "Child missing. Coyotes. No body. Seems straightforward."

"Not really."

Tallient recited a second address, and I read some more. "Wolf sightings."

My heart increased in tempo. Wolves had been Simon's

specialty; they'd turned into his obsession. Now they were mine.

"Where is this?" I demanded.

"New Orleans."

If possible, my heart beat even faster. Once red wolves had roamed the Southeast from the Atlantic to the Gulf and west to Texas. They'd been sighted as far north as Missouri and Pennsylvania. But in 1980 the red wolf had been declared extinct in the wild. In 1987 they'd been reintroduced, but only in North Carolina. So . . .

"There aren't any wolves in Louisiana," I said.

"Precisely."

"There's a legend, though. . . ." I struggled to remember it. "Honey Island Swamp monster."

"I doubt that Bigfoot-like footprints found thirty years ago have any relationship to death, disappearance, and wolves where they aren't supposed to be."

He had a point.

"Could be an ABC," I ventured.

The acronym stood for "Alien Big Cat"—a cryptozoological label given to reports of out-of-place felines. Black panthers in Wisconsin. A jaguar in Maine. Happens a lot more than you'd think.

Most of the time ABCs were explained away as exotic animals released into the woods when they became too hard to handle or too big to fit in an apartment. Funny thing was, no one ever found them.

If they were pets, wouldn't they be easy to catch? Wouldn't their bones, or even their collars, turn up after a truly wild animal killed them? Wouldn't there be at least one record of an ABC being hit by a truck on the interstate?

But there wasn't.

"This is a wolf, not a cat," Tallient said.

I was impressed with his knowledge of crypto-terminology but too caught up in the mystery unfolding before my eyes to compliment him on it.

"Same principle," I murmured. "Could be someone dumped a wolf in the swamp. Nothing special about it."

Except wolves weren't vicious. They didn't attack people. Unless they were starving, wolf-dog hybrids, or rabid. None of which were a good thing.

"There've been whispers of wolves in and around New Orleans for years," he continued.

"How many years?"

"At least a hundred."

"What?"

Tallient chuckled. "I thought you'd enjoy that. The disturbances don't seem to occur in any particular month, or even a common season. But they always happen during the same lunar phase."

"Full moon," I guessed.

No matter what the skeptics say, full moons drive people and animals wacko. Ask anyone who's ever worked in an emergency room, psych ward, or county zoo.

"Not full," Tallient said. "Crescent."

I glanced at the thin, silver, smiling moon visible from my window. "What was the date on those articles?"

"May."

I frowned. Five months ago. "Since then?"

"Nothing."

"Could be because the bodies weren't found."

"Exactly. Things that hunt under a certain phase of the moon do so every month. They can't help themselves."

I wasn't sure about "things," but I was sure about animals. They were nothing if not creatures of habit.

"A body was found yesterday," Tallient continued. "Hasn't hit the papers yet."

I looked at the moon again. Guess I was right.

"What's your interest in this?" I asked.

"Cryptozoology fascinates me. I'd love to go on an expedition, but I'm . . . not well."

I stood. My feet literally itched. I bounced on my toes as excitement threatened to make me jump at this chance. I had to remember: What seemed too good to be true often was.

"You want to pay me to find a wolf where a wolf isn't supposed to be. Once I do, then what?"

"Trap it and call me."

Not an unusual request in my line of work. The people who hired me usually did so in the hopes that they would become famous by revealing some mythical creature to the world, and they wanted to be the ones to do the revealing. I had no problem with that as long as the disclosure took place. All I wanted was to prove Simon hadn't been crazy.

"I can do that," I agreed.

"You do realize this isn't just a wolf?"

I hoped not, but my hopes weren't often realized.

"They call it a loup-garou," Tallient continued. "That's French for—"

"Werewolf."

The rush of adrenaline made me dizzy. Though I took jobs searching for any paranormal entity—beggars couldn't be choosers—the true focus of my quest should have been a lycanthrope. As Simon's had been.

The only problem was, I just couldn't believe. Even though my maiden name was O'Malley and my father's family hailed from the land of leprechauns and fairies, in

Boston, where I grew up, the only fanciful thing was the city's rabid belief in a curse on the BoSox.

In my youth there'd been no nonsense allowed—no Santa, no tooth fairy—I had to fight to read fiction. Which might explain why I fell so in love with a man who dreamed of magic.

I glanced around our apartment near the campus of the University of Chicago. I hadn't moved a book, hadn't given away his clothes, hadn't realized until just this moment how pathetic that was.

"I find it strange," Tallient continued, "that odd things happen under a crescent moon in the Crescent City, don't you?"

I found it more than strange. I found it irresistible.

"Are you interested?"

Why did he bother to ask? He had to have heard how Simon had died. He had to know Dr. Malone's sterling reputation had wound up in tatters. Tallient might not be aware that I'd vowed to make everyone who'd scorned Simon eat their words, but he had to suspect it considering what I'd been doing in the four years since my husband had died.

My gaze fell on the only picture I had of Simon—knee-deep in a Canadian lake, slim, scholarly, blond, and brilliant—his grin still made me yearn. My stomach flopped as it did every time I remembered he was gone forever. But his hopes, his dreams, his work, lived on in me.

"I'll be on a plane in the morning."

2

Tallient promised there'd be an airline ticket and a check waiting at O'Hare. He was as good as his word.

In the meantime, I looked him up on the Internet and remembered why his name was familiar. He wasn't Bill Gates, but he was close.

Tallient had invented a widget for computer modems and become a gazillionaire. At least he could afford me.

After an accident several years ago had turned him into a recluse, he'd become fascinated with cryptozoology. Interestingly enough, details on his accident were nonexistent, leaving me to wonder if Tallient had used his tech skills to ensure a little privacy. I couldn't blame him.

Heat slapped me in the face as soon as I walked out of Louis Armstrong International Airport. Mid-October and the temperature had to be in the midnineties. No wonder the wolves had long ago fled New Orleans.

Along with the plane ticket and the check, Frank, as he'd insisted I call him, had provided a rental car, a hotel room on Bourbon Street, and the name and address of a swamp guide.

"I could get used to this," I said as the agent handed me the keys to a Lexus.

Shortly thereafter I checked into the hotel and tossed my bag on the bed. I'd have the luxury of running water and sheets only until I found a base of operations. I couldn't look for a cryptid from town. I needed to be right where the action was at all hours of the day or night. Once I found such a place, I'd have my camping equipment shipped south.

I wandered to a set of French doors, which led to a patio. Under the heated sheen of the sun, the rot showed—sidewalks cracking, buildings crumbling, homeless people begging coins from the tourists.

One of the bizarre things about Bourbon Street, and there were a lot of them, was how a very nice hotel, like this one, could have a view straight into a strip joint on the opposite side of the street.

Two women danced on top of the bar. When they began to do more than dance, and the milling crowd began to cheer, I turned away from the spectacle. I wasn't a prude, but I preferred my sex in private and in the dark.

Or I had back when I'd had sex. Since Simon, there'd been no one, and I hadn't cared, had barely noticed. But alone in a hotel room on a street that advertised sex twenty-four hours a day, I felt both deprived and depraved. Hiring myself a swamp guide seemed like a good distraction.

I did an Internet search on the address provided by Frank, then drove out of the French Quarter to the interstate, over Lake Pontchartrain, and into Slidell—an interesting combination of commuter suburb and Victorian brick houses. I didn't have time to enjoy the contrast. I wanted the guide issue settled so I could get to work.

I headed past every fast-food joint and franchise restaurant I knew and some I didn't. Just beyond a strip mall, I took a left, trolling by new houses complete with Big Wheels in the driveways and swimming pools in the backyards.

These gave way to older and older residences, then mobile homes, and finally shacks. One more turn and *bam*—there was the swamp. No wonder I'd heard reports of alligators in people's yards. What did they expect, putting a backyard near an alligator?

I shut off the motor, and silence pressed down on me. The weight of a cell phone in my pocket was reassuring. I could always call . . . someone.

Climbing out of the Lexus, I thanked Frank in absentia. Whenever I was forced into any vehicle smaller than a midsize four-door, I felt as if I were driving a clown car.

My mother, also quite tall, was an annoyingly slim woman with ice in her veins and hair as dark as her soul. Though she'd had no patience for fairy tales, she'd insisted I was a changeling. Where I'd gotten light green eyes, bright red hair, and an intense desire to play softball no one seemed to know. My appearance had marked me as an outsider, even before my behavior had branded me the same.

Damp heat brushed my face along with the scent of rotting vegetation and brackish water. My eyes searched the gloom for something. Anything. Though my watch insisted I had a good hour of daylight left, the thick cover of ancient oaks shrouded me in chilly shadow.

I saw nothing but a dock and a tributary that disappeared around a bend. Across the water, hundreds of cypress trees dripped Spanish moss into the swamp grass.

"Hello?" I reached into my pocket and pulled out the note. "Adam Ruelle?"

The only answer was a thick splash, which halted my stride down the dock. How fast could an alligator travel on land?

Not as fast as I could. But what if that hadn't been an alligator?

Wolves are quick, as are big cats, and when dealing with new or undiscovered animals, anything could happen.

I took a deep breath. I might have been raised soft, but before Simon and I started spending so much time in the field we'd taken self-defense classes. You couldn't sleep under the stars in a dozen different states and not run into trouble sooner or later.

However, knowing how to disable a man who out-weighed me by fifty pounds wasn't going to do me much good with a wild animal. What had I been thinking to come here alone, without a gun?

I snorted. I didn't own a gun.

Slowly I backed toward land, keeping my eyes on the flowing water. The muted splashing came closer and closer. I should make a run for it, but I hated to turn my back on whatever lurked in the depths of the lily pad–strewn tributary.

I heard a rustle that wasn't a fish, wasn't even water. More like the whisper of weeds, the snap of a twig. Slowly I lifted my gaze to the far shore.

A single flower perched atop a waving stalk, the shade of a flame against the dewy blue-green backdrop, and the tall grass swished closed behind a body.

Could have been anything, or anyone.

"Except for the tail," I murmured.

Bushy. Black. I tilted my head. Canine? Or feline?

I walked to the edge of the dock to get a better look at

what had already disappeared. When water splashed across my shoes, I started, then slipped.

I was falling, my arms pinwheeling, my gaze focused, horrified, on the eight-foot alligator, jaws wide and waiting. Someone grabbed me and hauled backward. My heels banged loudly against the wooden slats of the dock, and the alligator let out an annoyed hiss.

I expected to be released once my feet touched dirt; instead, my savior, my captor, held on tight.

"Who're you?" His voice rasped, as if he rarely spoke, and carried both the cadence of the South and a touch of France. I'd never heard another like it.

"D-d-diana," I managed, despite a significant lack of breath and a near-painful increase in my heart rate. "Diana Malone."

There. I sounded cool, calm, in control, even though I wasn't.

"I need a swamp guide," I continued.

"No guide here."

"I was told there was."

"You were told wrong. Take an airboat tour down de way."

Cajun, I realized as I strained to understand the words past the sexy accent.

Sexy? What in hell was wrong with me? I couldn't even see his face. Guess I had a thing for accents.

I tried to recall what I knew about the culture. It wasn't much. The Cajuns, originally Acadians, had come to Louisiana from France by way of Canada. Most had settled west of New Orleans, become farmers and fishermen, but that didn't mean a few hadn't migrated closer to the Crescent City.

"Those folks will even let you hold a baby alligator," he murmured.

I shivered, remembering how close I'd come to an alligator holding me—and that hadn't looked like a baby.

"No," I managed. "I need—"

His chin bumped my head; I could have sworn he was smelling my hair. I tensed, trying to remember what I'd been taught to get out of this situation, but nothing came to mind.

He was taller, though not by much, and definitely stronger. With one arm he held me so tightly I couldn't move. I wondered what the other arm was doing until I felt his palm skim up my thigh.

"Hey!"

"Woman alone shouldn't come here," he whispered. "You might see t'ings you should not."

"Like what?"

Silence settled over us, broken only by the hum of the bugs skimming across the water. I could have sworn I heard a laugh. However, when he spoke, no humor colored his voice.

"Curious cats should be careful."

"Was that a threat?"

"An observation, *cher*."

Cher? I hadn't laid eyes on his face, and he was calling me *dear*? Talk about balls. Or maybe I shouldn't.

Twisting, I tried to get free, or at least see him. He tightened the steel band he used for an arm, and I couldn't breathe. My breasts—not large, but not bad—jiggled against his wrist. Something stirred against my backside before he released me with a shove.

By the time I'd caught my balance and whirled around, he'd escaped into the cover of the trees, moving with a grace that reminded me of the ABCs I'd been thinking of when he arrived.

His white T-shirt stood out in the encroaching night like a flare. The sleeves had been hacked off in deference to the heat, or maybe to reveal tanned, honed arms. Khaki pants hung on slim hips; he wasn't wearing any shoes. Dark, shaggy hair sifted across his shoulders. I still couldn't see his face.

"Who are you?" I whispered.

He didn't answer, instead lighting a cigarette, cupping the match in such a way as to keep the glow from reaching anything but tobacco. A bronze bracelet, the same shade as his skin, encircled his wrist. I'd never cared for jewelry on men, but on him the adornment only seemed to emphasize his masculinity.

"Seen any wolves?" I asked.

He took a deep drag, as if he hadn't a care in the world, or an appointment in this century. Nevertheless, I sensed a wary interest.

"Maybe a black coyote?" I pressed.

The very thought excited me. A black coyote just might get me that Ph.D.

"How about a big cat?" I continued when he did nothing but take another drag. "Cougar?"

He blew smoke through his nose. "No wolves this far south."

"Coyotes?"

"Got 'em now. Brought in to hunt nutria rats."

I'd read about those. Large rodents that resembled beavers but with a ratlike tail. I hoped the coyotes were winning.

"Cats?" I asked again. "What about bears?"

"Bobcat. A few bears. Don't see 'em much."

I was constantly amazed at how easy it was for creatures to hide in their native habitat.

"I've heard there've been disappearances. Tales of a wolf."

"There will always be tales."

"Where there's smoke there's fire," I pointed out.

His cigarette flared red on one end as he drew on the other. "You a cop?"

"Scientist."

Saying I was a cryptozoologist only confused people.

He grunted and tossed the butt to the ground. The resulting hiss revealed he'd hit water.

"Can you guide me?" I stepped forward. "Do you know Adam Ruelle?"

"No."

His voice was mesmerizing. I wanted to keep him talking—forever.

A mighty splash was followed by a thud on the dock. I spun around, remembering there were more wild animals in the swamp than furry ones, but there was nothing there.

Just as there was nothing when I turned back to the trees—no man, no beast.

Hell, I couldn't even find the cigarette butt.

3

As I stared at the place where the man had been, a long, low howl rose into the night. The hair on my arms lifted. I could swear the noise came from right in front of me.

I'm a zoologist. I know howls are funny that way. Not only is it virtually impossible for a human to gauge their direction or distance, but often a few wolves can sound like a whole lot more.

Of course one sounds like one, and that was one more than there were supposed to be around here.

"No wolves in the swamp, my ass," I muttered.

Nevertheless, I headed for my car at the fastest clip I could manage and not trip over my feet. I didn't plan on proving myself right by meeting a lone wolf—or whatever that was. Being right wouldn't keep me from being dead.

Since wolves are nocturnal, my best bet would be to return with the sun, a guide, a gun.

Maybe a gun wouldn't even help. Or at least not one that wasn't loaded with silver bullets.

The thought startled a laugh out of me. Since the sound was slightly hysterical, I started the car and headed to town, not slowing down until I planted my butt on a bar stool in a place called Kelly's. There was always a Kelly's.

Several blocks over, the music, the voices, of Bourbon Street increased as the night progressed. I waited until the tourists cleared out and the locals drifted in; then I started to ask questions.

"Ruelle ain't a guide, ye nuts?"

I frowned at an ancient man, so brown and wrinkled he must have bathed in sunlight for the past forty years. Why had Frank sent me to Ruelle if he was—?

I tilted my head. "What is he?"

"Crazy."

"I'm sorry?"

My companion stared into the bottom of his empty beer mug with an expression of such pathetic loneliness that I waved a finger, and the bartender filled it.

"He owns a mansion at the edge of the swamp, but the thing's all fallin' down. He lives in the wild."

"Then he *is* familiar with the area."

"Better'n anyone. But he ain't been seen for years. He's probably dead."

Strange. Maybe Frank had known Adam before he'd lost his mind.

"Why would Ruelle abandon the family home?"

"He went into the army right out of high school. Word is he joined some hotshot Special Forces group. When he came home he couldn't live in the world anymore, so he went into the swamp."

I found myself wondering why a young man with any other opportunity would enlist. Of course I'd turned my back on opportunity, too, preferring to sleep in a tent with the man of my dreams rather than make oodles of money working for Daddy.

However, I doubted Adam Ruelle had become a soldier because of a woman. Then again, maybe he had.

As I considered what Ruelle had to do with anything, I picked up a book of matches on the bar emblazoned with a spooky font that spelled out *Cassandra's*.

The old man leaned over and tapped the word with a nicotine-stained finger. "You wanna learn about voodoo and such?"

I frowned. "Why?"

"Priestess Cassandra bought Marie Laveau's old house on Royal Street."

"Marie Laveau the voodoo queen?"

"Yes, ma'am." He nodded, warming to his subject. "Most think Marie was actually two women—a mother and a daughter. When one died, the other took her place, which explains why folks believed Marie had power."

"Growing younger and not dying will do that," I agreed.

"No one knows where Marie lived for certain," the bartender interjected, "or where she's buried, neither."

"She's buried in St. Louis Cemetery Number One," the old man insisted. "Second most visited grave site in the country."

"What's the first?" I'd bet on the Tomb of the Unknown Soldier or maybe the Eternal Flame.

"Graceland."

Well, no one's ever claimed that Americans aren't bizarre.

"Priestess Cassandra lives at Marie's place," my companion insisted. "Set up a voodoo shop."

"Sounds kitschy."

"Catchy?"

"Touristy. Tacky."

"Not this one. She's got things you won't find just any-where. Even has a voodoo temple out back."

That I wouldn't mind seeing, but first things first.

"I hear there's been disappearances."

"In New Awlins?" He lifted a brow. "Don't say?"

His sarcasm was understandable. I'd discovered early on in my search for the paranormal that a lot more people disappeared than anyone realized. With the huge transient population in New Orleans—both homeless and tourists—as well as a river, a lake, and a swamp nearby, I bet they didn't even have an accurate count of the missing.

I motioned for a refill and tried a different approach. "Been talk of a wolf in the swamp, too."

"I saw a wolf on Jackson Square."

I blinked. "In town?"

The old guy nodded.

"You're sure?"

Wolves definitely didn't venture into highly populated areas—unless they were completely whacked.

"If ye don't believe me, ask Jay." He flicked a finger toward a young man who was quietly consuming a huge hamburger at the other end of the bar. "He works the Square."

"Works?" I eyed Jay. He was cute enough, but I couldn't see him trolling the streets.

"Po-lice."

Well, that made more sense.

I resisted the urge to rub my hands together in glee. An off-duty police officer. What could be more convenient?

If a werewolf walked right into Kelly's, but I wasn't going to wait around for that to happen.

"Was there a wolf in Jackson Square?" I asked.

Officer Jay looked up from his plate. "No."

I turned to the old man.

"I saw it," he mumbled.

"Folks see strange things around here every night," Officer Jay explained.

"Like what?"

Standing, he tossed some money onto the counter. "New Orleans is the most haunted city in America, and there's a reason for it."

"Ghosts?"

"Booze, drugs, loud music." He headed for the door. "Messes with the head."

A few moments later I said my good-byes, then meandered down a quiet, dark side road in the direction of Bourbon Street. Within minutes I had the distinct impression I wasn't alone.

Perhaps one of the ghosts had decided to follow me home. Or maybe it was just a mugger. I'd almost welcome the opportunity to kick some low-life ass after allowing myself to be embarrassingly manhandled by—

Who?

I paused and could have sworn whatever lurked behind me paused, too. How's that for paranoid?

I glanced to the left, the right, the rear, and saw nothing but shadows. So I walked faster, and as I did, I distinguished a *clackety-clack,* like nails tapping on a desk. Or claws clicking along the pavement.

Now I was really losing my mind.

Heated breath brushed my thighs, a growl rumbled the air, and my heart stuttered. I was afraid to turn, afraid of what I would see, or not see.

Up ahead, someone had left open the gate to a private courtyard. I pretended to head past, then ducked in.

Something scooted by, something low to the ground

and furry. I was so amazed, I scrambled forward to get a better look and caught my toe in a crack.

My knees hit the pavement, then my hands. I waited, expecting hot breath to brush my face instead of my thighs.

Nothing happened.

I climbed to my feet, using the wall for support, and stepped onto the street. A car whooshed past. Laughter drifted on the wind. A dog barked, but the sidewalk was deserted.

Except for the man who lounged against the building a block away. Beyond him lights flashed, music pulsed, people danced in the street. His bicep flexed as he leaned forward to light the tip of the cigarette just visible beyond the long, dark fall of his hair.

I started to run as he slid around the corner. By the time I reached Bourbon Street, all that remained was the milling crowd.

That night I dreamed someone climbed onto my balcony. I'd left the French doors open. I'd known he would come.

He moved to the bed with the grace of an animal. His eyes were so blue, they made me gasp, even before he reached out a rough, calloused hand and touched me.

In the dream I saw him, and he was beautiful. Full lips, sharp cheekbones, long eyelashes—an aristocrat's face and a workingman's body. No man of leisure would ever possess scarred fingers, bulging muscles, or tanned skin.

Naked he stood above me, the faint silver light shining across the ladder of his ribs, a taut, rippling abdomen. The desire to trace my fingers along the flow, feel the heat and the strength, press my mouth to those ridges, then move lower and taste him, nearly overwhelmed me.

"Goddess of de hunt, moon, and night," he murmured, his voice spilling down my skin like a waterfall.

I wanted to lose myself in that voice, in him.

The bed dipped. He did things I'd only imagined, whispered suggestions in a language I didn't understand. I cried out, "Loup-garou," and the breathy, hoarse rasp awoke me.

A breeze fluttered the curtains. No wonder I'd had a nightmare. Heat poured in, along with the rumble of the party that still rocked the street below.

I got out of bed, slammed the French doors, flicked the lock, still trembling with the memory of a dream that hadn't seemed like a dream.

I couldn't blame myself for an erotic fantasy. I was a young, healthy woman who'd denied herself sex for four years. Suddenly confronted with a mysterious man, unlike any I'd ever known, I'd have been worried if I didn't dream of him.

Nevertheless, I was annoyed with myself—frustrated, sweaty. Too wide awake for this time of the night, I didn't relish what was to come.

Hours in the dark, lonely and guilty, because even though Simon was dead, within my dreams he'd been alive. Until tonight, when another man had taken his place.

I spun away from the window, and suddenly I couldn't breathe.

At the foot of my bed, stark against the creamy satin bedspread, lay the bright red flower I'd seen on the far shore of the swamp that afternoon.

4

Not the same one. Couldn't be.

I stood near the window shaking my head, unreasonably spooked by a flower.

Well, maybe not unreasonably. I hadn't brought it here.

My gaze flicked around the room. There wasn't anywhere to hide, except—

I glanced at the floor, and the breath I'd been holding streamed out in relief. The wooden bed frame ended at the carpet. There was no "under the bed."

Slowly I crept toward the bathroom. Why I didn't just call security I'm still not sure. Perhaps I couldn't bring myself to say, "I found a flower. Save me!"

I'd left on the bathroom light as I always did when sleeping in a strange place. I hated walking into walls half-asleep.

The reflection in the vanity mirror revealed there was no one inside. Just as there was nothing in the closet. Which meant—

I turned toward the window.

The curtains, meant to block the sun so Mardi Gras partiers could sleep away the day, also blocked everything else. Unable to bear not knowing, I strode across the room and whipped them back.

Then stared past the empty balcony, studying the flickering neon across the street. My room was on the fifth floor. How could anyone scale the hotel without being seen from below?

But would the drunks even notice? If they had, would they care or merely cheer? However, if they'd cheered, I'd have heard them.

"Damn," I muttered.

Someone had been here. But who? How? Why?

All questions for a time when the sun was shining. Too bad they kept me up for the rest of the night.

Dawn found me dressed and swilling coffee from the complimentary urn in the lobby. If I could have positioned my mouth directly beneath the spigot without undue notice, I would have. I was so tired.

I showed the concierge the address on my handy dandy sheet of paper. Contrary to the opinion of the sexy-voiced Cajun with an attitude, the concierge confirmed it as the location of a trustworthy guide service—CW Swamp Tours.

I retraced my route to the dock where a man waited on an airboat. "Deanna Malone?"

I guess he was waiting for me.

"Diana," I corrected, and he grinned.

I wished that he hadn't. His teeth were nothing to write home about. They'd make a short letter, since there were so few left. A shame. He didn't appear a day over twenty.

"Mr. Tallient sent me."

The accent was Deep South—not a hint of France, and I missed it.

"I was here yesterday," I said.

His face, which resembled both Howdy Doody and Richie Cunningham, despite the bright white hair that shone beneath the morning sun like a reflector, crumpled with the effort of thought.

"Was I supposed to come yeste'day? I get confused."

Hell. I hoped he didn't get confused in the middle of the swamp.

"I met someone—" I began.

"No one but me comes to this place."

"Tall, dark." I left out "handsome," fearing I'd sound too much like Snow White. "Long hair."

My guide shrugged. "Don't bring no one to mind."

"Did Frank—Mr. Tallient—tell you what I need . . . ?"

I wondered if he was Adam Ruelle, except Ruelle was mysteriously missing. Besides, I doubted a man who had been raised in a mansion, however broken down, would let his teeth rot out of his head. Then again, I could be wrong.

"What's your name?"

"Charlie Wagner. Tallient said you wanted to look for the wolf."

"Have you seen one?"

Charlie's gaze slid from mine. "Can't say as I have."

I found his choice of words interesting. He *couldn't* say. Didn't mean he hadn't seen it.

"You gonna meet me here at dusk?" he asked.

"Dusk?" The last time I'd come at dusk I'd nearly been eaten by an alligator, and that had been the best part.

I remembered the voice, the scent of smoke, his breath in my hair, and his arm cradling my breasts. A long, long time had passed since a man's anything had been near them.

Maybe the alligator hadn't been the best part, after all.

"Wolves don't come out in the light," Charlie explained.

I knew that. "All right," I said. "Dusk."

He made no move to leave. After several silent moments, I asked the only question I still had: "Do you know Adam Ruelle?"

Charlie had been peering into my face, and now he glanced away. "Never met him."

"Know where he lives?"

"No one does."

"What about the Ruelle place?"

Charlie pointed to the far side of the water and the waving grass.

I had nothing else to do. Tallient had already hired Charlie. And I was curious.

"Take me there," I said.

Charlie's boat was a smooth, fast ride. I probably should have been wary. Airboats flipped in the swamp all the time. But the whip of the wind in my hair, the sun on my face, was too enjoyable to ruin with what-ifs.

In the daylight, the swamp was beautiful. A riot of colors, hardly any alligators, not a nutria rat to be had. I doubted the area would be as appealing tonight.

The red, stalklike flower grew everywhere. I jabbed my finger at a clump as we scooted past, but since we both wore earphones to drown out the blare of the boat, Charlie wasn't going to be answering my questions anytime soon. He merely flashed me his un-teeth and kept driving.

The Ruelle Mansion became visible as we slid wide

around a small island. The place would fit perfectly on a Halloween card.

The boards had gone gray; the windows were broken; the porch listed to one side. Despite its condition and obvious age, the word *stately* came to mind. In days past, music, laughter, life, had filled the rooms. If I concentrated very hard, I could imagine the Ruelle Mansion coming alive again.

Most plantations in this part of Louisiana were located on the Great River Road, which ran from New Orleans to Baton Rouge. Finding one here was as mysterious as it was fascinating. I felt as if I'd stepped through a time warp and into another century.

Charlie cut the engine, and we bumped against the decaying dock.

"How long since someone lived here?" I asked.

"Used to be a lot of transients in and out. But no one lately."

"Why not?"

"People got spooked. Ha'nts and such. Heard tell a few folks disappeared and no one ever saw 'em again."

I stared at the building. If any place looked haunted, the Ruelle Mansion did.

"I'd think the walls would have rotted in the damp."

"Made of cypress wood from the swamp. Never rots. House'll stand until the end of time."

While I should have been reassured that the structure was sound, instead I was a bit creeped out that the house would be standing here when the rest of the world had passed away.

"Come with me," I ordered.

I wasn't afraid of ghosts, but I had a hard time believing every homeless person in the area had been scared off by the rumors. I didn't relish running into a transient as I wandered through the place.

Charlie shrugged, tied up the boat, and followed.

"What're those flowers?" I indicated a patch that seemed to mark the end of the yard and the beginning of the swamp. "The tall red ones."

"Fire iris."

"Pretty." I took a step in their direction.

"Don't touch 'em!"

"Why?"

I had visions of hives, rashes, swamp warts. Hell. The thing had been on my bed.

"Bad luck."

"What kind of bad luck?"

"Hoodoo and such."

Hoodoo was an old-time, backwoods version of—

"Voodoo?"

His only answer was another shrug.

This was the second time voodoo had entered the conversation since I'd gotten here. Of course I was in New Orleans, the voodoo capital of America. I shouldn't be surprised.

I wasn't. However, I decided it might behoove me to make a visit to Priestess Cassandra after all.

Charlie climbed the steps, his boots thunking against the worn wood like distant thunder. The sun threatened to cook everything well done, yet he wore jeans, a long-sleeved shirt, and work boots. I suspected the latter had something to do with snakes. Glancing at my sneakers, I made a mental note to buy heavier shoes.

He opened the door, and I followed him in. Someone *had* stayed here once. Several hundred someones, by the size of the garbage pile. The smell didn't help.

Old food, new dirt, and . . .

I could have sworn I smelled blood.

I shook my head. The place was dim, dusty, dirty, but there wasn't any blood. Why would there be?

If there'd ever been any furniture, it was gone now, either stolen or maybe used as kindling—although I couldn't imagine the weather ever being cold enough to warrant a bonfire.

There weren't any holes in the roof or the floor, only the windows. With some elbow grease and a few pounds of soap and water, the place could be habitable again. Hey, I'd seen worse.

A board creaked overhead, as if someone had accidentally stepped on a crack, then frozen at the sound.

"Hello?" Charlie called.

No one answered.

I jerked my head toward the stairs and together we climbed them, splitting up on the second floor. Charlie took the right side; I took the left. I didn't find anything but dirt until I reached the last room near the back of the house.

There wasn't anyone there—at least no one alive. *Haha.* But there *was* a picture on the wall. A very old, very interesting picture. I was still looking at it five minutes later, trying not to hyperventilate, when Charlie found me.

"Who is that?" I asked.

"Ruelle."

"I thought you'd never met him."

Charlie cut me a quick glance. "Not Adam. That there's his granddaddy, several generations back." He tapped the corner of the photo where a tiny notation read: *1857.* I'd been too flipped out to notice.

"Name's Henri." Charlie spoke the name with a French

twist, dropping the *h*, putting the accent on the second syllable. "He's been dead nearly a hundred and fifty years."

Charlie's words reached me from a long way off. I couldn't stop staring at the photo.

The face was that of the man in my dream.

5

"I guess New Orleans really is the most haunted city in America," I murmured.

"Ye think it was a ghost up here?" Charlie's voice wavered, and he inched toward the door.

"What?" I dragged my gaze from the picture. "Oh. Maybe."

What did I know? I'd dreamed the face of a man who'd been dead for a century and a half. I'd found a bad-luck voodoo flower in my bed. I was in Louisiana searching for a werewolf, for crying out loud. I shouldn't be let loose without a keeper.

Charlie tugged on my arm. "Let's get outta here."

His hands were ice-cold. Poor kid. I took pity on him and went.

As we hurried across the grass, I wondered aloud, "The photo was the only thing left in the house. Wouldn't someone have stolen it by now?"

Charlie leaped from the dock to the boat. "I dunno."

Neither did I.

He drove the boat as if we were being chased, then dumped me back where he'd found me.

"We still on for tonight?" I asked.

"Sure. Swamp I got no problem with."

Charlie left with a roar of the motor, sending a huge wave over both the dock and my sneakers.

I returned to the hotel, where I discovered my flower was gone. I'd have figured the maid disposed of the thing, except my room hadn't been cleaned yet.

"No, ma'am," the girl insisted when I tracked her down. "I haven't gotten to your floor."

"Did anyone else?"

"No. That's my responsibility."

She could be lying, but why?

As I let myself back into my room, my cell phone rang. I glanced at the caller ID.

Frank.

I'd been meaning to call him but kept getting distracted.

"What did you find?" he demanded without the courtesy of a hello.

I wasn't sure what to say. I hadn't found anything except a voodoo flower and a picture of a ghost. Neither one had any bearing on what Frank had hired me to do. So instead of answering his question, I asked one of my own.

"Why did you write the name Adam Ruelle next to the guide's information?"

"I didn't tell you?" Frank sighed. "My mind is not what it used to be, I'm afraid. Ruelle land has been the favored territory for the loup-garou."

Considering Ruelle land was basically a swamp, except for the small area where the house had been built, I could see why.

"Could you rent the mansion?" I asked. "I'd like to use it as my base of operations."

"I bet I could," Frank said slowly. "Great idea. You're going to find the loup-garou; I'm sure of it."

"Thanks," I said dryly. "You understand, don't you, Frank, that the possibility of discovering a werewolf is pretty slim?"

Right up there with the possibility of there actually being one, but I wasn't going to tell him that. He was paying my salary.

"I understand," Frank said. "But there's something there. Something new and exciting. Can't you feel it?"

I could, and I was both frightened and fascinated.

"Did you see Ruelle?" he asked.

I wasn't sure.

"According to the locals," I murmured, "he's been missing for years."

"Bullshit! He's there, and he knows something."

I started to get uneasy about Frank. "Have you met this guy?" I asked.

He hesitated. "Not him. His . . . father."

"Does he have any information?"

"He's dead."

"That seems to be going around."

"Find me the werewolf, Diana. I need it."

Frank hung up, and when I redialed his number, I got voice mail. I wondered again about the accident that had made him a recluse. Had he fallen on his head? Why would he *need* a werewolf?

I shrugged and pocketed my cell phone. Until his checks became as bent as he was, I'd just keep doing what Frank had hired me to do.

With several hours until I met Charlie, I took a stroll

down Bourbon. My feet led me to Royal Street, and from there to a tiny shop tucked back from the others.

Cassandra's.

I stepped inside. The contrast between heated sunshine and cool shadow, frantic noise and a certain peace, made me dizzy. I caught the scent of herbs, spice, heard the trickle of water somewhere in the distance, and music.

Not jazz or even the blues. Something folksy with drums. A tune that was as ancient as time.

"Hello?" I called.

No answer.

I had a sense someone was watching me, which seemed to happen a lot lately, and was making me increasingly paranoid.

A doorway covered with beads of many colors led into the back. I saw nothing beyond their plastic sheen, which was, I'm sure, the whole idea.

I turned toward the retail section of the store, took three steps, and stopped. Some*one* wasn't watching me; some*thing* was.

A huge, coiled snake occupied a cage in the corner, its eyes black and unblinking. Eyes of the dead. Long, brown, with uneven black circles all over its body, the reptile appeared to be a python. Was that even legal?

I inched away. The cage looked secure enough, but I didn't want to get him excited. There were plenty of other items to view in the snake-free section of the store.

Shelves full of bottles, bowls, which were in turn full of . . . stuff. With none of it marked, I was clueless.

Several mini cloth sacks stuffed with Lord knows what lay on the countertop. I brushed my fingertip across one of them, and I could have sworn it shimmied on its own.

"Gris-gris."

I lifted my gaze to the woman standing in front of the beaded doorway. How had she come through without making them go *clackety-clack*?

"I'm sorry?" I said.

She moved behind the counter, picking up one of the bags. "A gris-gris, meaning charm or talisman. For good luck."

Her lack of an accent revealed her to be as much a stranger here as I was.

"Not bad luck?" In my memory banks *gris-gris* meant "cursed."

"Not in my shop."

My shop. *This* was Priestess Cassandra?

I'd expected her to be African-American, or perhaps Haitian, since voodoo had taken root and grown there. She'd wear a turban, a flowing dress, bangles on her wrists, huge hoops in her ears.

Instead, Cassandra was a tiny blue-eyed white girl with a single streak of gray marring the right temple of her short, black hair. Hair that appeared to have been hacked off recently, by someone who did not know what they were doing. To my amazement, the style complemented Cassandra's high cheekbones and pointed chin, softening them just enough to nudge her toward stunning.

She was dressed in ratty jeans, a pink T-shirt, and her feet were bare, except for the rings on two of her toes. If not for the premature gray, I would have mistaken her for a coed at Tulane.

"You have a question?" she asked. "Something bugging you?"

"You psychic?"

Her smile was sweet, as if I were a child, though I had to be older than her by several years. "Everyone is at times."

I snorted, then realized how rude that was. "Sorry."

She spread her hands. "We believe what we believe."

Even if I was in town searching for a werewolf, that didn't mean I bought into voodoo and other mind games. I had my standards.

"I do have questions," I said. "Doesn't everyone?"

"Some have answers." I lifted a brow and she laughed. "But not many. How can I help you . . . ?"

She tilted her head, waiting for me to introduce myself.

"I'm Diana."

"Moon goddess."

I stilled at the tickle of a memory. I'd heard that before, or something like it, in my dream last night.

Cassandra studied my face. "You didn't know the meaning?"

"I do, but my parents named me after my grandmother. Knowing them, there wasn't any discussion of the moon involved."

"Regardless, names have power and purpose. Cassandra means prophet."

"How . . . convenient."

She laughed again, as if I were the funniest person to come into her shop in years. I took in the herbs, the beads, the snake. Maybe I was.

Hissing erupted from beyond the chicken wire. "Relax, Lazarus. She's a friend."

"Lazarus? As in risen from the dead?"

"Names have power," was all she said. "What's your question?"

I frowned at the snake, which was staring at me again. The idea that the reptile might not die or, if dead, would rise, was a very creepy thought indeed. Weren't zombies a part of the whole voodoo thing?

And snake zombies . . . Well, I didn't even want to go there.

"There's a flower in the swamp," I said. "A fire iris?"

"Yes." Cassandra moved down the row of shelves and began to pull out a little of this and a little of that, sprinkling the unknown items into a gris-gris bag. "Very powerful."

"What does it mean when someone leaves one on your bed?"

She paused, fingers poised over a basket of what appeared to be dried chicken bones. Then, as if she'd had second thoughts, she took a pinch of red dust instead and scattered it on top.

"Not 'welcome to the neighborhood,' " she murmured. "Can you bring me the flower?"

I cleared my throat. "It's gone."

"Hmm." She turned to a completely different set of shelves and continued to mix and match. "Another question?"

She hadn't answered the first. Not really.

"Do you know anything about a wolf in the area?"

Her hand froze above a glass jar of what looked like black olives but probably weren't. "Who are you?"

"I told you. Di—"

"Not your name. Why are you here? In New Orleans?"

"I'm a cryptozoologist. I was hired to find the wolf in the swamp."

"Why?"

"That's my job. Finding unknown animals."

"A wolf isn't unknown."

"In Louisiana it is."

"What if there isn't a wolf? Or at least not a wolf as you know them?"

"Even better."

She cast me a quick glance, then busied herself tying a string around the top of the gris-gris. "There's a legend about the Honey Island Swamp."

"The swamp monster?"

Her derisive hiss was echoed by the snake in the cage. "Nothing more than an overgrown nutria rat, which scared some half-wits over two decades ago."

Interesting theory—and one that explained the legend nicely. Cassandra was both refreshingly levelheaded and disturbingly strange.

"I meant the legend of the loup-garou," she continued.

Now we were getting somewhere.

"The werewolf."

"You've heard the tale." She stared at me for a long moment. "But you don't believe there's any such thing, do you?"

I ignored her question to ask one of my own: "Have you seen a wolf?"

Cassandra moved to the front window and peered at the street. "There's something out there. Something that comes and goes. Something that kills and is never caught."

"Wolves don't kill people."

She turned, and her now-sober eyes met mine. "Exactly."

"What's the legend?"

In my world, legends often skirted the truth. I needed to listen, to analyze, to pick and choose what was real and what was not.

"Over a hundred years ago a man was cursed."

"Why?"

"He was a man. Isn't that enough?"

I smirked. I really shouldn't like her so much. If she wasn't nuts, she was at least a charlatan.

"Every crescent moon he runs as a wolf."

That much I knew; the question was— "Why not the full moon?"

"A loup-garou is special."

"Why?"

"You have an awful lot of questions for someone who doesn't believe."

"I'm curious."

"He was cursed," she repeated.

"Why?" I sounded like a broken record.

"Because he owned people, and he would not set them free."

Slaves. I should have known.

Voodoo came to this country with those brought here in chains. I had to say, if anyone had bought and sold me, I'd have cursed their ass, too.

"So his slaves voodoo-cursed him to become a wolf under the crescent moon?"

"Not a wolf, a werewolf."

"What's the difference?"

"A wolf is an animal, but a werewolf is monster. An evil thing, ruled by the moon and possessed by bloodlust. They're given life, but they can't live. They can hate, but they can't love. They think like a human and kill like a beast, no longer caring about anything or anyone but themselves."

I guess I didn't want to meet one in a dark alley.

"Why the crescent moon and not the full?" I asked.

"Besides the fact that this is the Crescent City?"

Frank had mentioned that. I'd thought it nothing more than an interesting coincidence. However, when dealing with curses, coincidences weren't always so coincidental.

Not that I believed in curses, but some people did. Obviously Cassandra was one of them.

"The full moon comes but once a month," she continued. "The crescent arrives twice."

"Double your cursing pleasure," I muttered.

Cassandra nodded. "A full moon is technically one night only, but each crescent lasts several days, bestowing multiple madness every lunar cycle."

"Who was this guy? Simon Legree?"

I hated that the first name of my beloved husband and that of the legendary bad guy from *Uncle Tom's Cabin* were the same, but I hadn't written the book and Harriet Beecher Stowe had died long before I had a chance to complain.

"Nobody knows for certain who the man was," Cassandra said. "In the way of legends, he was probably an amalgamation of every slave owner. Doomed to be damned for eternity by their own greed."

"Do you believe a werewolf is running around the Honey Island Swamp?"

"Maybe there is; maybe there isn't. But a wolf's been seen. People have been killed."

"What do the police think?"

"They're like you. Never believe until they see. No wolves in Louisiana, so the culprit has to be a wild dog, or a coyote."

I remembered something Simon had told me. "Wolves won't tolerate coyotes in their territory. Drives 'em nuts."

"OK." Cassandra appeared puzzled by my seemingly random thought. "But what about werewolves and coyotes?"

That I wasn't sure about.

Another thought occurred to me. "Don't those bitten by a werewolf become werewolves themselves?"

"So the legends say."

"Then if there's a werewolf in New Orleans—and has been for over a hundred years—shouldn't there be more than one?"

Cassandra pressed the gris-gris into my hand. "Who says there aren't?"

6

The tinkling of the shop bell interrupted our conversation.

"Excuse me," Cassandra said.

"I need to go anyway."

I tried to return the gris-gris, but she wouldn't take it.

"That's for you."

"I don't think so."

"It'll protect you against the mojo from the flower."

"Sure it will."

She tilted her head. "What can it hurt?"

"Depends on what you put in here. Bats' wings? Puppy dog tails? I'm allergic."

Cassandra laughed. "Nothing so ominous. Some herbs, red pepper. Dust from the grave of a believer."

I made a face.

"Kidding," she said. "I also put in a little something to keep the beasts of the swamp away."

"Right. That oughta work." Along with a gun and a baseball bat.

"If you're going to be working in the swamp, I doubt you'll want the alligators hanging around."

I shoved the gris-gris into my pocket.

"In the old days, people placed charms in their left shoes," Cassandra continued, "but the old days are the reason a lot of folks wound up lame."

"I can't imagine why."

"Just keep the gris-gris on you by day and under your pillow by night. Make sure you take it out before the maid sees. Some tend to get a little freaked if they find them."

I couldn't tell if she was teasing or not. Probably not.

"Let me know how things work out," she said. "I enjoyed talking to you."

I'd enjoyed talking to her, too. I didn't have many friends. Hell, I didn't have any. Once I'd found Simon, I'd let the few I had drift away. I was in a bizarre profession, which didn't lend itself to camaraderie. I disappeared at the ring of the phone, never knew when I'd come back, forgot lunch dates, could care less about movies. And the other cryptozoologists . . .

Well, they'd as soon steal your Loch Ness Monster as look at you.

Arriving back at the hotel, I discovered the maid had cleaned my room and departed. I dropped my clothes on the floor, left a request for a wake-up call for an hour before dusk, then shoved the gris-gris beneath my pillow.

After the dream I'd had last night . . . Well, as Cassandra said—couldn't hurt.

I slept like the dead, waking with a yelp when the phone shrilled next to my ear. A recorded voice reminded me of my wake-up call.

No gifts on the bed. My gris-gris was right where I'd left it. *Yay.*

I got dressed, pocketed the charm, grabbed my camera,

my cell phone, and a tote bag to put them in, then went to meet Charlie.

He was waiting when I pulled up at the dock. The sun cast orange rays through the trees and across his face. I blinked. For an instant the light had taken on the shade of fresh blood.

I pushed aside the disturbing thought. I was the moon goddess, not a prophet, if I believed Cassandra's name-dropping. But what did a moon goddess do? I probably didn't want to know.

The gris-gris weighed heavily in my pocket, and I was tempted to throw the talisman into the drink. But I didn't want Charlie to see it. The way he'd behaved this after-noon at the mansion, anything weird might spook him away for good.

"Ready?" he asked.

In lieu of an answer, I climbed into the boat, and we headed off. Night settled over us like a cool velvet cur-tain. The stars came out, and the crescent moon rose.

Charlie turned on the spotlight attached to the front of the boat, and I stared, transfixed, at what seemed like a hundred shining orbs in the water.

"Gators," he said. "They like the dark."

In the daytime it was easy to believe the alligators were slow and unthreatening. Not very many of them out here at all. But in the night, surrounded by their glowing eyes, every one of which seemed to stare directly at me, they seemed very threatening indeed. I longed to be back on solid ground.

"Where are we going?" I asked.

"Thought you wanted to see the place where the body was found."

"I do."

Charlie pointed straight ahead. "Right there."

"Who discovered it?"

"Me."

"You?" I stared at him incredulously. "You said you hadn't seen the wolf."

"Friend of mine did."

"So it didn't necessarily kill the man."

"Guy's throat was torn. Paw prints all around him."

"Not a coyote?"

"Coyotes are scavengers and cowards. They wouldn't kill a man."

"Neither would a wolf."

Charlie shrugged. "Me and my friend was huntin' nutrias, found the body. I stayed, while he looked around. Said he saw a wolf disappearing into the tall grass."

"He's sure he saw a wolf?"

"Huge, black, big head, long legs. He shot it, but the thing disappeared."

"He's sure he hit something?"

"Found a bit of blood. Nothin' else."

"Isn't it illegal to shoot a wolf?"

The species was still endangered in some areas, threatened or protected in others, though their numbers had increased sufficiently in a few northern states for them to be delisted. In other words, wolves could be killed by certain people with good cause, not by any old person whenever they felt like it.

"No law around here like that," Charlie said. "Ain't no wolves."

I went silent, thinking, as Charlie pointed the boat at the shore. "I'd like to get a peek at that body."

I didn't realize I'd spoken out loud until Charlie answered. "Already in the crypt, I'm sure."

"Crypt?"

"Whole city's below sea level."

Ah, the singular burial practices of New Orleans. While I wasn't an expert, I had read an entire guidebook that I'd bought at O'Hare before getting on the plane.

For hundreds of years, citizens of the Crescent City stacked their dead on shelves inside brick monuments known as ovens. After a year and a day, the body was decomposed enough to dump into a well with all the others who had gone before, making room for the next entrant on the assembly line of death.

Most people choose to be buried in a family crypt. Better to spend eternity mixed with Gramma than the psycho next door.

I was pulled from my thoughts when the boat bumped against the embankment.

"You stay here," Charlie said. "I'm gonna clear the gators out of the way."

"Swell." I contemplated the staring eyes. "What if one of them wants to climb aboard?"

My hand crept to the pocket that held my gris-gris. I sure hoped the thing worked, and wasn't that a change in attitude?

"I doubt they could, but—" He leaned over, flicked the catch on the cabinet beneath his seat, and pulled out a handgun. "There ye go."

Picking up a bat, he strode into the night.

The weight of the gun felt good in my hand. Not only had I taken self-defense classes, but I'd learned how to fire both a rifle and a handgun. I wasn't half-bad.

Water lapped against the boat in a rhythm that would have been peaceful if it weren't for the bobbing army of eyes. I began to feel chilled, and it wasn't lack of the sun. Something was watching me again.

I glanced at the tributary. A lot of somethings.

A rustle from the bank made me start. "Charlie?"

I waited, but Charlie didn't appear.

"Charlie?" I called a little louder, startling the alligators that had swum in close.

The brush seemed to be waving in a nonexistent breeze. I crept to the front of the boat and shifted the spotlight.

The glare blazed across the top of the grass, splashed off the crooked limbs of the cypress trees, and revealed an indentation in the flora, as if a large body was moving steadily toward . . .

"Charlie!"

His answer was a scream, a gurgle, then silence.

I jumped out of the boat, not even thinking about the alligators, not even caring. At least I remembered the gun.

The spotlight lit my way as I headed in the direction of the scream. Charlie must have gotten rid of all the alligators in the vicinity, unless they'd smelled my gris-gris, or maybe they'd slithered back into the water to avoid . . .

Whatever the hell had come after Charlie.

I paused, listened, caught a faint rumble to my left. Tightening my fingers around the gun, I barreled through the overgrowth, shouting Charlie's name.

Some animals will run if you startle them. Then again, some won't.

I'd come far enough that the light from the boat was fading. When I burst through a tangle of weeds and into a small clearing, I had to squint to see. Or maybe I just had to squint because I couldn't believe my eyes.

Charlie was on the ground. Dead from the appearance of the throat wound. A man knelt next to him, fingers pressed to Charlie's neck. At first I thought he'd been attacked, too.

Blood all over a bare chest will give that impression.

But with that much blood, I should see a gap, a tear, a great big hole. He definitely shouldn't have been able to stand, to move, to walk toward me. I panicked and lifted the gun.

"Stop." My voice sounded thick, as if I were speaking through swamp water.

The man kept coming—fast—his long, dark hair flying around his face, giving me tantalizing glimpses of a nose, a chin, teeth. He snatched the pistol, and the bronze bracelet on his wrist shimmered as he tossed the weapon aside. I'd never flicked off the safety, but he didn't know that.

Then he shook back his hair, and I couldn't think beyond the sight of the face I'd seen twice—in the picture on the wall of the Ruelle Mansion and in my erotic dream of the night before.

"You're—"

I meant to say *dead,* but the word froze on my tongue when he grabbed me.

Solid, warm, real. He wasn't a ghost.

So what in hell was he?

7

This close I could smell the blood. Not his, I realized. Charlie's.

The thought caused me to stiffen, then attempt to pull away. He only held on more tightly.

"Where you goin', *cher*? The police will want to talk with you, I'm thinkin'."

I couldn't seem to put the pieces of the puzzle that was him together quite right. I knew his voice, remembered the way he'd called me *cher,* recognized the bracelet surrounding his wrist and the drift of his hair against his shoulders. But his face was that of a dream man long dead.

He frowned, gave me a little shake. "You OK? Think you might faint?"

"Wh-what—"

I couldn't catch my breath to ask . . . Who was he? *What* was he?

"Happened?" I blurted.

"What happened?"

I nodded. He shrugged. If he hadn't been so bloody, I might have gone gooey at the sight of all those rippling chest muscles.

"Heard a scream. Found him. Tried CPR. Didn't work."

Emergency procedures *could* explain the blood. Made a lot more sense than this man having killed that one. Still, I was too spooked to trust him completely.

"You didn't see anything?" I pressed. "Anyone?"

He looked away, then back. His eyes were such a brilliant blue, I was reminded again of my dream. How could I have dreamed his face, his eyes, when, at the time, I'd never seen them?

That dream was starting to creep me out almost as much as the dead Charlie.

"Something big went crashing that way." He let me go to point into the depths of the swamp.

"How big?" I asked, and my voice shook.

He didn't answer, instead moving across the grass, then kneeling to get a better view of the body.

I didn't want to, but I followed.

"Animal, most like." He tilted his head, staring at the torn throat. "Men don't do that."

True, but—"What kind of animal would attack a man? Tear out his throat?"

"One you don't want to meet."

I was beginning to get used to his compact sentences and the cadence of his accent.

"Got a cell phone, *cher*?"

"Huh?"

That voice did funny things to my insides.

He smiled. Or at least I thought he did. His lips turned

up, but his teeth never made an appearance and the sadness in his eyes didn't lighten. Then again, what could lighten this situation? Charlie was dead.

"A phone. To call de police."

Good idea. Except my phone was on the boat.

"Damn," I muttered.

He merely lifted his dark brows.

"I left it on the boat. In my bag."

I didn't want to admit I was afraid to go back there alone, but I didn't have to. He gave a sharp nod and strode toward the sound of the idling motor and the blare of the spotlight.

Darkness closed in without him. The swamp was both damp and chilly. Even if it had been hotter than a Louisiana July, I'd still have shivered. There was something out here, and as Cassandra had said, it killed.

My gaze went to Charlie. I'd seen dead bodies before. But not like this.

Several quick splashes near the boat were followed by a low, warning growl that seemed to flow over the swamp grass. I swung in a circle, searching for movement, finding none. I missed Charlie's gun almost as much as I missed Simon. I was never going to find the thing out here. It had probably already sunk to the bottom of a murky, muddy hole.

I started for the boat, just as—hell, I didn't even know his name—burst into the clearing. The blood was gone; his skin still sparkled with moisture. His hair was slicked away from his face.

The splashing I'd heard must have been him washing off the blood in the tributary. But the growl?

"Did you see anything? Hear anything?" I seemed doomed to repeat myself.

"Gators." He handed me the phone. "Keep an eye out."

Did alligators growl? I couldn't recall.

"You'll need to call the St. Tammany Parish Sheriff's Department."

In Louisiana a parish is the equivalent of a county. Has been for over two centuries.

"Should you have washed up?" I asked. "Wasn't that evidence?"

He stiffened. "Evidence of what? You think I killed him?"

I didn't, not really. Charlie had been attacked by an animal, and while I was searching for a loup-garou—a werewolf—I didn't really believe one existed. The very idea that this man could have morphed into a wolf, killed Charlie, then morphed back into a human being and hopped into his pants before I got here was ludicrous. But something *was* strange about this place, the deaths, even him.

He wandered to the edge of the clearing and peered into the darkness. "What did you hear while I was at the boat?"

I hesitated. *Had* I heard a growl? Considering the nature of Charlie's wound, I thought so.

Black coyote, Louisiana wolf, ABC, or an undiscovered cryptid—whatever was out there, if it could kill, it could certainly growl.

"An animal," I answered. "Didn't sound like an alligator. More like something with claws and fur."

He continued to stare, and I took the opportunity to call information for the number of the St. Tammany Parish Sheriff's Department. I had them connect me and after I stated my problem and my location, I was promised help would arrive within minutes. Considering someone had died here not more than a few days ago, I wasn't surprised a police car cruised nearby.

I shut off the phone, dropped it into my pocket, then contemplated the distractingly gorgeous back of the man whose name I had yet to discover.

"Who are you?" I whispered.

"You know."

For an instant—in the swamp, in the dark—I had a vision of him turning, teeth bared, eyes wild, hair sprouting from his skin even as a tail sprouted from his spine.

I shook off the image. He wasn't the loup-garou, because there was no such thing.

Still, when he faced me, I tensed. But it was just him—whoever he was—his bright blue eyes fixed on mine as he waited for me to say something.

"Um—I do?"

"I'm Adam Ruelle."

Recluse. Soldier. Swamp native. Why hadn't I made the connection before? Perhaps because I'd asked him once and he'd . . . ignored me.

"You own this land," I said.

He dipped his head but said nothing.

"And the mansion." I suddenly remembered. "There's a picture on the wall upstairs."

He didn't react to the information that I'd been inside his family home. From the appearance of the place, who hadn't been?

Taking a deep breath, he let it out on a long, resigned sigh. "I favor my great-great-grandfather."

I opened my mouth, shut it again. What had I expected? That he'd admit to being a ghost? As amazing as his explanation was, it made a lot more sense than any other.

"*Favor* is too mild a word," I muttered.

"Got that right."

"Your family—"

"There is no family," he said sharply, eyes flashing.

"None?"

"Everyone is gone but me."

"Oh," I said faintly. "I'm sorry."

"I'm not."

I'd heard of people who did not get along with their families. Hell, I was one of them. But I didn't wish them dead. Then again, my parents were just stick-up-the-ass, judgmental elitists. Who knows what Adam Ruelle's had been?

"Did all the Ruelle men . . ." My voice faded. Why was I asking a perfect stranger about his family?

Because Adam fascinated me, and not merely his face, that body, his brooding, secretive manner. I had the distinct impression Frank had been right. Adam knew something; he just wasn't telling.

"Did all the Ruelle men look so much alike?" I finished.

He shrugged. "Some."

That answer was nearly as helpful as his usual lack of one.

Suddenly he stood right next to me, so close his body heat pressed against my damp, chilled skin. Why didn't the man wear a shirt? Although some might consider it a sin to cover such a magnificent chest with cloth.

"You should go," he said quietly.

His being so close reminded me of the first time we'd met—how he'd grabbed me, held, touched, frightened me—and I couldn't breathe. My dream came back, and my face flushed even as my body responded to the memory of sex we'd never had.

"Th-the police," I stammered, unable to tear my gaze from his.

"After they come. Leave de swamp. New Orleans. Louisiana."

"I can't."

"Why?"

"I promised—" I broke off, unable to voice my vow, my pain, my need.

He took my hand, and then I couldn't speak. Not that the touch was anything more than casual. Still, I felt it all the way to my toes.

I was a young, healthy woman, sure I wanted sex, but what I wanted even more was skin against skin for no other reason than comfort.

"What did you promise?" Ruelle tilted his head and his hair swung loose from his shoulder.

I had a sudden image of that hair drifting down my body, the tactile sensation more erotic than any I'd ever known. I glanced away. That *hadn't* happened.

"I took a job. To prove the unbelievable is true."

He stared at me blankly.

"The paranormal?" I tried again.

"Ghosts?" Adam's gaze lifted to the night. "You came to de right place."

"Not ghosts. Creatures."

"Monsters?" His sharp eyes returned to my face. "Why would anyone want to prove such a thing?"

I couldn't talk about Simon with a half-naked man who'd aroused the first dollop of lust in me since I'd lost him, but Adam's questions made me think.

Simon had been an intellectual with a splash of the fey. Only those who could believe in the unbelievable had any success in cryptozoology, which was probably why I hadn't.

Whenever I'd voiced my practical, scientific opinion Simon had smiled as if I were a deluded child and said, "We can't see air. We can't see love. But they're there. Always."

This justification had never quite cut it for me.

His original interest in wolves had turned into an obsession with werewolves that had been the one thing that lay between us. I wanted to do the work I'd been trained to do—seek out unknown animals—Simon just wanted to chase the magic.

Suddenly Ruelle tensed, and his gaze flicked to the shadowed, swaying grasses surrounding us.

"They come," he murmured.

I spun around, my mind conjuring images of a hundred possible things that might be coming. So when two policemen broke from the darkness, for an instant I couldn't remember why they were there. How could I have forgotten dead Charlie?

A howl split the night, fleeing toward the crescent moon. The officers glanced uneasily at each other. They knew as well as I did what a coyote sounded like, and that wasn't it.

"Thought you said there were no wolves in Louisiana," I muttered.

One of the policemen had pulled out a small notebook and started toward me. At my words, he glanced up with a frown. "Ma'am, I've never spoken to you in my life."

"I was talking to—" I turned.

Ruelle was gone.

8

The officers were more interested in my claim that I'd spent the better part of the last hour with Adam Ruelle than my tales of an invisible growling beast that might or might not have killed Charlie.

"No one's seen Ruelle in years. Most folks think he died in the swamp."

"I guess most folks are wrong," I said.

The officers—both young and buff, one white, one black—exchanged glances.

"What?" I asked.

"Some say he's a ghost."

I'd thought that myself, but did a ghost let off body heat? Could a ghost hold your hand? Or fetch a cell phone? I didn't know, and I didn't plan on asking these children. Although they were probably around thirty, like me, they seemed eons younger.

The two skirted the damp earth near Charlie, taking care not to disturb the evidence as they peered at the ground.

"Huh," said the blond, baby-faced officer with a name tag that read: *Cantrel*.

"Yeah," said the other, who went by the name of Hamilton.

I waited, but neither of them was forthcoming with any info.

"What?" I asked, a little more loudly than last time.

"Only tracks are the victim's and yours."

I hadn't thought to search for tracks. Hadn't thought beyond my fear and the strange feelings Adam Ruelle had engendered in me.

"There aren't any animal tracks?"

"Sure." Hamilton nodded. "Big dog maybe."

I joined them to peer at the light wreath of paw prints surrounding Charlie. "That wasn't a dog."

"How you know for sure, ma'am?"

"I'm a zoologist. I've seen wolf tracks."

"There aren't any wolves in Louisiana."

"Is that like the state motto or something?" I rubbed at the pain right between my eyes. "Wait a second." I dropped my hand. "No other tracks but mine, Charlie's, and the—" I waved at the canine impressions.

"None."

No wonder they didn't believe Ruelle had been here. The man hadn't left any tracks.

I frowned. Then again, he hadn't been wearing any shoes.

By the time the other officers arrived, I'd finished my statement. They cordoned off the scene, then began to gather evidence and prepare the body for transport. Cantrel offered to take me back to my car, and I gratefully accepted. I didn't want to go alone, even if I had been capable of driving an airboat.

A short while later, he deposited me at the dock. "We'll be in touch."

"Do you have any leads in these murders?"

"Murders?" Genuine surprise twisted the word.

"I heard another man had his throat torn out in the swamp."

"So?"

"Two men, killed the same way. I'd think homicide would be working overtime."

"Homicide?" He laughed. "By a dog?"

"That wasn't a dog, and you damn well know it."

The anger in my voice made him stop laughing. He glanced at the flowing tributary, then back at me. "My boss thinks there might be a rabies problem. Feral dogs. Even coyotes. Virus spreads like wildfire."

I lifted a brow. He could be right. Except a rabid animal wouldn't have run from Ruelle and me after killing Charlie. A rabid animal would have attacked us, too.

I knew a little bit about rabies. Certainly the infected animals were vicious, violent, but they were also as good as dead. If there were a rabies epidemic in the Honey Island Swamp, there'd be a lot more bodies. Both human and beast.

Cantrel climbed back on the airboat, sitting in the driver's seat with a confidence that revealed he'd been there before.

"You seem to know what you're doing." I waved a hand at the vehicle.

"I've been driving these all my life."

"You're from the area?"

"Right around here."

"Then you knew Charlie."

"Yeah." He sighed. "Decent guy."

We both went silent, thinking of Charlie.

Cantrel straightened—all business once more. "You'll need to stay out of the swamp now, ma'am. Too dangerous."

"I don't have much choice. I've been hired to—"

I broke off. I couldn't say I was looking for a loup-garou. Cantrel might just commit me to the insane asylum. Around here, they probably still had one.

"Hired to what?" Cantrel pressed.

"Research," I said, which covered quite a bit and usually bored people so much, they stopped asking questions.

"I thought you were a zoologist. Shouldn't you be . . . in a zoo?" He flushed. "I mean, working there."

I didn't want to explain what I really was. So I didn't. "I'm working here."

"It'd be best if you stayed out of the swamp." He glanced at the crescent moon slowly moving across the night sky. "At least for a few days."

Before I could question him further, he started the motor and whirled away.

Once I was alone, the silence surrounded me. I glanced toward the water and caught the glint of the moon off several sets of bobbing eyes, though none of them seemed interested in getting any closer.

I patted my gris-gris. For a bogus protection charm it worked pretty well. Nevertheless, I hurried to my car and returned to the city.

Bourbon Street was in full swing. I glanced at my watch. *Midnight.* Why did it feel so much later?

I wasn't hungry, but I hadn't eaten all day and while my body could definitely stand to lose a few pounds, I knew better than to skip food entirely. I enjoyed fainting even less than I enjoyed wearing Lycra.

I forced myself into the crowd and let them push me along the scarred, broken sidewalks, past the bars, the strip joints, the souvenir shops that sported T-shirts with obscene slogans, until I found a restaurant that wasn't too busy. Then, with a mighty thrust, I tore myself away from the throng and stumbled into a cobblestone courtyard filled with tables.

I chose one nearest the street. While I might not enjoy walking in a crowd, I definitely liked watching them. Though loud and mostly drunk, the Bourbon Street horde was fun. Cheery people visited New Orleans, and those who lived here loved it.

Sure there was voodoo and murder and something in the swamp, but this was also the Big Easy, and it had become that for a reason. New Orleans was the land of great music, good food, never-ending booze, hot sex. During the day, the rot showed. But at night, the neon camouflaged everything.

I ordered a zombie—why not?—and a po'boy. It wasn't until I was halfway through the food and all the way through the drink that the now-familiar sensation of being stared at came over me. However, there weren't any alligators on Bourbon Street, unless you counted the stuffed ones in the shop windows.

Uneasy, I glanced around, but all the other diners were busy with their own libations. The waiters were waitering; bartenders, bartending.

I slid my gaze toward the crowd, but it continued to flow by without any hesitation. I told myself I was exhausted from the combination of a drink, a full stomach, and a busy day, then paid my check and left.

The uncomfortable sensation continued. I glanced back every few seconds, but with hundreds of people on the street, I couldn't determine if any single one *meant* to follow me. Ducking into my hotel, I slipped behind a pillar and peeked out.

Nothing.

As I headed upstairs, I told myself I had good reason to be spooked. Someone had put that flower in my room. Someone had taken it out again.

I unlocked my door, checked the bathroom, the closet, a shady corner. No one here but me.

My gaze was drawn to the balcony. I found myself crossing the room, opening the French doors, stepping outside. I let my gaze wander over the crowd from above, and I saw him.

The revelers flowed around the man as if he were a huge rock in the middle of a river. He never glanced at them, just continued to stare at me. He was no one I'd ever met, yet somehow I knew him.

His clothes were dirty, torn, his hair wild; he wasn't wearing any shoes. What was the deal with shoes around here?

My phone started ringing—loud, shrill—and I spun toward the room, heart thundering. When I got myself under control, realized it was just the phone, I turned back, letting it ring.

He was gone, of course. No sign of him anywhere. Not that he couldn't disappear into the crowd, a bar, hell, maybe thin air.

The damn phone kept trilling. Wasn't there voice mail in this place? I snatched it up.

"Yes?" My heart still pounded fast enough to make black dots dance in front of my eyes. I needed to *breathe*.

"Diana."

Frank.

"I've been calling for hours. I was worried."

"Mmm," I murmured, staring at the wide-open balcony doors. Should have shut those.

"Is something wrong with your cell?"

Mechanically I patted my pockets, pulled out the phone, remembered shutting it off after calling the police.

"I was . . . in the field."

"I suppose it wouldn't do for you to sneak up on the loup-garou and have your phone frighten him away."

As if I could sneak up on a werewolf—I sighed—or any wolf, for that matter.

"What have you found?" Frank continued.

"Nothing really."

"What have you been doing with your time?" His voice was sharp, accusing, annoying as hell.

"My guide's dead."

A shocked beat of silence came over the line before Frank drawled, "That didn't take long."

"What didn't take long?"

"For the loup-garou to get him."

I frowned. "Why do you think a wolf killed him?"

"Didn't it?"

I was still on the seeing-is-believing plan, and I'd seen nothing but a tail. Could have belonged to anyone.

I meant any*thing*.

"I rented the Ruelle Mansion for the next month," Frank continued, letting the matter drop. "You can move in whenever you like."

"Great. I'll have my things shipped from storage."

"Let me know where they are, and I'll take care of it."

Usually I paid the owner of the storage facility to do that, but if Frank wanted to pay, I was all for it. I gave him the address.

I almost asked if Frank had rented the place directly from Adam Ruelle, but I recalled his reaction the last time I'd mentioned the name and decided to keep the question to myself. Frank thought Adam knew something, and maybe he did. But I'd find out what for myself.

"I'll arrange for a new guide," Frank said, as if his last arrangement hadn't died from a mortal throat wound.

"I'll take care of it."

In truth, I didn't plan on hiring anyone. I couldn't put another person in danger. I'd buy a gun; I'd done so before. Then I'd explore the swamp on my own.

"If that's what you want," Frank agreed. "I'll call you tomorrow."

"How about if I call you when I have some news?"

I couldn't work if he was going to check up on me all the time. He was already making me half-nuts.

"All right," he said slowly.

"I'll be out in the field a lot," I explained. "My phone will be off."

"Of course."

Frank still sounded a bit miffed, but he said good-bye without further comment.

I moved to the balcony, checked the crowd once more. No one paid me any mind, which was as it should be.

I began to think I'd only imagined being followed— again. I rationalized that even if the man had been staring at me, and I kind of thought he had, it was because he liked redheads, big girls, or balconies on Bourbon Street.

Still, I shut and locked the French doors before heading for my laptop. I had an idea.

Though wolves usually claim a fairly large territory, the proximity of the recent deaths made me think this wolf didn't. Although, for all we knew, the thing had been killing throughout the swamp—a distance of some 250 square miles—and only the bodies closest to civilization, i.e., on the Ruelle property, had been found.

I'd bookmarked the articles Frank had originally given me, and I brought them up on the screen, clicked through, made a few notes.

I was just about to do a search for other mysterious animal killings under the crescent moon when a tiny photo of one of the swamp victims caught my eye. I clicked on the enlargement feature, and then I couldn't move, speak, even breathe.

Hell, I could barely think.

9

I leaned closer, squinting at the screen. The man was dead; he couldn't have been standing outside my hotel room watching me. I knew that as well as I knew my bra size. So why were my hands shaking?

"Place is getting to you," I muttered. "Haunted houses. Werewolves in the swamp. Voodoo priestess."

Maybe I should talk to Cassandra. If anyone would know why I'd seen a dead man walking, that someone would probably be her.

Except it was well past midnight and there was no way I was going out on the street in the dark—even if it was lit up like Mardi Gras.

Instead I returned to my research, found several articles about dead people in the swamp, cross-referenced them with the phases of the moon, and came up with a list.

I found no mention of rabid animals, rogue beasts, or a serial killer. Which struck me as odd. Had no one but me and Frank noticed bodies were piling up under the crescent moon?

I studied the dates. Over the past ten years there hadn't been more than three bodies found per annum. Which was probably why there hadn't been an outcry. Especially in an area where death lived everywhere and had for a very long time.

According to my Internet sources, my guidebook, and my memories, New Orleans could have been called the Big Epidemic instead of the Big Easy. As it was located below sea level, between Lake Pontchartrain and the Mississippi River, yellow fever had loved the place. From 1793 to 1905 there were twenty outbreaks.

Besides the plagues, they had starvation, war, pestilence. The usual. However, in New Orleans the troubles seemed multiplied. Which is probably why when they partied, they did so for days.

I continued to search for deaths, disappearances, locations. About 2:00 A.M. my eyes drooped. I was so tired, I barely got my clothes off before I fell into bed. The next thing I knew, the sun was up.

No dreams. No visitations. No flowers. A good night.

I took a shower, snagged some coffee, and headed for Cassandra's. On the street, shopkeepers sprayed the sidewalks, flushing away the refuse left over from the nightly celebration. Water dripped from balconies and onto my head as residents watered their plants. I dodged people meandering down Bourbon Street with cocktails in plastic glasses. Had they ever gone home?

The door to the shop was locked. I glanced at my watch, then the sign on her window. Two hours until she opened for business. I needed to talk to her *now*.

I'd just lifted my hand to knock when she opened the door. My eyes narrowed. "How did you know I was here?"

"How do you think?"

She turned, leaving the door open. I stepped inside.

"Lazarus?" she called.

I froze, one foot in, one foot out.

"You mind shutting that?" she called. "If he sees the daylight, he'll bolt."

I cringed at the thought of Lazarus bolting over my sneakers, or maybe up my leg, and slammed the door. "How does a snake bolt?"

"You'd be surprised."

"Why is he out of his cage?"

"I let him out at night." Cassandra went down on her knees, peeking under one of the display cases. "Would you want to be stuck in a cage every minute of your life?"

Lazarus was a snake. Did he have wants and needs?

Something skittered across the open space. "There he is," I said, just a little too loud.

Cassandra started, bumping her head on the case before giving me a disgusted glare. "I thought you were a scientist. How can you be afraid of snakes?"

"Who said I'm afraid of snakes?"

She snorted.

"Call me crazy," I said stiffly, "but I don't like being in a small confined space with a freaking python."

"He's not interested in you."

A slight thud caused me to turn. Lazarus was right behind me. I stared at the odd growth in his throat. Or was that his neck? Maybe his body?

"There you are!" Cassandra hurried over and snatched him up, popping the snake into his cage, then flipping the lock.

"Does he have a tumor?" I asked.

"What?" Horrified, she bent and peered at him.

"That big bump."

"I thought you were a zoologist."

"Crypto."

"Still—didn't you study reptiles?"

"As little as possible."

She put a hand on her hip and tilted her head. "What do snakes eat?"

"Rodents." The light dawned. "That's what's in his throat."

"Another reason I set him free at night. He's much better than a cat. Never, ever, brings me a present." Cassandra shuddered.

I'd never had a cat, never had a pet. Can you imagine my mother allowing an animal to walk on her winter-white carpet? She'd rarely allowed *me* there.

However, I knew cats liked to share. Or maybe brag. I could see Cassandra's point, though I'd stop short of be-friending a python.

Cassandra turned away from the snake. "What brings you here?"

I hesitated. It was one thing to consider asking the advice of a voodoo priestess in the middle of the night and quite another to actually do it in the daylight.

"Tea?" She pushed through the beaded doorway without waiting for my answer, which would have been "ack" if I hadn't known that was rude.

I followed her into a quaint kitchen. "Don't suppose you have coffee."

"You suppose right. The stuff will stunt your growth."

I lifted a brow at her petite form.

"Never mind." Cassandra set the tea on the table and motioned me into a chair. "What happened?"

I found myself telling her everything. Since Simon's death I'd had no one to confide in, no one to bounce ideas off of, no one to trust. Why I'd chosen Cassandra I wasn't sure. She just had a way about her.

Despite her youth, she seemed wise. Her eyes were a little sad, as if she'd seen more than she should. I sensed she'd lost someone, too, someone she'd loved. Despite our differences, I felt a kindred spirit and I responded.

She listened to all that I told her, not speaking until I was through. "Comparing a news photo and a man you saw from pretty far away is a stretch."

"I know."

"He could be a relative of the deceased. Resemble him just enough to throw you off."

"Most likely."

Cassandra took a sip of her tea, swallowed, set the cup down with a *click,* and met my gaze. "Then why are you here?"

"Exactly."

She blinked. "What?"

"Why *am* I here? I'm not the spooky type. I don't believe in this stuff. Yet here I am, asking a voodoo priestess why a dead guy was following me down Bourbon Street. Why?"

"You've lost your mind?"

"I'm starting to wonder."

"Maybe you just need a friend."

I lifted my gaze. "That pathetic, am I?"

Cassandra smiled. "Not at all. You travel a lot. How could you make friends?"

"Even if I was any good at it."

"You seem pretty good at it to me." I half-expected her to reach over and pat my hand. "Anyway, you came to the right place."

"For a friend?"

"That, too. I like you, Diana. I think I have something that'll help you out."

Cassandra stood, then headed into the shop. I followed. A quick glance into the snake cage revealed Lazarus at work on his breakfast. At least cats ate their prey, eventually; they didn't wear it.

"If you see the guy again, blow this into his face." She handed me a tiny burlap bag.

"More gris-gris?" I asked, my fingers searching for, then finding the one I'd stuffed into my back pocket.

"No. This'll tell you if he's dead."

I frowned at the sack. "It'll tell me if the man who's following me down the street is dead?"

"Yes."

"Cassandra, what are you talking about?"

Her brow furrowed. "Zombies."

"Zombies!"

She winced. "You don't have to shout. What were you asking me about?"

"A dead guy."

"Who was walking. Add them together and that equals zombie."

"In New Orleans maybe."

"In any damn place."

She was right. I *had* come to ask about zombies; I just hadn't wanted to ask. But now that she'd answered . . .

"How are zombies raised?"

"I'm not exactly sure." Her lips pursed. "There are a lot of theories, spells, but I've never been able to raise one."

"You've tried?"

She shrugged. "It takes a lot more power than I have."

"Power?" I couldn't believe I was talking about this.

"Raising the dead is serious business."

"No shit," I mumbled.

"You don't believe, even though you've seen."

"We don't know what I saw. Probably the guy's cousin, uncle, twin."

"Use the powder; then you'll know."

"What happens if I blow this stuff into a zombie's face?"

"The one who raises the zombie gives it purpose and strength. His or her power keeps the zombie moving physically. Mentally they just aren't right."

I was starting to get the drift.

"If I blow this in his face—"

"The magic dies. He'll revert to a corpse right before your eyes."

IO

"Cassandra, this is ridiculous."

"Try the powder; then tell me it doesn't work."

"Fine." I stuffed the bag into another pocket. "Thanks."

"That's what I'm here for."

"I'll—uh—be staying at the Ruelle place from now on."

She lifted her brows. "How did you manage that?"

"My boss." I shrugged. "You know where I can get some camping equipment?"

There were a few things I didn't have—like mosquito netting. It had been a while since I'd gone anywhere this tropical.

Cassandra gave me an address. I wrote out my cell phone number. "In case you need me."

Although what *she'd* need *me* for, I had no idea. Still she smiled as if I'd just given her a gift beyond rubies and walked me to the door.

"You aren't going to be there alone?" she asked.

"Probably not," I muttered, and headed for the hotel.

I checked out, got directions to the address Cassandra

had given me, charged what I needed, and drove to the mansion. On the porch sat my camping equipment. I don't know how Frank had gotten the stuff here that fast, and I didn't care. He was the greatest.

As soon as I'd unloaded, a sudden compulsion to do something proactive made me head into the swamp. If I was going to take a look around, I wanted to do it in the daytime.

I found the location of last night's "incident" without too much trouble. Yellow crime scene tape stands out pretty well amid the swaying grass and cypress trees. I resisted the urge to tear it down. Behavior like that could earn me a few days in a cell.

I spent far too long in the swamp. The place was both wild and tranquil, steamy with heat, yet filled with cool water. I saw birds I'd never seen before, plants, trees, flowers, fish. I was captivated, entranced, mesmerized, which was the only reason I didn't notice the sun falling down.

I discovered a field of fire irises and used the pocketknife I'd just purchased to saw through a few stalks. As I gathered them into my arms, something caught my eye. Thinking I'd see the tip of a tail once again disappearing into the swamp, I gaped at the shape of a man in the shadows of a cypress tree.

I knew that silhouette—the broad shoulders, the slim waist, the tousled hair.

"Adam?"

I blinked and he was gone.

Which was impossible. Nobody could move that fast.

I tightened my fingers on the knife, then hurried to the tree and walked around the huge trunk. There was nothing, no one, yet still I felt . . . something, and it wasn't friendly.

I stared upward, cringing at the idea of a man dropping from the tree and landing on me. All I saw was branches and moss; nevertheless, I cursed. Dusk hovered on the horizon.

With one last wary glance at the swamp, I folded the knife and put it in my pocket, then clasped the irises close to my chest and headed for home at a near run. Along with the thunder of my own frantic feet—now encased in unfashionable but practical hiking boots—I could have sworn I heard footsteps behind me.

I was officially paranoid.

As I burst out of the foliage and into the yard, the house seemed to stare back at me with a smirk. Not only was I paranoid but a little crazy also.

I ran inside and slammed the door, locking it behind me. No wonder the house seemed to be laughing. What good would a locked door do me when all the windows were broken? Why on earth was I out here without a gun?

From what I'd gathered on the Internet, it wasn't hard to buy one. No waiting period, no registration, no background check. God, I loved the South. First chance I had, I was using some of Frank's money on a pistol.

A thud from the second floor had my heart racing as fast as my feet had. I should have stayed in the city, but then I'd never find out anything. With a sense of déjà vu, I turned toward the steps.

Adam Ruelle stood at the bottom, holding the lantern I'd bought, wearing the usual frayed khakis. This time a white tank top covered his chest, the lack of sleeves only emphasizing the ropy muscles of his arms.

Confused, I glanced out the window, toward the swamp, where I could have sworn I'd seen him not more than fifteen minutes ago. "What are you doing here?"

"I could ask you de same thing." He set the lantern next to my backpack, sleeping bag, and portable stove. "This is my house."

"Not while I'm renting the place."

He frowned. "You rented it?"

"My employer did. I need to be close to the area where the—" I broke off.

He didn't seem to notice, staring at the flowers I clutched to my chest. "You shouldn't have brought those."

I lowered my arms, stared at the crushed blooms. "Why?"

"They attract—" He yanked them out of my hands. "Animals."

Before I could say anything, do anything, he opened the front door, walked to the dock, and tossed the fire irises as far away as he could before striding back inside.

"You're kidding," I murmured.

"I don't kid."

I wasn't surprised. The man hadn't cracked a smile since I'd met him.

"Someone left one on my bed at the hotel."

Had that someone been him? If so, why leave the flower then and take them away from me now? I was so confused.

Adam appeared deep in thought, more worried about the fire iris on my bed than I had been. Which couldn't be good.

"I was told those flowers were bad luck," I said. "I figured someone didn't much care for me."

His eyes flicked to mine, the bright blue a beacon in the hazy light from the lantern. "Who you think it was?"

"No idea. I'd just gotten into town at the time. How could I have pissed off anyone that fast?"

"It's a gift," he muttered.

"Thanks."

I plucked a stray red petal off my shirt and rubbed it between my thumb and forefinger. A spicy aroma arose, like cinnamon atop a bonfire. I could understand why an animal might be attracted to them. I was.

"At least I'm not nuts," I murmured.

"No?"

I narrowed my gaze. "I could have sworn someone was following me just now. But maybe it was . . . something."

He scowled. "What did you see?"

"Well, I thought I saw you, but that must have been a trick of the light. You were here. Right?"

"Right," he agreed, though he didn't sound convinced. Which was as bizarre as my seeing him in the first place. Didn't he know where he'd been?

"The police think you're dead."

"They aren't the only ones."

"You like being a ghost?"

A long moment passed, the silence broken only by a faint splash from the swamp. He went to the window and his whisper came out of the darkness. "I don't mind."

He seemed so sad, so alone. I'd been there, hell, I still was, and while sometimes I liked it, more and more lately I didn't.

I couldn't help myself. I inched in close and touched his arm. "You seem real enough to me."

He stiffened and I yanked my hand away, but he caught it in a swift, catlike movement as he turned. I didn't have time to think, let alone escape, even if I'd wanted to. He wrapped his long, strong arm around my back and kissed me.

I was so shocked, I let him. Or maybe I let him because the man kissed as if he did little else but.

Tongue, lips, teeth, he devoured. Nothing gentle in this kiss, all wet heat and lust. He twined his fingers in my hair; I dug mine into his shoulders and held on.

He tasted of mint, as if he'd just brushed his teeth. I ran my tongue along the straight, white expanse and he moaned, then nipped my lip.

A shudder ran through me. His kiss was as rough as his hands, and I relished it. I didn't know why. Simon had been gentle in all things, especially lovemaking.

Maybe that was why.

He wasn't Simon, and this wasn't love. I didn't want it to be.

I'd had my shot. One man, one woman, forever. I believed that. A woman like me didn't get two soul mates. Did anyone?

Since Simon was dead, I was doomed to be alone. But that didn't mean I couldn't have this.

I ran my palms over his arms, let my thumbs trace his collarbone, tangled my fingers in his hair. His skin was so soft over muscles so hard. I wanted to trace every inch of him.

I was overcome with a sudden urge to drop to my knees and score the ripples of his abdomen with my teeth. I'd never seen a man put together so well, not that I'd seen all that many.

His erection brushed my stomach; my gasp was captured by his mouth as his hand dipped inside my shirt, slid under my bra, his palm cupping my breast, testing the weight, thumb teasing one nipple even as his lower body skimmed softly against mine.

He kept kissing me; I couldn't think. I wanted nothing more than to feel his heat, his strength, his life. How could I ever have thought him a ghost?

Suddenly he tore away; I nearly fell. He stared at me wide-eyed, his mouth wet and swollen, as he shoved a hand through his tangled hair.

I'd tangled it. I wanted to do so again.

"I shouldn't have . . ." He made a vague gesture in my direction.

I swallowed. I could still taste him. "Why did you?"

He snorted. "Have you looked in de mirror lately?"

"I don't— I mean, I'm not—"

"You are."

"What?"

"Sexy."

I laughed. "You must be more deprived than I am."

The corner of his mouth lifted. "I'm sure that's true."

No one had ever called me sexy. Simon had loved me, but he'd been more interested in my mind than my body. We'd been colleagues, friends, then lovers. The sex had been good. This had been—

Catastrophic?

Mind-bending?

Life altering? Or just—

Wrong.

I didn't know this man. Not really. Everything I'd heard about him should make me wary.

Most, if not all, of the bodies had been found on his property; why wasn't he a suspect? Then again, the police were blaming animals. Unless Adam Ruelle planned to shape-shift beneath the crescent moon, he was innocent. At least of the Honey Island Swamp killings.

"Diana?"

I started as Adam brushed my hair from my face. His fingertips grazed my cheek, and I resisted the urge to rub my skin against his and purr. What was the matter with me?

"You should take your things and go back to wherever it is you came from."

That was the second time he'd told me as much.

I stared into his bright blue eyes. "It didn't feel like you wanted me to go."

"What I want and what's best for de both of us are two different things."

"I don't understand."

I waited for him to explain. When he didn't, I let out an exasperated sigh and turned away. He grabbed my hand and yanked me back, catching me when I stumbled, aligning our bodies just right all over again.

His jaw tightened. "What I want is to lie you down on de ground, right here, or maybe shove you against de wall, right there, and take you until you can't argue with me anymore."

As if he couldn't help himself, he leaned forward, brushed his lips to the swell of my breast exposed by our acrobatics.

"I want to mark you with my teeth." He scraped the sensitive skin just under my collarbone. "Bury myself in you."

He pulled me more tightly against him. I should have been insulted; instead I was interested.

"Over and over and over again. Me, you. You, me." He punctuated each hoarse whisper with a thrust of his hips.

"I'll be inside you day and night until you don't know where you begin and I end."

Leaning over, he nuzzled my cheek, put his mouth to the curve of my neck, and suckled my skin hard enough to leave the mark he'd spoken of. Then he lifted his head and his whisper brushed the moist imprint, making me shiver. "Are you afraid enough to run now?"

Afraid?

No.

Aroused out of my mind?

You betcha.

He stilled against me—hard, hot, his pulse beating out of time with mine. The intimacy of our position, his words, my feelings for a stranger, should have made me bolt. Instead I lifted my gaze and let him see that I wanted the same thing, too.

He cursed and swung away to stare out the window once more.

I wasn't sure what to say. Had the entire interlude been an attempt to make me flee? If so, he was the best actor on the planet. I could swear I'd tasted desire, and how could he fake a hard-on?

Dumb question. He was a guy. They could get a hard-on in a stiff breeze. Or so I'd heard. A man like Adam Ruelle was not only out of my league but also out of my realm of experience, seeing as I'd only known one man intimately in my life.

"You intend to stay?" Adam murmured.

"Damn straight." He couldn't get rid of me that easily.

He took a deep breath, let it out slowly, and faced me. "You'll need another guide."

"I don't need anything."

Except you, my treacherous body whispered. I ignored it; I'd gotten very good at that over the past few years.

"I'll do it."

For an instant I thought he meant do *it,* and why wouldn't I? We had, after all, practically done *it* standing up. Then I understood he was talking about guiding me into the swamp.

"No."

"You want to see my land, you go with me. Always. Never alone. You understand, *cher?*"

I understood. There were things out there I didn't want to meet alone. But did I want to meet them with Adam Ruelle? I wasn't sure. Still, what choice did I have? As he'd pointed out, this was his land. My boss might have rented the house, but I didn't recall anything about the swamp.

"Don't call me *cher,*" I said between my teeth.

His mouth lifted into a ghost of a smile. "I guess that means yes."

II

"You know what I'm looking for?"

I couldn't remember what I'd told him and what I hadn't.

"An animal that does not belong."

Which was as good of an explanation as any.

Something was out there. Something that did *not* belong—be it a wolf in Louisiana, a big, black cat in the swamp, or an animal that no one even knew about yet. Any one of them would be a coup for me to find.

The *snick* of a match returned my attention to Adam as he lit a cigarette. I considered protesting, but—

The place was trashed, and it was technically his place. What harm could one more cigarette butt do? Still . . .

"Those things'll kill you."

He stared out the window, his pose contemplative as he lifted the cigarette to his lips, took a long, slow drag, then blew smoke through his nose. "Something will kill me, but I doubt it'll be this."

I frowned at the statement, a variation of "we all have to die sometime." Except there was a vast difference between dying and being killed. Had his time in the military changed his thoughts on death?

I wanted to ask, but I wasn't sure how. This man's tongue had been in my mouth, his hand on my breast, his body pressed intimately to mine, yet I was uncomfortable questioning him about his past. Which only made me vow not to let his tongue anywhere near me ever again.

A vow easier made than kept, I was certain.

He glanced over his shoulder as he took another drag. "How did that flower get on your bed?"

"Someone put it there while I was sleeping."

His hand, halfway to his mouth with the cigarette, froze. He flicked the stub to the floor and ground it out. He was wearing shoes for perhaps the first time since I'd met him. Combat boots. Figures.

"You're sure?" he asked, the softness of his voice belying the tension in his body.

"Sure it was a fire iris or sure someone left it while I was sleeping?"

"Both."

"I went to bed without a flower, woke up with one at my feet."

Speaking about what had happened, I was creeped out all over again. Someone had been in my room while I was asleep and vulnerable. I didn't like it.

Adam's lips tightened and his hands clenched. He stared out the window again, and the silver light from the moon filtered over his face. He really was quite beautiful.

As if the glow pained him, he winced and stepped away. "Did you get rid of the flower?"

"Didn't have to. The thing disappeared."

He tilted his head, and his hair swung free of his shoulders. What was it about his hair that made my stomach all warm and jumpy? "So you think you may be losing your mind?"

I didn't answer, because I wasn't sure.

He faced the window, and though his next words were muffled, I could have sworn he said, "Join de club."

Before I could ask what he meant, a chorus of howls split the night. More than one this time and very close.

I raced across the room, but—surprise!—I saw nothing.

"Here." He pressed something cool and heavy into my hand.

A gun. *Oh, goody.*

"Do you know how to use one?"

"Yep."

"Use it." He headed for the door.

"Wait! I'll go with you."

Adam didn't pause, didn't look at me, didn't answer, just slipped outside. By the time I reached the porch, he was gone.

"How does he *do* that?" I muttered. And why had he given me his gun? What was he going to use? His bare hands?

Why not? According to local legend he was Cajun Commando. Of course, according to local legend he was also dead and there was a werewolf in the swamp.

Considering what I'd just heard, maybe there were a whole bunch of them.

My gaze swept the thick grass. This was the first time I'd discerned more than one, and I was excited. More than one would be easier to find.

Still, I hesitated. Adam had told me not to go out there

without him. But I was here to find the wolf or wolves, and they were close.

I checked the weapon—a .45-caliber Browning—fully loaded. Should be enough. I just needed one more thing.

Hurrying inside, I retrieved my camera. No one believed there was a wolf? I'd forgo the thousand words and take a picture. I needed the actual animal for proof positive, but a photo wouldn't hurt.

The night settled around me, damp and hot. The swamp grass whispered, though there wasn't even a flicker of a breeze.

I wished I could imitate the call of a wolf. Wolves howl for a number of reasons: to assemble the pack, warn of danger, locate one another, communicate. If I howled, they'd answer, and I'd know where I was going.

I continued in what I thought had been the direction of the howls. I couldn't be that far behind Adam, yet I didn't hear the muted thud of his boots or catch even the slightest hint of a cigarette.

I hadn't realized where I was headed until I broke into a clearing and found the yellow crime scene tape hanging limply in the no-breeze.

The blood had soaked into the ground, the moist nature of the land removing every stain. If not for the tape, no one would know something horrible had happened here last night.

A low, rumbling growl made me tighten one hand on the gun, while the other reached for the camera I'd slung around my neck.

The moon ducked behind a cloud, and I couldn't see more than a few feet. However, the grass rustled all around me, as if animals approached from several directions. But that couldn't be right.

Wolves didn't move in as if they'd learned military formations at West Point, and they didn't attack humans. Or at least they hadn't until they'd turned up in New Orleans.

Who was to say the wolves hadn't changed their hunting tactics along with their geography?

The lack of sight, the plethora of sound, made my nerves jump beneath my skin. I *had* to know what was coming. So I hit the flash on my camera, and the swamp lit up like a lightning strike.

Eyes stared back at me from the swamp. Alligator? Nutria? Wolf? Psychopath?

Turning to my left, I took another picture. The flash revealed what I already suspected. I was surrounded.

However, this time, before the light died, I saw not only eyes but also the outline of an animal. Too tall for a rat or an alligator, too short for a human being. But not a dog, not a coyote. An animal with longer legs and a bigger head than either a coyote or most dogs. In Zoology 101 those things added up to a wolf.

Amid the tension of being surrounded, a tiny bit of excitement filled me that I'd found something weird. That was, after all, why I'd come.

A growl rumbled to my right, another to my left, one behind. They were closer. I could almost feel their tepid breath. The hair on the back of my neck tingled and adrenaline rushed through me.

"Get lost!" I shouted, hoping I could make them run— the other way—hoping I wouldn't have to shoot them. Not only would it be difficult in the dark, but for proof a live creature was always better than a dead one. Still—

I lifted the gun. If they insisted.

Their measured tread came near, along with their panting, canine breath. I flicked the safety, and the night stilled, as if they'd heard the sound and knew what it was.

My arms shook with the effort of holding the gun, of forcing myself not to run. Predators chased prey. There were many zoologists who subscribed to the theory that if a rabbit didn't flee, a fox wouldn't even be interested. I'd never come down on one side or the other—until now. In the swamp, in the night, I kind of agreed with that theory, too.

How long I stood frozen, frightened, I'm not sure. But the moon danced out from behind the clouds and sprinkled just enough light over the clearing to reveal the truth.

I was alone.

"Shit."

I'd heard *something,* seen a lot of things.

"I am *not* crazy."

Then why are you talking to yourself?

Excellent question. One I didn't care to answer.

Diana.

I swung around. "Who said that?"

Déesse de la lune.

I'd taken Latin at my high-class prep school. But I knew French when I heard it. Too bad I couldn't understand it.

"Who's there?" I whispered.

There was a flash of movement in the grass. A rush of air, sound, the scent of evil.

Evil?

The moon disappeared again, as if someone upstairs had thrown a big switch, and all I saw was a shadow darting toward me. Bigger than a wolf, smaller than a man.

No true form, but enough substance that I felt the ground shake beneath its . . . feet? Paws?

I pulled the trigger.

The report of the gun was so startling, so loud, I took a step back and stumbled over a root, or maybe a rock. I hit the ground on my tailbone. My camera thumped against my chest so hard, I coughed. I waited for a scream, a moan, the thud of a body. I heard nothing.

I sat stunned, shaking, until the moon came out again; then I got to my feet, and I went searching.

No blood, no wolf, no man. Had I imagined everything?

I didn't think so. But I was alone in the clearing where Charlie had died. Just me, my gun, and—

I glanced down at the camera around my neck and smiled.

The pictures I'd taken.

I hurried back to the mansion and waited for dawn.

12

I hadn't planned to fall asleep. Hadn't realized I had until the pounding woke me.

"Adam," I mumbled, too tired to consider why he would bother to knock on his own front door. He certainly hadn't last night.

The man standing on the porch couldn't have been more opposite of Adam Ruelle if I'd created him myself. Six-foot-five and about 250, he had blond hair shorn close to his head. His muscles were big, his hands even bigger, and when he spoke I was reminded of home and not of hot sex, damp sheets, and jungle nights.

"Diana Malone?"

I blinked at his electric yellow tie, complete with a navy blue New Orleans Saints insignia. The sun sparked off his shiny shoes and straight into my brain. I grunted and walked away, leaving the door wide open.

He took the gesture for the invitation it was and followed. The place was still trashed and I didn't bother to apologize. I hadn't done it.

I also hadn't had time to do anything but get rid of the refuse. I'd figured on using the better part of today on a little cleaning, but now I needed to drive to town, find a one-hour photo shop, then hit the library and do a little research.

Though the Ruelle Mansion might appear to have come through a time warp from the Civil War, in truth the utilities had been updated in the last decade. However, the years of neglect had not been kind. The utilities weren't working.

I'd told Frank not to bother getting them fixed. I didn't want repairmen hanging around, asking questions, scaring away the wildlife. Besides, I'd camped out in worse places than this. I tugged out my battery-operated coffeemaker and got down to business.

"I'm Detective Conner Sullivan—New Orleans PD."

I'd already figured him for a cop. No one showed up this early in a suit and tie unless they were badge happy. What I couldn't figure out was what a guy like him was doing in a place like this. So I asked.

"Why is the New Orleans PD in St. Tammany Parish?"

I managed to get the coffee grounds into the proper container, then poured distilled water into the carafe and waited. I'd learned a long time ago that shaking the thing only made a mess. It didn't make the coffee come out any faster. More's the pity.

"I'm not squatting," I said when he didn't answer right away. "I rented this place fair and square. Or my employer did."

Sullivan stared at me for several seconds. His eyes were brown, which didn't seem right, but then, not every person of Irish descent possesses the blue or green gene.

"I'm not here to roust you," he murmured. "We don't usually send detectives for that."

"Good point." I picked up the coffeepot and lifted a brow in his direction.

"No thanks. I've already had so much I might jump out of my skin."

My lips twitched at the thought of this laconic man jumping anywhere over anything. I wondered if he were trying to make a joke, except he just kept staring at me with his curious cop eyes and flat, unsmiling mouth. Guess he was serious.

I poured myself a cup, then sat on my sleeping bag, leaving the only chair, a foldout canvas model, for him. He ignored it, choosing to stroll around the room peering into corners.

"I know you rented the place," he said, "but why?"

"I'm investigating reports of a wolf in the swamp."

"In Louisiana?" He cast me a quick glance. "I don't think so."

"I'll find that out and be on my way."

"What do you know about Adam Ruelle?"

I hid my surprise behind a sip of coffee. Why was everyone so interested in him? "According to the locals, he's dead."

Sullivan turned quickly for such a big man. "According to you, he isn't."

Hmm. He'd been busy this morning, checking my rental status, reading Cantrel and Hamilton's report.

I slurped more coffee, took my time swallowing, then lowered the cup. "A man who says he's Ruelle has been around."

"Where is he now?"

Good question. I had no idea where Adam lived. He just turned up wherever I was. Which was downright odd now that I thought about it. "Why do you care?"

Sullivan kept his dark gaze on my face. "A man was killed."

"Charlie. I know."

"Not him. Another man. Last night."

The cup halfway to my lips again, I had to tighten my fingers quickly before I dropped it into my lap. "Where?"

"Not far from the incident with Charlie Wagner."

I'd sworn I'd heard a growl, seen an animal, but what if I'd killed a person?

My hands started shaking, and coffee nearly cascaded over the edge of my cup. I set it on the floor as I took several deep breaths and forced myself to think.

I'd walked around, hadn't found anything. Not a person, not an animal, no blood. But it had been dark, and I wasn't Outdoor Girl no matter how much I liked to pretend that I was.

"Shot?" I blurted.

He gave me a strange look. An animal had killed the others. To know the man was shot—well, basically I'd just confessed.

Sighing, I ran through the names of everyone I knew. Not a lawyer among them. Hell.

"Not shot," Sullivan murmured.

Since I'd already fitted myself for a pair of handcuffs, my mind groped for meaning and quickly found one. "Another animal attack?"

I started to get to my feet, intent on seeing the body, checking the tracks, but his next words had me sitting right back down.

"Strangulation."

Now my mind was really groping. "Strangled? How?"

"Bare hands are the usual method."

I blinked at the repetition of my own thoughts of the

night before. Adam had given me his gun. He'd had only his hands for protection. Had he used them?

"Fingerprints?" I asked.

" 'Bare hands' was just a figure of speech. A rope was used. Probably gloves. Not much evidence." He took a deep breath. "There've been more disappearances than usual in and around New Orleans."

I narrowed my eyes. "And you're starting to think serial killer."

His face went blank. "I never said that."

He hadn't said much, including what he was doing out of his parish. But I could figure it out. Tourists and locals disappearing, some of them turning up in the swamp. When St. Tammany police found a body, it was natural they'd call the man in charge of the original case, see if their corpse matched any of his missing.

"Why do you want to talk to Adam?"

Sullivan lifted his brows at my use of a first name, but he didn't comment. "Dead people keep turning up on his property."

"The others were killed by animals."

"True. But this one is murder, and despite what you see on television, strangling someone isn't easy. You have to be strong and you have to be quick. There's a bit of an art to it. One someone like Ruelle would know."

"I heard he was in the Special Forces."

"He was in something," Sullivan muttered.

"What's that supposed to mean?"

"There's a block on his file that requires higher security clearance than I have."

"Bummer," I muttered.

Sullivan scowled. "Do you know where he is or don't you?"

"Don't," I answered with complete truthfulness.

The detective stared at me for several seconds. His stoic glare probably worked on most people, but not on me. He hadn't spent eighteen years with my mother.

"Fine." He reached into his jacket, pulled out a card. "If you see him, call me. Better yet, tell him to call. If he doesn't have anything to hide, we should be able to clear this right up."

"Uh-huh."

Sullivan cut a glance in my direction, but I just smiled as if I hadn't been being sarcastic.

"Who was the victim?" I asked as I walked Sullivan to the door.

"We don't know."

"Come on, Detective, the name's going to get out eventually."

"I hope so; then I'd know it." He shook his head. "This guy had no ID."

"Stolen?"

"Maybe. But his money clip was still in his pocket. His fingerprints didn't pop. There isn't a missing persons report that fits his description."

"If he's a tourist, it might take a while for anyone to notice he's gone."

Sullivan seemed about to say something more, then tightened his lips and kept further comments to himself. Considering this was shaping up to be a murder investigation, I didn't blame him.

"If you think of anything that might be useful," he stepped onto the porch, "let me know."

With a nod, I shut the door. I probably should have told Sullivan I'd been in the swamp last night, but I hadn't killed the guy and I hadn't seen anything.

Except a wolf or something like one.

A lie was a lie, even if it was by omission. However, I didn't want to be dragged downtown for questioning when I had an appointment with a one-hour photo shop.

"If there's anything on that film that'll help, I'll take the picture directly to the police station." I put my hand over my heart. "Swear."

Since there was no one to hear my vow, it wasn't really binding, but I felt better anyway.

I took a sponge bath, brushed my teeth in a bowl. I didn't mind camping, but the lack of a shower was a definite drawback. I'd have to rent a cheap hotel room once, maybe twice, a week, or I wouldn't be able to stand myself.

Grabbing the gun and my camera, two things I did not want to lose—though from the age of the garbage I'd removed from the inside of the house, no one had stayed there for months—I went out the door.

What could have spooked the homeless away from such a good flop spot? Had word gotten out that people were dying?

I shivered despite the early-morning heat. Not for the first time I questioned the wisdom of remaining in the swamp alone.

After tucking the pistol into the trunk with my computer, I headed for town. I probably should have unloaded the weapon—I wasn't exactly clear on the transportation-of-firearms rules around here—but the idea of having the bullets in one place, the gun in another, a rabid wolf or even a serial killer chasing me around and around and around . . . I decided I'd take my chances with the police.

I easily found a one-hour photo shop, dropped off the

film, and headed to the library for a little research. This early in the morning the place was cool and deserted. Just the way I liked it.

A quick trip through the search engine netted me nothing. Unless the Ruelles had written a book or had one written about them, that usually didn't work, but it was always a good place to start.

My next stop was the desk of the reference librarian. When in doubt, ask questions.

"I'm looking for information on a local family."

Short, thin, ancient, with granny glasses, clunky shoes, and—wait for it—a shawl, the woman's nameplate read *Mrs. Beasly.*

"Oh! Are you researching your family tree?"

Since she seemed so excited about the prospect, I said, "Sure."

"What's the name?"

"Ruelle."

Her bright, helpful smile faded. "Oh, no, dear, you must be mistaken."

"Why's that?"

"There hasn't been a female born to the Ruelles for at least a century."

I didn't miss a beat. "My connection is much older than that."

If I was going to lie, I might as well lie big.

"I see."

Mrs. Beasly contemplated me over the top of her wire rims. I wondered if she'd been an English teacher with a penchant for rulers before she'd migrated to the library. I hid my knuckles behind my back and tried to appear angelic, always difficult with my devilishly red hair.

"Isn't that a bit strange?" I asked. "No females."

"That isn't the only thing."

"Oh, really?"

She glanced around as if someone might be listening, but we were still the only people in the library. To help her out, I leaned over the desk and craned my ear in a conspiratorial manner.

"The poor family," she whispered. "It's as if they're cursed."

Cursed? my mind mocked. *As in . . . cursed to run as a wolf beneath the crescent moon?*

Couldn't be. Because I didn't believe in werewolves or curses. However, I didn't believe in coincidence, either.

How many curses were there around here?

13

"What kind of curse?" I managed.

"Oh, not a *real* curse." Mrs. Beasly laughed, veiny white hand pressed to her concave breast. "Just extremely bad luck. Or maybe insanity."

Insanity? Well, this kept getting better and better.

"You're talking about Adam?" She cut me a quick, sharp glance and I shrugged. "I read some before I came here. He was in the army. Flipped out."

"So they say." Her lips went prim. "But I wasn't referring to him."

I resisted the urge to shake her until all the secrets spilled out. Mrs. Beasly was the type of woman who wouldn't talk if you pissed her off—kind of like me. I'd bet my next hot shower that the info she would impart couldn't be found in any book. Instead, I held my breath and I waited.

After another glance around the echoing, cavernous library, she lowered her voice until I practically had to crawl over the desk to hear her.

"Suicide." The word seemed to slither across my neck like Lazarus.

"Who?"

"Both Adam's father and his grandfather."

I frowned. No wonder Adam had escaped to the army.

"The police were certain it was suicide?"

"They both . . ." She paused, uncomfortable. "Well, there's really no other way to say this except straight out. They blew their heads off."

"*Both* of them?"

She nodded. "There was an investigation. But the angle of the gun pretty much told the tale. The sons were always suspect, of course."

"Sons?"

"Adam's father was a suspect for his father's death, and Adam for his."

"Why?"

"The police thought there was money."

"But there wasn't?"

"Not only are the Ruelles cursed with insanity and sons, but everything they touch . . ." She spread her hands.

"Turns to shit," I muttered.

Her mouth pruned again. "If you must be vulgar."

I must.

"They're land-poor," she said. "The mansion, the swamp. Keeping that in the family takes a lot of money."

"Why is there a mansion near the swamp anyway?" I asked. That had always bugged me.

"The first Ruelle came to Louisiana from France by way of Canada."

Acadian. I thought so.

"Those people, the Cajuns, they kept to themselves,

but the Ruelles even more so. They bought that land for a song, and they refused through centuries of bad luck to let it pass out of the family."

I'd never understood the obsession with land, but wars had been fought, countless lives had been lost, over just that.

"Was there any indication of why the senior Ruelles killed themselves?" I continued. "A note?"

"Nothing."

"I'd like to read the articles on those deaths, but . . ."

I glanced at my watch. First I needed to pick up my film.

"I'll find them for you," Mrs. Beasly said. "I can make copies. A dollar a sheet."

"That would be great." I handed her ten dollars.

"I'll leave them at the desk. If I'm not here, someone will be. What's your name?"

"Diana Malone."

She gave me her English teacher stare. "I've never heard of the Ruelles having Irish relatives."

"Wrong side of the blanket," I said. "Hush-hush."

For an instant I thought she might refuse to help me, and why? She was a librarian, paid to impart information. What difference did it make who I was?

I guess not much, because she pocketed the money and said good-bye.

I hurried outside, surprised at what I'd learned. However, the real surprise awaited me at the photo shop.

I paid for the prints, anxiously drew them from the envelope, then nabbed the clerk and shoved one under his nose. "What happened?"

Since he was about ten years younger, four inches shorter, and twenty pounds lighter than me, he got that deer in the headlights look as his prominent Adam's apple began to bob. "I . . . uh . . . what?"

"There's nothing here."

"But—" He peered at the picture. "There is."

"I don't mean the swamp, the grass, the trees. There was something there."

"What?"

"I don't know!" I practically shouted. "That's why I took the picture."

The kid appeared more confused than ever. "You took a photo of something, and it isn't on the print?"

"Yes."

"That's impossible, ma'am. If there was something there, it'd be," he pointed to the lovely picture of night-time in the swamp, "there. Unless it was a vampire."

He snorted at his own wit. "No, wait, that's a mirror. Vampires don't have a reflection. It's werewolves that don't show up on a photograph."

I frowned, blaming the shiver that passed over me on too much air-conditioning for a steamy autumn day.

"What did you say?"

My voice must have alerted the kid to the fact that I was not amused, because he stopped snickering and retreated behind the counter. Like that would keep me from following him if I wanted to.

"Werewolves don't show up on film," he repeated.

"And you know this why?"

"I've lived in New Orleans all my life," he answered, as if that explained everything.

"There's no such thing as vampires or werewolves."

"No?" he murmured, the word taking on a faint French twist. "Maybe you should spend some time alone in the

Quarter after midnight. Or walk through the swamp under a full moon. You know why there are no cemetery tours after dusk?"

"People get robbed."

"Sure they do. And the dead also rise."

I stared at the young man who'd seemed so harmless, almost shy. Now he just seemed nuts.

"Ooookay." I backed toward the door.

"The only way to tell if a wolf is a werewolf is to shoot it with silver."

"Makes sense," I said. "Thanks for the tip." Was this guy for real?

I fumbled with the door, got it open, and fled into the heat.

"Not going back *there*," I muttered. Even if they hadn't screwed up my pictures.

It was only a coincidence that my photos showed nothing but grass, and werewolves didn't show up in a photo. Because there was no such thing, no such thing, no such thing.

And maybe if I clicked my heels together three times I'd be in Kansas and not in the middle of this mess. I was tempted to try, but I was fresh out of ruby slippers.

Instead I bought new film, telling myself the airport X-ray machines had ruined mine, then headed for the swamp. Not until I'd parked in front of the mansion did I remember the articles I was supposed to pick up at the library.

A rumble of thunder in the distance turned my gaze to the west. Huge, dark clouds billowed on the horizon. Looked like we were in for a doozy of a storm. Since I was used to wussy Midwestern thunderstorms, rather than Southern hurricane-force winds, tomorrow seemed as good a time as any to return to town.

Besides, if I dug out some soap, I could take a shower right in the front yard. Considering the heat index of the last couple days, the idea had too much merit to pass up.

I locked my camera and photos in the trunk with the gun, then hurried inside and grabbed what I needed, along with my gris-gris.

"When in Rome," I murmured as I shoved it into the pocket of my pants. I left the zombie-revealing powder behind, afraid the stuff would disintegrate, or worse, if wet.

The sky opened up when I stepped onto the porch. Though the rain was warm, steam rose when the drops hit the ground.

I dragged off my jeans, socks, shoes, and through an acrobatic maneuver managed to slide my bra from beneath my tank top. Then I walked into the storm.

I was drenched in an instant, my top and underwear plastered against me like a size 4 Lycra bodysuit. Quickly I made use of the soap and the shampoo. Needles of rain washed everything away; rivulets of water ran down my face so fast, I could barely see. When I was done, I continued to stand under the clouds, lifting my hands to the sky as I let nature cleanse me.

Déesse de la lune.

My eyes snapped open. Slowly I turned a circle in the yard. Why did I keep hearing those words murmured in French as if they were the whisper on the wind? Was I losing my mind?

I frowned at the Ruelle Mansion. Did everyone who lived in that place eventually eat lead?

Refusing to be spooked, I stalked to the porch, rubbed the towel over my body, and stepped into my jeans. I lifted my head, glanced toward the swamp, and saw someone watching me.

The rain beat down; the mist drifted up. I had a hard time focusing, but there was definitely a person, a man, leaning against a cypress tree about a hundred yards from the house. Spanish moss hung from the branches, nearly touching the ground, obscuring his face. But the outline of the body was familiar, as were the hair, the jeans, the bare chest.

"Adam?"

He didn't answer.

"I'm sick of this," I muttered.

I was going to confront him, ask all my questions, and demand answers. Tossing the towel on the porch, I headed into the storm.

The figure didn't move as I approached. He seemed wilder somehow—his eyes brighter, his hair more tangled, his body tense as a stalking beast. Without the shirt, skin slick with rain, I could see every ridge, every curve. He wasn't wearing his bracelet. I couldn't remember ever seeing him without it.

Why was he here? Did he want the same thing that I did? Mindless sex until I couldn't remember the questions anymore?

I reached the edge of the yard, the cusp of the swamp, and still he waited. Lightning flashed; water ran into my eyes. Impatiently I swiped at my face, and when I looked again, he was gone. Had I seen him or only wished that I had?

And why would I wish? The police wanted to talk to Adam Ruelle about strangling the life out of someone. I shouldn't go near the man, let alone lust after him.

Though he disturbed me in ways I didn't want to examine, had scared me more times than I wanted to count, I couldn't wrap my mind around the idea that Adam had killed someone with his bare hands.

I'd felt those hands on me, and while they'd been desperate, urgent, and rough, they hadn't been violent. However, that didn't mean they couldn't be.

Beneath the tree I found the slight indentation of a bare foot in the dirt. Then another and another, leading deeper into the swamp.

I wasn't crazy. He *had* been here.

I should turn back; I might get lost and wander for days. But I followed the tracks anyway.

Why I was so obsessed I had no idea. The man was a mystery, and I liked my life neat. Perhaps that explained my difficulty believing in the paranormal. The paranormal didn't make sense, hence the name. I hated things that did not make sense. I was obliged to make sense of them.

After a half an hour of traveling at a pretty fast clip, the trail petered out. I paused, ears straining, eyes searching. All I saw was the swamp in the rain; all I heard was that rain coming down. Then I smelled the faint, acrid scent of a cigarette.

As I blinked the water out of my eyes, my gaze was caught by what appeared to be a roof on the other side of a slight rise. I had no choice but to head in that direction, even when my bare feet sank to the ankles in muck.

I pulled them out, wincing at the disgusting sucking sound they made popping free of the greenish-brown goo. Luckily, once I hit solid ground, the rain washed away the slime.

I topped the hill and stared at the shack, which seemed to have sprouted from a bayou. The building resembled something straight out of *The Beverly Hillbillies III: Elly May Does Louisiana*.

"Good title for a porn flick," I murmured, peering at

the figure on the porch, one that could put pornographic thoughts into the mind of any woman.

A shirtless Adam Ruelle leaned against the railing, smoking as he watched the storm rage.

I glanced at the swamp, suddenly tempted to go back. A flicker of movement somewhere in the depths had me hurrying into the slight valley, stopping at the edge of the overgrown front yard.

The instant I appeared, Adam's attention fell from the sky to me. He took one last draw on his cigarette, then flicked the thing into the grass, where it hissed as the ember met rain.

He walked slowly down the steps and across the ground, stopping so close, the heat of his body battled the chill of mine. I half-expected steam to rise from my soaked clothes.

His gaze wandered over me; desire rolled across his face like thunder rolls across the sky. His eyes locked on my breasts, and I glanced down, my face heating at the sight.

I'd removed my bra, spent nearly an hour in the rain. Being topless would be less suggestive than wearing the soaked tank, which outlined the weight and fullness, seeming to accent the thrust of my nipples, magnifying the darkness of the areola.

He reached out, the tanned skin of his hand stark against the white shirt as he cupped one breast gently, almost reverently. Testing the weight, he skimmed a single thumb over the tip.

I opened my mouth to ask . . . something, and he yanked me against him. My breath caught, the sound both fear and excitement. I tilted my head, an offering, and his lips captured mine.

Our tongues met; his tasted of smoke and I liked it, which only showed how far gone I was. I'd never cared for cigarettes, but when Adam smoked them, I could only think of how I'd feel if he wrapped his beautiful lips around my nipple the way he wrapped them around a cigarette and suckled.

His arousal rubbed against me. My hands flitted over his skin, kneading the muscles, learning the curves and the dips. I couldn't think, could only feel both his desperation and my own. I should have protested, pulled away, but I didn't.

From the moment I'd first seen him we'd been headed for this. I could no more have stopped what was about to happen than I could have stopped the moon from growing larger with each passing night.

He lifted his head, glanced into the trees, frowned. I tangled my fingers in his hair; then I frowned, too.

He'd been out in the rain as long as I had, yet his hair was almost dry.

14

Adam licked my chin, nuzzled my neck, then captured my rain-puckered nipple in his mouth and gently bit the tip. I decided his hair didn't matter. Right now, neither would an earthquake.

I had questions, yes. But they weren't going anywhere and neither was I. I'd save them for after I'd had sex with a perfect stranger.

Well, not exactly a stranger. I skimmed my palms over his biceps. But damn close to perfect.

He didn't speak, which was fine with me. I wanted sex, not chatter.

His body slid along mine as he went to his knees and lifted my shirt. Mouth hot against my damp skin, he traced my rib cage, then swirled his tongue around my belly button.

The rain beat down on us both. I had a sudden urge to feel the droplets everywhere, so I pulled the tank top over my head and tossed it aside.

He looked at me and smiled—the first smile I'd ever

seen on his face—and my heart did a funny sort of stutter. Why did he have to be so beautiful?

Reaching up, he tugged the end of my hair. "Come."

I cast a confused glance at the house.

"Nah, *cher,* right here. I wanna see your red hair against de grass. I wanna be inside you with de rain comin' down."

Suddenly I wanted that, too. My knees gave way, and I joined him on the ground.

As I lay back, I expected an unpleasant, damp chill. But I was as wet as the earth and the afternoon as hot as the sun. When he dragged at my jeans, I merely lifted my hips and let them go.

Somehow he managed to lose his pants, too. No doubt he'd had a lot of practice. I pushed that thought out of my head. Who he'd done in the past, even *what* he'd done, had nothing to do with this.

The sky swelled above us, heavy with clouds and the rain. The wild vegetation shielded us from anyone who might walk by. As if there were anyone but the two of us this far into the swamp.

The thought made me bold. I wasn't Diana Malone; I was merely a woman who wanted a man. This man. And she could have him. No one would ever know.

His hard, clever hands skimmed over me, both insistent and reverent, arousing even as they soothed. His breath brushed my breast as he licked a drop of water from the curve.

"You're so wet," he murmured, the rumble of his voice a sensation all its own. "Are you as wet here," a finger traced my hip, my thigh, "as you are here?"

My legs fell open, expecting that clever finger to discover the answer. Instead he slid down my body in a movement so fast, it left me gasping, even before his tongue swept into me.

"Mmm-hmm," he said. "Wet both inside and out."

I wanted to protest. I'd never been much for oral sex, which always seemed so personal—maybe because it was. I barely knew this man. But when I shifted uneasily, he grabbed my hips in his big, hard hands and held me still as he continued what he'd started.

Within seconds I was beyond protest, tongue-tied. Thank goodness he had no such problem.

My body tightened, quivered, and he entered me in one smooth movement. As I was already convulsing, the press and release, the enticing rhythm of flesh into flesh, skin against skin, caused a desperate moan to escape. Horrified, I bit my lip, choked it back.

He gazed at me, the clouds swirling behind his head, both the trees and his hair whipping madly in the wind.

"Don't stop, *cher*. Make all de noise you want. No one'll hear you way out here. Besides," he flexed his hips and stroked me deeper, leaning down to nuzzle my neck, his now-wet hair tickling my cheek, "I'm not gonna quit until you scream."

"Th-that might take a while."

I wasn't much of a screamer.

"A man's gotta do what a man's gotta do. I don't care if it takes all night."

He began to move again, murmuring encouragement, telling me to touch him, take him, fuck him. The latter disconcerted me, but something in his voice, a note of desperation, a tiny quiver of need, made the word less a profanity and more of a plea.

I did as he asked, clenching around him as the tremor in his voice spread through both his body and my own. I felt him come as the rain swirled around us, and I got so caught up in the depth of sensation, the scent, the sound, the feel of him and me together in the half-light, that I forgot I'd already had one orgasm and went ahead and had another.

I forgot a lot of things while I lay there, Adam's head on my shoulder, his body still buried in mine. He shifted, sprawling half on the ground, half on me, his cheek pressed into my breast, his breath tickling my still-aroused nipple.

He traced a lazy finger across my belly. "You do that a lot?"

I stiffened. "Are you insinuating that I'm loose?"

"Loose?" He raised up on one elbow, using the hand that had been caressing me to shove his hair out of his face. His bracelet caught the light of the moon and turned from bronze to silver and back again. "You felt pretty tight to me." His fingertips skimmed the curls between my thighs, and my skin danced. "What I meant was, come twice in ten minutes."

My face went hot. I wasn't sure what to say. Was that slutty?

I'd been with one man before today. I'd loved him with all of my heart. We'd had a good sex life. The best. I'd never wanted anyone else. Until now.

Suddenly I felt as if I'd betrayed my best friend. I guess I had.

I started to get up, reach for my clothes. Adam yanked me back, and when I struggled he rolled his body on top of mine, capturing my legs between his and pinning my wrists above my head with one hand. The other held my hip still as I tried to buck him off.

"You keep that up, we'll go again. I'm game."

I could feel that he was. How could he be aroused so fast? What was he, superstud?

Dumb question.

"Don't be embarrassed, *cher*. You think a man doesn't want a woman to come every time he touches her? I liked it."

I had, too, but I wasn't used to discussing sex in such detail with my body still humming from his. I wasn't used to discussing sex at all. I'd learned the facts of life in the locker room of my private girls' school, and to tell the truth . . . they'd gotten a couple of things wrong.

"Where you come from that you make love like a wild thing and get all red in de face when you talk about it?"

"Love?" I blurted.

This hadn't been love, at least not for me. Not for him, either, I was certain. He didn't seem like the kind of man who fell in love.

"Figure of speech," he murmured, his voice trilling down my body, leaving goose bumps in its wake.

"Find another," I snapped, unreasonably annoyed at his cavalier attitude. Though why, I had no idea. I wanted him to be that way. I couldn't bear anything else.

"You'd rather I say 'you fuck like a wild thing'? How about 'screw'? 'Bang'? 'Boink'? None of them seemed de right word at de time."

My lips trembled, and he stared at me, horrified. Then I burst out laughing. I couldn't help myself. " 'Boink'?"

He smiled, too, then shrugged, the movement making his slick chest rub against mine in new and enticing ways. "See what I mean? Not de right word."

The laughter had been good, had made me feel almost closer to him than the sex had.

Almost.

Rain dotted my cheeks, sparkled in his hair. Suddenly my hands were free, and I drew a finger down his face. "There's so much about you I don't know."

Amusement fled as wariness took its place. "There are things you don't wanna know."

He rolled off me and to his feet in a quick feline movement. Leaning over, he dug his cigarettes out of his pants, then glanced at the still-dripping sky.

"Did you kill someone?"

I hadn't meant to ask that, wasn't sure why I had. Like he was going to tell me.

The pack of cigarettes crunched as his hand clenched, then he took a deep breath, and as he let it out, his muscles relaxed, his fingers unfurled, and the shiny crumpled paper thudded to the ground.

"You know I have."

I blinked. "Wh-what?"

"Why you ask if you don't want to hear? I was in de army. I did what I had to do."

"I wasn't talking about the army."

Slowly he turned, his eyes eerily light in the encroaching night. "What *were* you talkin' about?"

Adam might feel comfortable standing in the swamp buck naked, but I didn't. I reached for my shirt, drew it over my head, and started hunting for my underwear.

"A detective came to see me." Had it only been this morning? "There was a man killed in the swamp."

"Another animal attack," Adam murmured.

I found the white scrap of cotton and shoved my legs inside. My jeans were soaked. I debated trying to put them on and decided against it.

"Not an animal this time." I looked up. "Guy was strangled."

Adam's face revealed nothing; however, he didn't seem surprised. "You think I did that?"

"Did you?"

"Who was this man? Why would I kill him?"

I didn't know the answer to either question. "The detective wants to talk to you."

"He can want all he likes."

"You aren't going to talk to him?" I asked.

"When I get around to it."

"He seemed pretty determined."

"He'll have to be a lot more than determined to find me out here."

He had a point.

I jerked my head toward the shack. "This is where you live?"

"Yeah."

"Why?"

He lifted his brows. "Why not?"

"You've got a perfectly good house, if you'd only take care of it."

Adam's face became shuttered. "I hate that place. I wish it would rot, but de damn thing never will."

His vehemence surprised and confused me. "You moved out here because you hate the house, not because you—?"

I stopped abruptly.

His mouth quirked. "You heard I lost my mind, huh? Why you come here if you think I'm nuts?"

I hadn't *come* here—actually I had, but not the way he meant; I'd followed him. Or at least I thought I had. "Why were you watching me at the mansion?"

He'd been leaning over, reaching for his clothes, giving me an eyeful of his terrific backside. At my question, he stilled for just an instant. If I hadn't been admiring the view, I wouldn't have noticed.

"Watching?" He straightened, but he didn't face me. Instead, he seemed to be scanning the swamp.

"By the cypress trees. When I called out, you left, so I followed you. Didn't I?"

"Mmm," he murmured, then scooped up his clothes, my jeans, and grabbed me by the arm. "I've had enough of de rain. Let's go inside."

I hung back, uneasy, uncertain. "Why did you lead me here?"

He stared at me from behind the tangled curtain of his hair. "I'm a man. Why you think?"

For some reason the idea that he'd led me into the swamp for sex annoyed me, which was stupid. I hadn't followed him for a tour of the area. I wasn't that delusional.

We were mature adults who were attracted to each other. There was no reason we shouldn't act on that attraction. Just because Adam gave voice to the truth shouldn't make me feel slutty and guilty and bad. But I did.

"I should go," I said.

"Not tonight."

"But—"

He kissed me, lips, tongue, teeth, and I forgot again. Where I was, who I was, the other questions I wanted to ask.

He lifted his head, and his gaze flickered to the swamp, then back to mine. "Stay with me. At least until de storm ends."

I found myself nodding, even though I got the distinct impression he meant something other than the wind, the rain, and the thunder.

15

Adam's place definitely looked better on the inside. Not much furniture, but tidy and dry—what more could anyone want?

Hot water and a shot of whiskey—Irish, to be sure. I was suddenly so cold, my bones ached. Which made no sense. The storm hadn't done one thing to dissipate the heat.

"I'll put your clothes in the dryer." Adam held out a hand. I stared at it, confused. "Your shirt, *cher.*"

He wanted me to strip in the living room?

His mouth quirked at my sudden shyness, but he didn't point out that he'd already seen everything, touched and tasted it, too. Instead he nodded to the nearest door. "Bathroom's right there. Take a shower; toss out your things."

"Hot water?" My voice quivered with hope.

Adam nodded. "I live here year-round. Could do without electric, but why? Bought a generator first thing."

I practically ran into the bathroom, which was small but functional. I turned on the water, tossed my clothes through the door. As I waited for the steam to rise, my gaze flickered over the countertop.

Shaving cream, razor, toothbrush, toothpaste, blow-dryer. I guess that solved the mystery of the un-wet hair, though why Adam had taken time to dry his locks while I wandered the swamp, I had no idea. Maybe he caught chills easily. He should try wearing a shirt and shoes.

Climbing into the shower, I nearly moaned as the water hit my skin. Though I would have liked to stand under the stream for an hour, I made do with fifteen minutes. Then I dried off, wrapped my hair in one towel and my body in a second, and went searching for Adam.

He stood at the front window. Night had descended completely. The thought of going out in that storm, walking alone through the dark, was too much. I would never be able to do it.

My clothes were gone, presumably whirling around the dryer with his. The image of our things all tangled together and warm made me think of other warm things that should be tangled together.

What was the matter with me? Was I suddenly obsessed with sex because it had been so long since I'd had any, or was I obsessed because I'd had it with him?

"Hey," I murmured.

He turned, and our gazes met across the tiny room. He'd donned gray sweatpants and a bright yellow T-shirt, which made his skin appear more bronzed and his eyes more blue. I was so out of my league.

"Hey," he returned. "I'll get you somethin' to wear while de dryer does its thing."

I didn't protest. There was no way I could be in the same room with Adam wearing only a towel and not be distracted by thoughts of him tearing it off of me.

Then again, would that be so bad? What were we going to do all night? Play chess?

I followed him down the hall, standing in the doorway as he rooted through a dresser. The bedroom was as sparse as the living room—nothing but a queen-size bed and a place to store clothes.

I lost the towel. The swish of the terry cloth down my legs, the slight *thunk* as it hit the floor, were faint, yet his head went up like a deer sensing danger in the forest. His eyes widened, and he dropped the T-shirt in his hand back into the drawer.

"The bed looks comfortable," I observed.

He crossed the floor, stopping just in front of me. Reaching up, he tugged the towel turban from my head. My damp, wildly curling hair tumbled free.

"Better than de ground," he whispered.

Lightning flashed so brightly, I still saw the flare after it faded. Thunder shook the earth; the windows rattled.

"Gonna be a long night, *cher.*"

"I hope so."

He led me to the bed, and we passed the long night together.

I awoke in that hour when the moon dies and the sun is born—the darkest time. The storm had raged outside, wild and primitive. Inside we'd done our best to imitate nature. I was both exhausted and exhilarated. Achy and alive.

I turned my head. Adam's face was so close, his breath caressed my cheek. I resisted the urge to brush back his hair and kiss his brow.

Just sex, I reminded myself. I had a job to do, a vow to fulfill, a life to lead. One that did not include a reclusive former Special Forces officer with too many secrets.

I didn't believe he'd murdered a man with his bare hands. How could he, and then touch me so gently in the night? There was violence in him certainly, but not insanity. At least not yet.

I frowned at the thought and shifted to glance out the window. My heart seemed to leap into my throat. I wanted to call for Adam, but I couldn't speak.

A wolf stared through the glass. Huge, black, beautiful. A shaft of excitement, of joy almost, shot through me that I'd at last found something I was searching for. And then I saw the beast's eyes.

Wolves have brown eyes—dark, light, sometimes hazel. They do not possess orbs of blue.

But what really freaked me out was the white surrounding the iris. I could swear those eyes were human—and familiar.

They were Adam's eyes.

I sat up with a gasp, trying to catch my breath, finally succeeding. I looked to the right. The wolf was gone.

Bracing myself, I looked to the left. Adam continued to sleep undisturbed.

I put my palm to my chest; my heart threatened to burst through my skin.

A dream, that was all. There hadn't really been a wolf with human eyes staring at me with just a hint of desire—though I had to say his expression had been more famished than carnal.

I lay down, spent a few moments breathing in and out, trying to make my heart return to a normal pace, hoping I didn't wake Adam with my foolishness. After his performance, he had to be more tired than I was.

The memory calmed me. I shifted closer, enjoying the warmth, the scent of his skin, the rhythm of his breathing. I hadn't realized how much I hated sleeping alone.

I drifted, perched on the precipice of sleep, when a tap

at the window brought me wide awake again. My eyes snapped open. I expected the wolf; I did not expect Simon.

A soft sob escaped my mouth. Just a dream again, had to be. Simon was dead. He could not be outside Adam's window.

I cringed at Simon seeing me in bed with another man, even if it was a dream Simon.

He tapped on the glass, crooked his finger, so I slipped from beneath the covers and padded naked across the floor.

Simon appeared exactly the same as he had the day he'd died. Tall and a bit gaunt—he'd always forgotten to eat unless I reminded him—his blond hair and blue eyes appeared almost Nordic. I hadn't known he was British until he opened his mouth. That accent had been my undoing.

When I'd met him he was well respected in his field. By the time he died he was a laughingstock, referred to as "The Wolfman" by people who'd once admired him.

A few days before his death he finally told me why he was willing to risk everything to find something no one else believed in. He'd seen a werewolf as a child in England—out on the moors, in the fog—and ever since, he'd been unable to forget.

I'd rationalized away the sighting as too much *American Werewolf in London* for a twelve-year-old mind. He'd been understandably angry that the one person in the world who should believe him, didn't, and when he'd received a call that a werewolf had been seen in northern Wisconsin, he'd gone alone.

I hadn't believed him, and he'd died for it.

Simon laid his palm against the glass. Droplets of rain ran down, skirting his fingers. I lifted my hand and pressed it to the windowpane, too.

God, I missed him.

"D-baby," he murmured.

Only the two of us knew that nickname.

"I'm here, Simon."

"I'm not."

"I know."

He glanced over his shoulder as if someone had called him, then returned his gaze to mine. "I have to go."

"Not yet."

He stepped back. Weird. He wasn't wet, and the rain was still coming down. Or maybe not so weird after all.

"You promised," he said.

I'd sworn till death do us part, but in my heart that meant forever. A love like ours just didn't go away.

I felt it now, swelling inside of me, making my eyes tear and my chest tighten. "Don't leave me."

"I never have. I'll be with you until the end of time. You took a vow, D-baby. Remember?"

He'd come to remind me of the vow and not our love? Dream Simon or not, I wanted to slug him.

"I haven't forgotten," I snapped. "Why do you think I'm here? I've been chasing legends every which way ever since you died. I haven't found one damn thing."

"You have to believe in order to see, not the other way around."

He'd told me that countless times, but faith, for me, was tough. I was a scientist; I needed proof.

"Be safe," he whispered; then he was gone.

I jolted as if I'd been startled awake. However, I wasn't in bed; I was standing at the window. I couldn't have been sleeping. Unless I'd been sleepwalking.

As I leaned close, my nose brushed the glass. Nothing was out there but the night. I inched back, and my gaze caught on the imprint of a hand.

My heart gave one hard thud before I came to my senses. I'd touched the window in my sleep, that was all. To prove it, I fit my palm to the outline.

The fingertips on the glass extended half an inch past my own.

16

"Who's Simon?"

I spun toward the bed. "Where did you hear that?"

Adam rested his head on one palm, his face shuttered. "From you."

"I never told you about him."

"Not told, no. You said de name in your sleep. And since you're sleeping with me, I want to know who he is."

Had I dreamed Simon or not? I wasn't certain. If I had, was that good or bad? If I hadn't, what the hell?

I glanced at the window, but the handprint was gone. Had it ever been there in the first place?

"Who is he?"

Adam sounded as if he was speaking through clenched teeth. When my gaze returned to his, I saw that he was.

"Simon's my husband."

A flicker of violence passed over his face. "You didn't think you should mention a husband? I might do a lot of things, but I try not to fuck another man's wife if I can help it."

"No. I'm not— I mean we're not— He isn't—"

Adam got out of the bed and crossed the floor so fast I barely had time to take a step back. When I did, I hit the wall. He grabbed me by the forearms and dragged me onto my toes. His grip hurt, but I was too bewildered to protest.

"He isn't *what*?"

"Alive."

Or at least I didn't think so.

Adam released me as if I were a hot potato; I would have fallen if I hadn't had the wall to hold me up.

"Sorry." He shoved a hand through his hair.

I wasn't sure if he was apologizing for Simon's death or for manhandling me, but I understood his anger. In fact, his fury at the idea I was married made me view him in a different light.

Adam Ruelle hadn't seemed the type to respect marriage vows, to take to heart the myth of one man, one woman, forever. If I'd been wrong about that, I'd been wrong about him. Which only confused me more.

"Never mind," I said. "Forget it."

"You haven't forgotten."

"No."

"You still love him. I could tell by de way you said his name."

I wanted to ask how he knew so much about love, but I didn't. The conversation only emphasized that we were practically strangers, and I wanted to keep it that way.

"I'll always love Simon. Death can't change what I feel."

He stared at me so hard, I got the feeling he wanted to open my head and peek inside, find out what made me tick. "How did he die?"

I didn't want to talk about this, especially naked, so I yanked the sheet off the bed and headed for the bathroom. Adam caught the tail end and held on.

"You dream of him," he whispered.

I wasn't so sure it had been a dream, but I couldn't tell Adam I'd seen my dead husband outside his window.

"I saw a wolf," I blurted instead.

"Dreams aren't real."

I wasn't so sure anymore.

"There." I pointed. "At the window. Big, black, with weird blue eyes."

If Adam hadn't been nude, I wouldn't have noticed him tense. His gaze flickered to the window and back. Nevertheless, I was distracted by the ripple of muscle beneath skin, the wave along his abdomen like a softly flowing river.

"There was no wolf, *cher.*"

"What about the howls in the swamp? The deaths? The tracks?"

"What about them?"

"Why do you keep denying even the possibility that there's a wolf or ten out here?"

"Because there isn't."

I gave a frustrated little shriek and resisted the urge to kick him.

"You want me to prove it? Tonight I take you. I know this swamp like I know my own name. If there's anything here that doesn't belong I'd have seen it."

Unless he was hiding something, and I kind of thought that he was. Maybe I shouldn't go tripping off merrily into the swamp with him in the dark. I might never be heard from again.

Be safe, Simon had said. What had he meant?

From the loup-garou? From my feelings? Or from Adam?

But what choice did I have? If I was going to fulfill my vow, I needed help. And the only help available was the only man who'd made me feel alive since my whole world died.

Life certainly was a vicious bitch.

I blinked as another thought occurred to me, one that made me dizzy with dismay. Cursing, I collapsed on the bed. "I'm no damn good at this."

Sex required responsibility. Protection. My celibate lifestyle had kept me free of disease. I was also free from birth control, being both a widow and an idiot.

The bed dipped as Adam sat beside me. His hip brushed mine, but he touched me nowhere else, and for that I was grateful. When he touched me I couldn't think.

Obviously.

"You're pretty good at this, if you're askin' me."

"What?" My mind wasn't keeping up very well with the conversation.

"You said you were no damn good, but you are."

I smiled before I could stop myself. "Thanks. But I meant at technicalities." His blank stare made me continue. "Protection. We didn't use any."

I saw the understanding spread across his face. I waited for the horror, the panic, the escape, but it didn't come.

"You don't have to worry."

"I think I do."

"You wanna ask me have I been with a lot of women?"

I shrugged. My lame-ass equivalent of "Hell, yes!"

"Once I fucked like rabbit, my father said."

"How . . . flattering."

"He thought so."

Now would be the time to ask about his father. Then again, what did it matter how, when, or why Ruelle Senior had died?

"Me, I was lookin' for love. What's that song? In all de wrong places."

The sadness on his face made me want to touch him, but I knew where that would lead.

"Those days are gone," he murmured. "Love isn't for me."

"Why not?"

Adam contemplated my face. "You aren't lookin' for love. We both know that."

He was right, so I dipped my head.

"I want you. Shouldn't, but can't seem to help myself. I see that red hair," He picked up a strand and rubbed it between his fingers. "Smell your skin, stare into your pretty green eyes, and I lose my mind."

Being wanted for my body was something new, and I kind of liked it.

"Since I left de army, there's been no one."

"No one?" I found that hard to believe.

"No one," he insisted. "And in de army, they tested us regular for every old thing. I came out clean, *cher,* and clean I still am. Right?"

He quirked a brow and my face heated. I'd never had a conversation like this before, although if I planned to spend the rest of my life alone, with the occasional lover to take off the edge, I'd have to get used to them.

"There was never anyone but Simon," I whispered.

The words *until you* hung in the air unspoken.

Adam touched my hair again. "Why not?"

"He was everything, and when he died—" My throat closed.

"A part of you went with him," he finished.

I didn't bother to answer. Couldn't, really.

"It's not natural to be alone."

I cleared my throat. "I'm fine."

"Sure you are. You'll fall in love again."

"No," I snapped.

"No?"

"I don't ever want to feel the way I felt when he died."

"So you feel nothing?"

"I had my shot. Simon was it for me."

"You don't think you can love twice in one lifetime?"

I lifted my head, looked him straight in the eye. "No."

He studied me for a second to ascertain that I meant what I said. He must have seen that I did, because he gave a sharp nod, as if we'd sealed a bargain. I guess we had.

"You're like a wolf," he murmured, "mating for life. If one dies, de other is forever alone."

"How do you know so much about wolves?"

"Common knowledge, no?"

I stared at him, suspicious though I wasn't sure why. He was right. The whole mating-for-life thing *was* common knowledge.

"Never mind," I muttered. I'd had another cheery thought. "There's more to be concerned about than STDs."

All I needed was a baby. I could barely take care of myself.

I glanced around the sparse bedroom. Adam wasn't doing much better.

In truth, I wasn't crazy about kids. I didn't long to be a mother. Maybe this made me a freak of nature, but that's how I felt.

I was an only child. I'd never played well with others. Without brothers and sisters, nieces and nephews, I'd had neither a reason nor an inclination to babysit. Kids just made me twitchy.

Simon and I had decided all we needed was each other. We'd planned to travel the world, sleep in tents until we couldn't anymore, then retire. Besides, if I wasn't going to have Simon's child, I certainly wasn't going to have anyone else's.

"I can't," Adam murmured.

To make sure we were talking about the same thing, I asked, "Can't what?"

"Have children."

"No kidding." I lowered my gaze to his lap. "You aren't exactly equipped for the process."

"I meant I can't get you, or anyone else, pregnant."

I wasn't sure what to say. I could ask what was wrong with him, but since he hadn't offered to tell me . . . should I? What was the etiquette for something like this? I didn't have a clue.

Adam stood and turned away, as if the conversation upset him. Maybe he'd been wounded, although I hadn't seen any scars and I'd seen pretty much everything.

Perhaps, unlike me, he'd wanted children one day. Learning he'd never have them would hurt and might account for some of the sadness in his eyes.

The question was: Did I believe him?

I studied Adam's tense shoulders. A better question might be: Why would he lie?

Since I couldn't come up with an answer, I went to him and slid my arms around his waist. "It doesn't matter."

"No?"

The way he said the word, with that French twist, always made him sound just a tad sarcastic, which was probably the whole idea.

"For us, that's a good thing."

He turned in my arms, taking me into his. "Whatever you say."

"We're having a—"

Adam tilted his head. "A what?"

An affair sounded too long-term and old-fashioned, *a fling* too flippant for the intensity of what we'd shared.

"I'm not sure," I said. "But whatever it is, it's about sex, not love, or kids, or anything but the moment. Right?"

"What man would say no?"

Lowering his head, he kissed me, putting all of himself into the embrace. Only later, when we were back in bed, my heart still pounding, my chest still heaving after another bout of exactly what I'd wanted, did I consider his response. Or rather his lack of one. Adam had the habit of answering every one of my questions with a question of his own.

And that wasn't really an answer at all, was it?

17

I awoke to the sun and an empty bed. I tried not to be hurt. This wasn't a relationship. We'd both made that perfectly clear. So why did I feel as if I'd been screwed in more ways than one?

The only indication that Adam had been here at all were his jeans on the floor and my dry clothes, neatly folded on the dresser.

My gris-gris perched at the apex. I wondered what he'd made of that. Probably nothing. Having lived here all of his life, he'd no doubt seen a thousand of them.

Would it still work after being soaked by rain, then scorched by electric heat? I had to hope so, since I needed to get through the swamp without being eaten by alligators. I couldn't believe I was putting such store in a bag of herbs, except I hadn't seen a gator since Charlie died.

I got dressed and shoved the gris-gris in my pocket. My hair was a mess, or at least it felt that way to my fingertips. I couldn't find a mirror anywhere.

There was something odd about that, but I couldn't figure out what without coffee. There wasn't a pot in the house, either. Maybe Adam was just a guy's guy—didn't care to primp. And really, what could he do? He was gorgeous wearing tattered pants, a two days' growth of beard, and twigs in his hair. I wish I could say the same about myself, minus the beard, of course.

In the kitchen, I pounced at a scrap of paper on the counter, frowning at the map, which detailed a path from the shack to the mansion. There wasn't a single personal word on the page.

What had I expected? A declaration of everlasting love?

"A little praise would be nice," I muttered as I made my way to the door. " 'Hey, Diana, rabbits pale in comparison to you.' "

I snorted at my own wit. Might as well, no one else would.

The storm was gone, leaving behind a bright blue sky through which the sunshine blazed. Shards of light sparkled off the glistening droplets of rain that lingered everywhere. From the position of the sun, I'd missed not only breakfast but lunch.

In the night, the cypress trees had seemed to blot out the moon and the stars. Against the sun, they weren't any help at all.

I glanced about hopefully, mind cursing my own stupidity when I realized I was looking for Adam. Why would he leave a map if he was going to be around? Even stupider was wanting so badly to see him.

If I wasn't careful I'd forget every vow I'd made. I'd stop searching for the loup-garou and spend all my time in bed. The idea was far too tempting.

Annoyed with the wishy-washiness of my resolve, I forced myself to march toward the bedroom window to search for tracks. The ground was damp; there had to be something. Unless there'd been nothing.

Coming around the corner of the house, I stopped dead. The earth beneath Adam's bedroom window had been turned up, as if someone had considered planting flowers or a shrub, then changed their mind.

Except the yard was a swamp. Anything planted there would be overtaken in a month. What would be the point?

There wasn't one, unless the ground had been dug up to hide something. The tracks of a man or a beast?

I wanted to see Adam more than ever. Instead, I followed the map, returned to the mansion, changed my clothes, and left for town.

I planned to head straight to Cassandra's. Something weird was going on—in either the swamp or my head or both. She was the only person who'd given me any sort of answers. Bizarro as they might be.

However, as I was trolling for a parking place, I remembered the library and the newspaper articles I'd already paid for, so I swung the car around and made a slight detour.

The clippings were at the desk as Mrs. Beasly had promised, but she wasn't. When I asked for her, the girl who'd handed me the packet whispered, "You don't know? She never came in to work."

Now why would I know that? People ditched work all the time, though Mrs. Beasly didn't seem the type. She was more the type to have fallen and she couldn't get up.

"Did someone check her house?"

The young woman, who looked nothing like a librarian in the low-slung pants that barely covered her crack and the high-cut shirt, which barely extended beyond her breasts, nodded. "She's just . . . gone."

"Gone?"

"Her car, her purse, her suitcase all right where she left them, but no Mrs. Beasly."

That was new. No animal attack, no death by strangulation. Just *poof*. Maybe Mrs. Beasly's disappearance was unrelated.

I glanced at the manila envelope in my hand. But I doubted it.

I thanked the girl and took a chair in the library, then dumped the clippings onto the table.

Local Man Commits Suicide at Home read the first headline. The only thing different about the second was the date—about twenty-two years later.

This went a long way toward explaining why Adam loathed the place. I wasn't wild about the idea of multiple suicides there myself.

The information was remarkably similar in the two deaths. Law enforcement theories ranged from self-termination to murder and back again. The family was investigated. The angle of the gun, lack of motive, and concrete alibis exonerated them.

"Survived by one-year-old grandson," I read in Grampa's obituary, earning a scowl from the student at the next table. If she put her finger to her lip and told me to "shh!" I'd be tempted to shout. I always was.

I searched through the clippings, looking for the obituary of Adam's father, but there wasn't one. Odd.

And that comment Mrs. Beasly had made about the lack of girls born in the last century, I should really determine if that was true—though what it had to do with anything, I couldn't decide.

I checked it out anyway, and unless someone had managed to birth a girl at home and keep the child off the records completely—a Herculean task even without the recent practice of assigning Social Security numbers in the nursery—there *hadn't* been a Ruelle girl born in over a hundred years.

I also couldn't find any obituary for Ruelle senior.

"Too weird."

But not impossible.

I hadn't asked Adam about any of this. When was the appropriate time to bring up an unfortunate tendency toward suicide in the family or their strange genetic anomaly?

When he was making me come the first time? Or maybe after the third?

I left the library, hurrying toward Cassandra's, dodging tourists, every one of whom seemed to be headed in the opposite direction. The wail of a saxophone hovered on the humid air, the mournful sound drawing me along with the crowd to Jackson Square.

Located near the river, Jackson Square had once been a military parade ground. Now it was a civilized garden spot, bordered by shops, restaurants, and the towering St. Louis Cathedral. Artists had set up booths to sell their wares, but a good share of the tables belonged to psychics and Tarot card readers as well.

In front of the cathedral, there appeared to be a party in progress. Musicians played, and if they weren't playing they danced, while tourists tapped their feet or tossed change into the open instrument cases placed strategically on the street.

Everyone was having so much fun, I wanted to. Inching closer, I let myself be carried away.

I'd never been much for jazz, but this was something special. How could they make such spectacular music when people appeared to join and leave the band at will?

"Does this happen every day?" I asked the man next to me.

"Pretty much. The players change—whoever can make it does. Isn't it amazing?"

Definitely.

Two police cars were parked right behind the musicians. The officers listened to the music, too, but they were also watching the crowd.

"What's with that?" I asked.

"Trying to keep the drug dealing to a minimum. Puts off the tourists."

Such a pretty place, such beautiful music—of *course* there was something rotten beneath the surface.

As I watched, one of the officers separated from the others and strolled toward Muriel's, a famous local restaurant, complete with the requisite ghost.

A preppy couple was engaged in conversation with a grubby young man. When he caught sight of the cop heading his way, he took off. The couple's eyes widened, and they disappeared almost as fast as the dealer had. The officer didn't even spare them a glance.

Though I would have liked nothing better than to walk into Muriel's, take a table on the terrace, sip a glass of wine while I waited for a glimpse of their ghost, I wasn't on vacation. I was working.

I glanced at the sky. While I'd been listening to the music, the sun had fallen down, leaving dusk in its wake. I'd lost an entire day and gotten very little accomplished. Nevertheless, I really should check in with Frank.

As I exited Jackson Square, headed for Royal Street, I pulled out my cell phone. Before I could dial, I caught a glimpse of a familiar face walking toward me.

I smiled, opened my mouth to speak, and froze.

How did one greet a dead man?

18

My stopping in the middle of the sidewalk had screwed up the flow of people, but since this was New Orleans no one shoved or cursed me. Most of them had drinks in their hands, and at this time of the day were mighty mellow.

Except for Charlie, who took off like the drug dealer had only a moment ago.

I wasn't much for running, but I leaped into the narrow street, dodging cars, horse-drawn carriages, and people who'd gotten sick of stumbling along the crowded, broken cement.

I might have been mistaken about the identity of the last dead man I'd seen walking. Him I hadn't known personally.

Besides, why would Charlie run if he didn't have something to hide? And being a zombie? Big secret.

I couldn't believe I was even considering such a thing, but hey—this was New Orleans and he was a dead guy.

As I ran, I reached for my zombie-revealing powder,

sending up a murmur of thanks when I found it in my pocket. Now all I had to do was catch him.

Easier said than done. My chest tight, my lungs burned. I might be able to kick ass in a self-defense class, but jogging I sucked at. Charlie was pulling away from me.

He turned a corner several blocks ahead. By the time I got there, he was gone.

I'd chased him out of the touristy section and into a slightly run-down area where small jazz clubs lined the street. Mostly empty now, a few stood open as employees prepared the places for the evening. All of them had interesting names like The Spotted Cat.

A thin, elderly black man swept dust out the front door of a building without a name. As I passed he nodded, smiled, and murmured, "Ma'am."

"Did anyone run through here just now?"

He shook his head but kept his eyes on his broom. I frowned. He had to have seen Charlie. Unless my quarry could just up and disappear.

For all I knew, he could.

I retraced my steps to Jackson Square, where the party continued. I no longer had any desire to linger. The sun was completely gone.

At Cassandra's, I burst in, then stared. Detective Sullivan appeared as surprised to see me as I was to see him.

"Ms. Malone. What are you doing here?"

"Funny, I was going to ask you the same thing."

"I have questions for Ms.—" He broke off with a scowl and turned back to Cassandra. "What's your last name?"

"Priestess Cassandra is good enough."

"I am *not* calling you Priestess."

"Cassandra's fine, too."

Detective Sullivan's face got so red I was tempted to help him loosen his tie. However, I didn't think he'd appreciate the gesture. The man probably slept in a suit.

Although—my gaze lowered to that tie, imprinted with a tiny Lucy holding a football for a clueless Charlie Brown—I was starting to think Sullivan wasn't as humorless as he pretended to be.

"You two know each other?" he managed.

"Yes," Cassandra and I said at the same time.

"How?"

"I came in to shop."

"For what?"

"What are you, a cop?" I quipped.

He blinked, a confused expression replacing his annoyance. "Well, yeah."

Cassandra laughed, then turned the sound into a cough. I took pity on the man and answered his question—kind of.

"I heard this was an interesting place. Came in, looked around, and—"

"We bonded," Cassandra put in.

"Bonded," he repeated.

"I liked her; she liked me. Pals." Cassandra crossed her middle finger over her index finger. "We're like this."

Now I was the one who choked on a laugh.

Sullivan didn't appear convinced, but he let the matter drop. "I'm investigating a missing person."

I thought of Mrs. Beasly. The New Orleans PD was really on the ball.

"Well, not exactly a person," the detective said, and Cassandra and I exchanged glances. "At least not anymore. There's a body missing from the morgue."

I started, but the detective was staring at Cassandra and not at me. He didn't notice my reaction. Cassandra did, but she was savvy enough not to ask why that information disturbed me.

"Whenever that happens," Cassandra murmured, "the voodoo priestess is always the first suspect."

"Because?" I asked.

"Zombies." Cassandra rolled her eyes. "What else?"

"You can't believe Cassandra is raising zombies," I demanded, even as my mind raced.

I'd come here halfway believing I'd chased a zombie out of Jackson Square. I should tell Detective Sullivan, but I couldn't get the words out of my mouth.

"I don't believe it," he muttered.

"He's from out of town." Cassandra smirked.

I didn't bother to point out that she was, too. Cassandra seemed as much a part of New Orleans as the humidity and the jazz.

"His superior ordered him to come," she continued.

Sullivan made an impatient sound. "I don't understand this place."

"You're not supposed to." Cassandra patted Sullivan's arm. "Since you didn't find the body in my closet, is there anything else I can do for you?"

"No," he snapped, and headed for the door. He stopped with his hand on the knob. "I was going to come and talk to you tomorrow, Ms. Malone. Have you seen Adam Ruelle?"

"Yes."

"And you gave him my message?"

"Yes."

"He didn't call."

"Sorry."

Sullivan cursed. "I don't have the manpower to beat the swamp for him. All I want to do is ask a few questions."

"You really think Adam strangled a perfect stranger with his bare hands?" I asked.

"Someone did."

True.

"Funny that you should call the victim a stranger," he continued.

"Funny ha-ha? Or funny weird?"

Sullivan's lips didn't even twitch. "The victim had no ID, he doesn't match any missing persons report; no record of anyone of his description entering by public transportation; fingerprints don't pop in the FBI files."

"Maybe it was a plain old robbery on Bourbon Street," Cassandra said, "and someone dumped the guy there so they'd have enough time to get out of Dodge."

"Tourists have hotel rooms, rental cars. One thing they don't usually have is a fully automatic rifle."

My mouth opened, then shut. "Isn't that illegal?"

"Extremely."

"How do you know the gun was his?"

"His fingerprints were all over the thing. Besides, if it was a robbery, why leave a gun like that lying around? Thing has to be worth some money, even without the weird bullets."

"What kind of weird?" I asked.

"Silver." He opened the door. "Who uses silver bullets?"

Without waiting for an answer, the detective left.

Cassandra and I stared after him, then looked at each other. "Uh-oh," we both said at the same time.

"Appears you aren't the only one searching for a loup-garou," Cassandra murmured.

"I am now," I said dryly.

"You should be careful. Someone doesn't want the beast found."

"Seems to me like someone doesn't want the beast killed."

Cassandra's lips pursed. "You've got a point."

I shook my head, gave a little laugh, even though I didn't find much of this funny. "Is everyone around here nuts?"

"That's rhetorical, right?"

"Silver bullets, missing bodies, zombies."

"Welcome to New Orleans." She tilted her head. "You look like you haven't slept at all. Did something happen in the swamp?"

I'd planned to tell her of Charlie; I'd forgotten about the wolf and Simon.

"It was probably just a dream," I muttered.

Cassandra's eyes sharpened. "Dreams have meaning. Tell me."

So I did.

"The wolf sounds like a dream."

"My dead husband at the window doesn't?"

"In this town—not so much."

A chill passed over me that had nothing to do with the overactive air conditioner. Simon was dead. I'd buried him years ago. I didn't believe in ghosts or zombies or werewolves. *Really.*

"You said there weren't any tracks."

"There could have been. The ground was all turned up."

Cassandra frowned. "Odd, but maybe it was like that even before your dream."

Maybe. But I doubted it.

"You're intent on finding a loup-garou," she continued. "You see one at the window. Simple wish fulfillment."

"And Simon?"

"Could be the same thing. You miss him, he's there."

I wrinkled my nose. "His ghost?"

"Why not?"

"Why now?"

"Guilt?"

I stilled. I hadn't told Cassandra about doing the horizontal mambo with Adam Ruelle, but from the lift of her brow, she knew anyway.

"You shouldn't feel guilty, Diana. Your husband's gone; you're not."

"I understand that here." I pointed to my head. "But here?" I patted my chest. "Not so much."

Her sigh was long and sad. "I know."

From the expression on her face, she did know, and I wanted to ask who she'd lost, how long it had been. After all, we'd bonded. But she shook off the sadness, smiling brightly, and I got the distinct impression her past was off-limits.

"You want to tell me why you came careening in here like something was chasing you?"

"Oh, yeah! Charlie Wagner."

Cassandra's smile faded. "How did you—?"

"What?"

"His body is the one that's missing."

"Which might be why I saw him on Jackson Square."

Her gaze sharpened. "Did you use the powder?"

"He took off. Disappeared." I paused. "Can a zombie disappear?"

"Not that I know of."

Was I *having* this conversation?

"Where did you lose him?" Cassandra demanded.

"Frenchmen Street."

She grabbed a huge purse from under the counter, then

chose items from the shelves and shoved them inside. "Let's go."

"Where?"

"Frenchmen Street."

"Because . . . ?"

"Zombies aren't the smartest beings on the planet. They follow orders, then return to their master."

"I don't believe this," I muttered.

"You do, or you wouldn't be here."

The woman was right too often for her own good.

"You have the powder?" she asked as she locked the door behind us.

"Yep."

"OK. We find him, reveal him, put him back where he belongs."

"Which is?"

She frowned. "Good question. I've never heard of a zombie being raised before they were buried. But then again, they aren't exactly buried around here. Encrypted. Is that a word?"

"Got me."

Cassandra led the way, moving at a fast clip down Royal Street, then turning on St. Peter and heading for Jackson Square. Night had fallen; the moon that rose was just over half-full. Where had the time gone? I'd need to wait over a week to search for the loup-garou again.

And was I really adjusting my job because of the phases of the moon? Yes. The unbelievable became more believable with every passing hour.

"Can't we do this in the daytime?" I asked.

"No."

"I saw him in the daytime." I frowned, remembering. "Well, not exactly daytime, but it wasn't night, either."

She stopped, turned, and put a hand on my shoulder. "It isn't that we can't wait; it's that we shouldn't. Zombies are rarely raised for the good of mankind. The longer Charlie's waltzing around, the more trouble he'll cause."

"You're the expert."

We started walking again.

"What did he look like?" she asked.

"Charlie."

"I mean was there any decay? What about his throat wound?"

I shook my head. "He looked the same as the day I met him."

She stopped again, right inside Jackson Square. The artisans and psychics were still there; the music had stopped.

"You're saying his throat wasn't bloody and gaping? His body hadn't started to rot?"

"I think I'd have noticed." Along with everyone else on the street.

She bit her lip and stared at the ground. "Weird."

"What are you getting at?"

Cassandra lifted her troubled gaze to mine. "Ever seen *Night of the Living Dead*?"

"No."

"Zombies aren't supposed to appear alive. They're a walking corpse."

"The movie could be wrong. And wouldn't that be a shock?"

She didn't answer, which was answer enough.

"You don't think so."

"No." She cut past the cathedral, and I followed. "Maybe Charlie is too newly dead to decay."

"Then how did he heal his throat wound?"

"Yeah." She glanced at me. "How did he?"

"You're the voodoo priestess."

Cassandra scowled. "Whoever did this has power beyond anything we can imagine. Not only was Charlie raised; he was healed." She shook her head. "I don't like it."

I had to say I wasn't crazy about it, either.

19

Frenchmen Street was deserted except for bartenders, waitresses, and local musicians ready to play a set for tips.

"Won't get busy here until after nine or ten," Cassandra said. "If you like, once we're done, we can hang out and listen to the best jazz in town."

I wasn't sure what to say. We'd come after a zombie, and once we put him back . . . wherever . . . Cassandra wanted to listen to music and drink wine spritzers.

When in Rome, I guess. By then I probably *would* need a drink.

"Now what?" I asked.

"Now we start walking through alleys, peeking in bars."

"Seems a little half-assed to me."

"You got a better idea?"

Actually, I did.

"Hey, Charlie!" I shouted. "Chaaaaaaarlie!"

One bartender and two waitresses stepped onto the sidewalk, saw us, shrugged, and went back to work.

I glanced at Cassandra. "You said names have power."

"I did, didn't I?" She took a deep breath and shouted, "Charlie!"

Farther down, past the jazz clubs, a head poked out between a grocery store and an abandoned building. I recognized that head even before Charlie stepped into the flare of a streetlight.

"Bingo," I whispered.

"Get the powder."

I did as she said, and each of us took a little into our hand.

"Remember, blow it right into his face."

We took one step in Charlie's direction and he ran.

"Hell!" Cassandra snapped, and started to run, too. "He isn't supposed to run."

I hustled after her. I had longer legs, but Cassandra had less weight on hers. "Why not?"

"Because it should be all he can do to shuffle. This guy is weird."

"This guy is dead."

She didn't bother to answer. Charlie was too fast to keep up a conversation and keep up with him.

He led us away from the dewy lights of Frenchmen Street, down roads I couldn't name without a sign, past signs I couldn't see without a light. Cassandra didn't seem disturbed, but then, she probably knew where we were going.

Nevertheless, I didn't think it was a good idea to chase a corpse all over New Orleans when all we had for protection was a zombie-revealing powder that might or might not work.

"Maybe we should let him go," I wheezed.

"Not on your life." Cassandra wasn't wheezing, of course. "This is the closest I've ever gotten to a zombie. I'm not giving up the chance to—"

Ah, she *did* have to take a deep breath. I felt so much better.

"To what?"

She frowned, her gaze flicking past me. "That's Louis Armstrong Park."

I stopped running.

Louis Armstrong Park was not a place we wanted to be after the dark. The only place worse was—

"He's going into St. Louis Cemetery Number One."

That.

All the guidebooks said, in big, bold, red letters, not to enter any of the cemeteries at night. And not because of a zombie problem, either. There was a certain diceyness, even in the daytime, that made it best to visit in groups.

Up until about eighty years ago, this part of New Orleans had been known as Storyville and was the only legal red-light district in the country. Customers could peruse a book that listed the bordellos and even had pictures of the prostitutes. Jazz flourished, too, since the musical movement was not considered legitimate until much later.

Even after prostitution became illegal again, Storyville remained the place to find a certain kind of girl well into the 1960s.

A police station had been built nearby. However, the area still had a dangerous aura that never seemed to go away.

"Let's go back to your place." I tugged on Cassandra's arm.

"No." Her mouth thinned into a stubborn line.

"Why are you so obsessed with this?"

Her face took on a faraway expression, and for an instant I thought she might confide in me; then the stubbornness returned. "I have my reasons. You still have your powder?"

"Yes. But I'd feel better if I had a gun."

I thought about the one Adam had given me, which was still locked in the trunk of my car, where it was going to be of *so* much use to us.

Without commenting, Cassandra reached into her bag and withdrew a very long knife. I gaped. Who was this woman?

"Uh, it probably isn't a good idea to walk around with that."

She lifted a brow. "Believe me, in this neighborhood, it is."

"There's no one here but us."

"You're wrong. They're all over the place." She headed for the cemetery.

The back of my neck tingled. Who were "they"?

Not wanting to be left alone, I scurried to catch up just as Cassandra reached the front of St. Louis Cemetery Number One. Barbed wire lined the top of the stone fence. The front gate was iron and sported a big lock.

I breathed a sigh of relief until Cassandra reached out and gave it a shove. The gate slid open.

"Damn it," I muttered.

She cast me an amused glance. "How do you think Charlie got in?"

"He couldn't just slide through the walls?"

"He's a zombie, not a ghost."

"You're sure about that?"

Cassandra lifted a palm filled with powder. "Let's find out."

Without waiting for me to agree or disagree, she slipped through the gate. I glanced longingly at the street, which was lit up like the Superdome on Super Sunday. There were lots of cars and even a few non-zombie people; I wanted to stay.

"Diana!" Cassandra snapped.

I couldn't let her go alone, so I followed her inside.

The half-moon only shone enough light into St. Louis Cemetery Number One to make the shadows dance and the white stone gleam. Other than that, darkness reigned.

"Watch your step," Cassandra murmured. "A lot of the old markers are crumbling. Easy to trip."

"Where are we going?"

"Best place to look for a zombie would be Marie Laveau's tomb."

"If you say so."

The crypt of the New Orleans voodoo queen wasn't very far from the front gate. Tall but otherwise unimpressive, it was tucked among many others. I wouldn't have taken the white boxy monument for anything special if not for the flowers in front of the door and the Xs drawn on the walls.

"What are those?" I whispered.

"People believe if they mark three Xs on Marie's tomb, scratch the ground three times with their feet, or rap three times on the grave, their wish will be granted."

I started to hum "Knock Three Times."

Cassandra snorted, then moved closer to the tomb and rapped on the door. Once. Twice. Three times.

I froze as the sound echoed in the stillness of the night. As I half-expected someone to answer, my head snapped around when a bell began to ring somewhere in the cemetery.

"Dead ringer," Cassandra murmured, and started in the direction of the sound. Since I had no desire to stay behind and see if her rapping had woken the voodoo queen, I followed.

"What the hell is a dead ringer?"

"You never heard the expression?"

"Sure. But it means someone who resembles someone else. What does that have to do with a bell in the cemetery?" I rubbed my arms against a sudden chill. "In the dark, in the night."

"This place was opened in 1789, back when they didn't know yellow fever was spread by mosquitoes. People thought it could be passed from person to person, be they living or dead."

"Understandable."

"So they placed the cemetery outside the city limits in an attempt to keep the fever away. But so many died, and so many panicked, sometimes people got buried before they were dead."

"Bummer."

She turned and lifted a brow in my direction. "Times ten. Because of the unique burial practices here, the tombs are opened to inter new bodies. When they started to find fingernail furrows in the doors, they came up with a brilliant idea."

The bell suddenly stopped ringing, and the ensuing silence was so loud, I could hear both of us breathing.

Cassandra pointed to a crypt. "They installed a bell on top, with a string leading inside. People were told if they suddenly awoke in a dark, enclosed space all they had to do was find the string and ring the bell. The cemetery attendant would come and let them out."

"Pretty smart."

"Not bad," she agreed. "Except when people began to see the folks they'd only buried a few days ago walking around on the street they were understandably freaked. They coined the term *dead ringer* to explain the phenomenon."

I contemplated the now-silent bell. "So who was ringing this one?"

"Let's find out."

"Let's not." I grabbed at her arm, but she was already gone.

The door to the tomb faced away from us. Before we could turn the corner, a loud *thunk* split the night.

Cassandra stopped so fast, I ran into her back. "Sounded like a door," she whispered.

"Are there still cemetery attendants?"

"No."

"That's what I was afraid of."

Together we peeked around the corner and discovered Charlie helping a woman out of the crypt. The name on the tomb read: *Favreau.* I filed that away for later use.

"You take him; I'll take her," Cassandra ordered, and stepped out of hiding.

Both Charlie and the woman growled at us.

"Mrs. Beasly," I blurted.

She gave no indication that she heard me or that she knew her name, just continued to snarl in tandem with Charlie. I hadn't thought a person could snarl, and while Cassandra and I were too far away to be sure, I could swear both of them had fangs.

Cassandra cut a quick glance in my direction. "You know her?"

"Missing librarian."

No wonder they couldn't find her. Why search in a crypt marked: *Favreau*?

"Is she dead?" I asked.

"You see a lot of live people climb out of tombs snarling?"

"Not lately."

When the two stalked in our direction, Cassandra hurriedly lifted her palm and put her lips near her wrist. I did the same.

"Now," Cassandra ordered.

We exhaled; the powder flew, coating their faces in pale yellow particles. Slowly my arm dropped back to my side as Charlie and Mrs. Beasly stopped walking and started coughing.

I waited for them to shrivel, disintegrate, disappear. But they didn't.

Charlie smacked me in the chest with the flat of his hand. Any air I had left in my lungs rushed out as I sailed backward and slammed into a crypt wall. I collapsed, too stunned to move.

Cassandra's knife flashed; Mrs. Beasly hissed as smoke rose from the cut in her forearm. She recovered quickly, backhanding Cassandra hard enough that she joined me on the ground. Mrs. Beasly was far too strong to be a live little old lady.

The two advanced. I tried to get up, but I was still loopy. Cassandra didn't look much better; she was going to have a shiner in the morning.

She glanced around for her knife, but the weapon had clattered in another direction when she was hit. Not that it had done her any good against a superhuman zombie librarian.

Was that redundant?

The two paused a few feet away, their bodies blotting out the light of the half-moon so that a silver halo appeared behind their heads. I couldn't see their faces, but the mumbles coming from their mouths were more animal than human.

"I don't think that zombie powder works," Cassandra murmured.

Two sharp reports split the night. Charlie and Mrs. Beasly jerked once and then exploded in blazing balls of fire.

"I don't think they're zombies," I said.

20

Cassandra and I managed to get to our feet with the aid of the tomb at our backs. My head felt as if it might split in two. The scent of burning flesh wasn't helping.

I tried to catch a glimpse of whoever had shot Charlie and Mrs. Beasly, but I saw no one.

The moon shadowed more than illuminated, and the graveyard was chock-full of tombs. Go figure. The shooter could be hiding anywhere. However, if they had meant us harm, they wouldn't have stopped at two bullets.

"Let's get out of here." Cassandra bent to snatch her knife out of the gravel.

"*Now* she wants to leave."

"Don't you?"

"I never wanted to come here in the first place."

She ignored the comment, tugging me toward the rear of the burial ground. I hung back, peering longingly at the streetlights. "What's wrong with the front door?"

"Those gunshots are going to bring cops, if not thugs. I know a less public way out."

"Of course you do."

But she had a point, so I went with her. I didn't want to explain why there were two flaming dead people in the middle of St. Louis Cemetery Number One. I doubted I even could.

Besides, if the police found Cassandra here they'd definitely think she'd been stealing bodies, and then some. I needed her free and able to help me figure out what was going on, not locked up for body snatching and desecration of the dead. If they even locked people up for that anymore, although I kind of thought they did.

She led me past a huge monument, which I recognized from the film *Easy Rider*. Peter Fonda had climbed up to sit in the lap of an angel. I'd thought the scene a bit sacrilegious even then. Now, in the silver-tinged night, I thought it more so.

This was a sacred place, a haunted place, a place where the living did not belong, and I wanted out of here as fast as I could go.

We left the white stone monuments behind and stepped into a small rectangle filled with more traditional markers.

"What's this?" I whispered.

"Protestant section."

No wonder it was so small.

"There." Cassandra pointed to a path that seemed to cut through someone's backyard.

"We shouldn't—" I began.

"What the hell!"

An exclamation from the front of the cemetery was followed by more voices and the patter of feet. Flashlight beams began to flicker round and round. I practically dived out of the city of the dead.

Cassandra and I emerged onto Robertson Street, which divided St. Louis Number One from St. Louis Number

Two. From the guidebooks, I knew that where we were now was even rougher than where we'd been. But after what I'd just seen, I had a hard time caring.

We cut down the side of the cemetery, headed for the lights, but when we reached Basin Street we turned in the opposite direction of the increasing number of police cars. A fire engine and an ambulance passed within minutes. They weren't going to be much help.

"What do you think they were?" Cassandra asked.

"You first."

"Not zombies. The powder didn't work and—" She shot me a sideways glance. "As far as I know, zombies don't explode when they're shot."

"What does?"

"No clue. But did you see . . . ?"

"The fangs?"

She let out a sigh of relief. "I thought I was nuts."

"Of course you aren't. It's perfectly sane to see dead people with fangs."

And I wasn't even being sarcastic.

"I saw the same thing you did," I said. "But I don't know *what* I saw."

"I think I do."

"Explain it to me."

"Dead people rising, growing fangs, and acquiring superhuman strength. You do the math."

I'd never been very good at math, but I could see where she was headed. "Vampires?"

"This *is* New Orleans."

"You keep saying that. It's still planet Earth, last I checked."

"Ever hear of Anne Rice?"

"She writes *fiction*, Cassandra. Vampires aren't real."

"Then what the hell was that?"

I didn't know, but I was damn straight going to find out.

"What do you know about vampires?" I demanded.

"Bram Stoker, Anne Rice, Laurell K. Hamilton." She shrugged. "I like vampire books."

"And you call yourself a voodoo priestess."

"Voodoo and vampires, not the same thing," she said.

"I'll take your word for it." I went silent as we made our way to Royal Street. "What's the common thread in all of the books?"

"The undead live forever. Coffins. Crucifix. Biting on the neck."

"Charlie was bitten on the neck. By an animal."

"According to legend, vampires can take the form of a wolf."

"Bingo," I whispered.

I couldn't believe in the short time since I'd arrived in New Orleans I'd gone from searching for an out-of-place wolf in the swamp to chasing zombies and considering vampires. Then again, this *was* New Orleans.

We reached Cassandra's shop.

"Do you have any books?" I asked.

"On the paranormal?" She unlocked the door and flicked on the lights. "I think I might."

I followed her across the shop, skirting the snake cage, even though Lazarus appeared fast asleep or dead. Considering his name, I doubted either one was a permanent condition.

Cassandra opened a glass-fronted case and pulled out one, two, three huge old volumes. Dust puffed as she set them on the counter. Then she bent and yanked another from a bottom shelf.

"We can start with these."

I glanced at my watch. "You care if I take them with me?"

"Got an appointment?"

"Kind of."

"Ruelle," she guessed.

I was supposed to head into the swamp with Adam tonight. And while I'd already decided to forgo that trip in favor of researching the vagaries of the vampire nation, that didn't mean I didn't want to do other things with him once I was through.

My face must have revealed my intentions, because she frowned. "Be careful."

"Why?"

"Have you ever seen him in the daylight, Diana?"

I opened my mouth, shut it again. Thought hard.

Hell.

"That doesn't mean anything," I insisted.

"Seems odd to me."

Now that she mentioned it, seemed odd to me, too. Still— "If Adam wanted to hurt me he could have a hundred times over."

"Maybe hurting you isn't what he's after."

"What's that supposed to mean?" I demanded.

"I don't know. You still have the gris-gris?"

I tapped my pocket. "Yep."

"I doubt that'll work against a vampire." She turned away. "But this should."

Cassandra reached into the display case near the register and withdrew a long gold chain. "Can't hurt, right?"

"How will that help, hurt, or anything else?"

"A crucifix a day keeps the vampires away."

I stared at the fancy chain. "What crucifix?"

"Well, not a crucifix, exactly. A cross. Times a hundred."

She held the necklace in front of my nose. The links themselves were in the shape of tiny fleurs-de-lis.

"This should work even better in theory," she continued. "The fleur-de-lis is the symbol of the Virgin Mary and, in some cases, the Trinity. Every little bit helps."

I hesitated, but in the end, I took the gift and put it on.

"That doesn't go around your neck," Cassandra murmured.

"Where else would it go?"

Cassandra reached out and lifted the thing over my head. "Pull up your shirt."

"What?"

"Relax. I'm not hitting on you. Though if I were gay, you'd definitely be my type."

I frowned, uncertain if I should be flattered or insulted. I decided on flattered.

"Haven't you ever seen a belly chain?" she asked.

"With a belly like mine? You've got to be kidding."

"There's nothing wrong with your belly. Pull up that shirt."

The idea of draping jewelry across my gut, of accenting a part of me that did not need any accenting, went against everything I'd learned as a big girl.

"Can't I just wear it as a necklace?"

"Too easy to yank off. A protective amulet is supposed to be hidden."

She seemed so certain—and really, what did I know about protective amulets?—I gave in and tugged up my shirt.

Cassandra quickly secured the chain. The cool links slid across my skin. Looking down, I was surprised the jewelry wasn't tight, had in fact disappeared below the waistband of my jeans. Knowing it was there, I felt kind of sexy.

"Thanks," I said, and really meant it. "What does *fleur-de-lis* mean?"

"Flower of the lily. Represents perfection, light, and life. Christian symbolism again—always in threes."

"Understandable. Do you have a computer?"

She blinked at my speedy change of subject. "In back. Why?"

"I want to know if Mrs. Beasly was ever found. I also want to research the name on that tomb."

Cassandra smiled. "You *are* good at this."

I wasn't so sure. I'd never found anything I was searching for. But as dream Simon had told me, I needed to believe. After tonight, I believed, all right. I just wasn't sure in what.

However, this time I wouldn't let anything escape my attention. I was going to find a paranormal entity—be it a loup-garou, a vampire, a zombie, or something I'd never heard of—and expose it to the world. Maybe then Simon could rest. Maybe then I could.

I followed Cassandra to her office. Huge, old, and slow, at least the computer worked. Arianna Beasly's name popped up in today's obituaries.

" 'Heart attack after being bitten by a vicious dog,' " I read.

"Sure she was."

"Her maiden name was Favreau, which explains where she was buried."

"Although it doesn't explain how she got dumped in the tomb so fast."

I glanced up. "What?"

"I don't know how they do things in your neck of the

woods, but down here a funeral takes a few days. And that's if there are no suspicious circumstances to warrant the police or an autopsy."

"True." I frowned. "Did you see any bite marks on her?"

"As many as I saw on Charlie."

"Weird, but I guess that answers my question."

"Which was?"

"They were both killed in basically the same way."

"Wound inflicted by a mystery canine," Cassandra murmured. "With said wound miraculously disappearing before the body rises and takes a little walk. So what does that mean?"

"As soon as I know, you will." I picked up the books and headed for the mansion.

I didn't realize how much I wanted Adam to be waiting for me until I came through the door and discovered the place empty.

Do not get used to him, Diana. You have to leave, and he doesn't want you to stay.

I made a peanut butter sandwich and coffee—you'd think the way I ate, I'd waste away to nothing, but no such luck—then I settled onto my sleeping bag and began to read.

Unfortunately, the events of the evening had worn me out, and I didn't get much done before I succumbed to sleep. As soon as I awoke, I spent the next day and well into the night researching.

The books were antiques, worth a small fortune. They were also full of great stuff.

"Crucifix, holy water, the Eucharist," I murmured.

All Christian items, which was fascinating considering the idea of night-flying, bloodsucking demons was not only pre-Christian but also a belief held around the world.

"How did they protect themselves B.C.?"

Sunlight, salt, and—

"Garlic."

Of course.

"A member of the lily family." I fingered the fleur-de-lis chain at my waist, feeling better about it already.

I continued to read, eating another peanut butter sandwich, drinking way too much coffee. I was hyped beyond belief and chattering to myself nonstop.

"Photos not a problem."

Which made sense. According to the photo shop kid, *werewolves* couldn't be photographed. But then, what had I seen in the swamp? Lord knew.

"However," I continued reading, "reflections are."

I considered the annoying lack of mirrors at Adam's cabin.

I didn't really believe the man I was sleeping with was a vampire, did I?

"No."

The sound of my own voice was getting on my nerves. But it was better than the sound of silence warring with the whirring confusion in my head.

I'd discovered how to kill them, how to slow them down; what I hadn't been able to find was—

"How do I know for certain I'm dealing with a vampire?"

A shadow at the corner of my vision made me gasp and spin in that direction so fast my neck cracked painfully. Adam leaned against the wall.

"You think I'm a vampire, *cher*?"

21

I glanced at the door—still closed. Then the windows—broken but not open. How had he gotten in without my hearing him?

I wasn't sure I wanted to know. If he was a vampire, did I plan to put a stake through his heart? I was fresh out.

"Well," he drawled. "Do you?"

While the appropriate response to that question would be *Of course not!* instead, I snapped, "How long have you been there?"

Adam shoved away from the wall and stalked toward me. His hair tangled when he shoved it out of his face; his bracelet caught the moonlight and sparkled. He wore a powder blue short-sleeved dress shirt, unbuttoned, and his chest rippled beneath a sheen of sweat that should have been unattractive but wasn't. Combined with the ragged jeans and bare feet . . . I wanted him so much I couldn't think straight.

He stopped directly in front of me. I had a perfect view of his crotch, which didn't look half-bad, either.

Because I wanted to lean forward and pull down the

bulging zipper with my teeth, I stood. On the way up, my breasts brushed his chest, and he hauled me against him.

"You think I'm a vampire, Diana?"

The question should have been foolish. We should both have been laughing. But we weren't.

His fingers bruised my skin. His erection pressed against my stomach. His blazing blue eyes seemed to pierce my brain.

"Are you?" I whispered.

"No."

The word came off his tongue sounding French. When he kissed me, there was a lot of French in that, too.

He tasted of hickory coffee—no, wait, that was me. Thick cream, heavy sugar—definitely him. I licked his teeth, wanting more of that taste, since I never dared drink my coffee anything but black.

With Adam I got all of the flavor and none of the calories. Only later did I realize, I'd also been checking those teeth for a razor-edged sharpness. I'm not sure what I would have done if I'd found some.

We were frantic again, pulling at each other's clothes. My top flew one way, my bra the other; his shirt slid from his shoulders and onto the floor. Why was it that every time we came near each other we couldn't seem to stop this from happening?

I was on fire, barely able to stand still, desperate for a release that I wasn't going to get from a kiss, when he backed me against the wall. How had he known I was weak in the knees?

I murmured my approval, lifting my arms around his neck as he ran his palms from the outside of my breasts to my hips.

He started, stilled, and stepped back, taking his hands and his mouth with him. I nearly fell on my face without his support.

"What's this?" He unbuttoned my pants, and the fleur-de-lis chain spilled out.

Oops.

I studied his face, but, as usual, I couldn't get a read on him.

"I—uh—got it today."

His eyes lifted from their solemn contemplation of my jewelry. "Why?"

"Protection."

"From vampires?" Adam's lips curved. "There's no such thing, *cher.*"

"Then why did I see Charlie in town?"

His lips flattened. "Dead Charlie?"

"Not anymore. Or maybe again. He blew up."

Adam glanced out the window, then back. "You're not makin' any sense."

"I saw Charlie, chased him to St. Louis Number One—"

"You nuts? Never go there alone."

I hadn't been alone, but that was beside the point.

"Charlie released a woman from her crypt. According to the obituary, she died two days ago, but she was walking pretty well last night."

"No one gets buried so quickly."

"That's all you've got to say?"

He touched my forehead. I slapped his hand away. "I'm not feverish or insane."

"You saw Charlie and a dead woman walk; then they blew up."

OK, when it was spoken out loud, I did sound nuts.

"And you think they were vampires?"

"Maybe. Cassandra said they weren't zombies."

"Who de hell is Cassandra?"

"Voodoo priestess."

He stared at me for several seconds. "My, you have been busy."

Why did his words sound like a threat?

Because I was paranoid as well as crazy. Oh well, the two went together like franks and beans.

"You don't believe me," I said.

"It doesn't matter what I believe; it's what you believe."

"I don't know anymore."

He brushed my hair from my cheek, and this time I let him. "New Orleans would spook anyone. There are ghosts here, can't help but be. But de things you're speaking of . . ." He shook his head. "I don't think this little old chain will protect you from them."

My chin tipped up. "You have a better idea?"

"No." His gaze lowered. "I like this one."

In a surprising movement, he dropped to his knees and tugged my jeans over my hips. His breath brushed my thighs, warm and inviting. My underwear followed the same path to the floor.

"Would you tell me if you were?" I asked.

"What?" When he glanced up, his eyes were unfocused, his mouth still swollen from mine.

Having him kneel at my feet, so gorgeous and tousled and aroused, filled my mind with too many possibilities. Nevertheless, I managed to choke out the question: "Would you tell me if you were a vampire?"

"Of course not, *cher.*"

Leaning forward, he pressed his mouth against the fleur-de-lis chain, against my belly, and suckled. Skin, metal, tongue, and teeth—the sensation was exquisite.

If he were a vampire, wouldn't he be—

Catching fire? Disintegrating into dust? Howling? Crying? Running?

He did none of them. But he did do other things.

The chain—both hot and damp, dry and cool—slipped from his mouth. He kissed me again. Lower.

My legs wobbled, and he cupped my hips with his big hands, pinning me to the wall as his tongue did amazing things.

Maybe he was a vampire? Maybe I didn't give a shit.

My fingers tangled in his hair, holding him closer, urging him on. How could a tongue be so hard and yet so soft, so clever and yet so tentative? Whenever I was on the verge of orgasm, he retreated just enough so I never came, driving me closer, higher, with the next stroke.

"I think you've had enough."

My eyes snapped open. He stood in front of me.

"No." I reached for him, and he took my hand, tugging me to the sleeping bag.

"We're not done." He gave me a little shove, and I toppled onto the covers.

As he stood over me in the faint moonlight, I memorized every ripple and curve. Just looking at him made me breathe a little harder.

He followed me down, brushed a stray strand of hair from my breast. "When you come, it's all I can do not to come, too, just watchin' you."

I wasn't sure what to say, so I said nothing.

"You're so alive." He laid his palm against my chest, dark against light, and pressed until I was supine. "So warm and soft and—"

He broke off, took a deep breath, and let it out. "I can't sleep nights thinkin' of being inside of you."

In one swift movement he covered my body with his and slipped in. I bit my lip to keep from making an embarrassing yummy noise at the contact.

"You're so tight." His forehead dropped against mine as he struggled for control.

"Sorry."

"No." A puff of air that was laughter hit my cheek. "That's good, so good."

I tried to relax, but I couldn't keep still. I had to have friction. My hips had a will of their own, pumping against him.

He cupped my breast in one hand, pressed his thumb to my skin. "I can feel your heart beat." His eyes seemed to reflect the three-quarter moon, glowing silver, fading to blue. "Makes me want to do all sorts of bad things."

"Just do me." I clenched around him. "Now."

I could feel his heart beat, too, in a completely different place. The pressure, the rhythm, the *thud, thud, thud,* made me shatter at last.

When I could see again, breathe again, we lay side by side, him tracing patterns across my stomach and breasts with one finger. "You still want to search for de wolf that isn't there?"

"You're awful accommodating for a man who doesn't believe we'll find one."

"I'll be as accommodating as you like, *cher,* if you keep accommodating me."

I pinched his arm and he laughed. I got a warm, squishy feeling right above the fleur-de-lis. This was nice.

Too nice.

I took his hand, meaning to push it away, but something flickered in his eyes, almost a wince. Instead of letting go, I held on.

"Of course the wolf isn't there," I said briskly.

His eyebrows lifted.

"The moon's nearly full. This is a crescent moon loup-garou."

If I hadn't been holding his hand, I wouldn't have felt the slight jerk of surprise. "Where you hear that?"

"I can read the newspaper, Adam."

An odd expression came over his face.

"What's the matter?"

"No one's called me by my given name for a long time."

"Why?"

"I don't see many people."

I tightened my fingers on his. "Why me?"

His lips curved. "Why not you?"

Well, that was flattering.

I suddenly remembered something I'd meant to ask. "When I left your place, I—uh, walked around a little."

"Mmm," he said, rubbing his thumb over my palm. I found it hard to think when he did that.

"Under the bedroom window it looked like you were going to plant something."

"Really?" His expression was as bland as his voice.

"I just wondered what."

"You a big gardener, *cher*? I never would have thought."

Well, what had I expected him to say? *There were wolf tracks there and since I'm hiding one, I didn't want you to see them.* Like that would happen.

Why didn't I just ask him straight out? He already thought I was loony because of the zombies. If I started talking about my dead husband walking, a mythical black wolf, tracks that weren't there, Adam might go away and never come back. I wasn't ready for that yet.

"You want to wait to search de swamp until de crescent moon returns?" he asked.

"I'm not sure."

His free hand played with the fleur-de-lis chain. At least he could touch it without bursting into flame.

He pulled me against him, spoonlike, and I was so shocked, I let him. With his breath in my hair and his hand at my hip, I drifted on a cloud of satisfaction and exhaustion.

Right before I fell into the abyss that was sleep I heard him whisper, "Better if you wore a silver chain. Two birds, one stone, that way."

I tried to stay awake. Tried to make sense of the comment.

Silver. Was that a hint? Or a warning?

I was too tired to ask. Too tired to do anything but fall.

22

I shouldn't have been surprised when I awoke to sunshine and an empty bed, but I was.

I'd suspected Adam of being a vampire, a foolish thought in the bright light of day. However, in the bright light of day, he was also gone again.

Perhaps the crucifix test was as worthless as the zombie-revealing powder. Although maybe the zombie-revealing powder worked just fine—on an actual zombie.

A thought tickled the edge of my mind. Adam had told me I should wear a silver fleur-de-lis chain. Two birds, one stone.

For a guy who was skeptical about vampires, were-wolves, and zombies he had an awful lot of paranormal advice to give.

I threw on some clothes, didn't bother with coffee, going directly to the books Cassandra had lent me. Maybe I'd been barking up the wrong tree after all. Pardon the horrible pun.

I flipped through one, found nothing. A second yielded the same result as the third. But the fourth—

"Bingo," I whispered as the book fell open to an entire chapter on werewolves.

Why is everything always in the last place we look?

Werewolves and vampires are alike in that they are both created by the bite of one similarly afflicted. A vampire can take the form of a wolf, and a werewolf can take the form of a human. However, silver will not harm a vampire and a crucifix will not harm a werewolf.

"One stone," I muttered, and kept reading.

If a werewolf is touched by silver, fire results.

I paused, remembering Cassandra's knife and the smoke that had risen from Arianna Beasly's arm. Had that knife been silver? I wouldn't be surprised.

If shot with a silver bullet, a werewolf will burst into flames.

"I guess we had our vampires and our werewolves all mixed up."

But someone didn't.

Both the person who'd saved us last night and the dead man in the swamp who'd come to New Orleans carrying an automatic rifle and silver bullets.

Had Detective Sullivan ever discovered the identity of his strangled swamp victim? If Sullivan had, the information might lead me to the second silver bullet–shooting believer. I really wanted to talk to that person.

I pulled out my cell phone and saw several messages

from Frank. I'd almost forgotten I was working for the man.

Detective Sullivan wasn't at his desk, so I left a message, then dialed my boss.

"Diana?" He must have caller ID. "Did you capture it?"

"Uh, not yet."

His sigh was both annoyed and disappointed. "I expected better of you."

Now I was annoyed. "I'm doing the best that I can."

"Do better. I need that loup-garou."

There was that word again.

"Why do you *need* it?"

"That's what I'm paying you for. I hate to waste money."

"What are you going to do with a werewolf if you get one?"

"Werewolf?" Both surprise and delight lightened his voice. "You told me there was no such thing. What have you seen to change your mind?"

I hesitated. There was *something* in the swamp—but was it the same something walking the streets of New Orleans?

"Diana? Tell me."

Frank's tension, his urgency, communicated itself over the miles. Not for the first time did I wonder if he were playing with a full deck. But since he was, as he'd so rudely pointed out, paying me, I told him what I knew.

"Disappearances, deaths, walking dead, silver bullets," he mused. "How can you doubt what you've seen?"

"I haven't seen a wolf."

I didn't tell him about my dream of the beast with Adam's eyes or about Simon. My dreams were none of Frank's business.

"You will," he murmured. "Then make sure you capture the loup-garou alive."

"I hadn't planned on killing him. Her. It. A dead cryptid won't help my reputation or Simon's."

"Of course." Frank cleared his throat. "Is there anything else you need?"

I'd planned to ask for a motion sensor camera, but considering the invisible nature of werewolves on film, such a request would no longer do me any good.

That werewolves couldn't be photographed was an interesting factoid and could explain why there wasn't much evidence on them. Cryptozoologists are often sent to investigate a photo, which leads to the real thing. But without that picture, no investigation.

My heart danced with excitement that I might be the first scientist to prove the existence of a werewolf.

"A cage," I said. "And a tranquilizer gun. I'll need the dosage of the darts based on the size of a large male timber wolf. About a hundred and twenty pounds."

"That's Alaskan size."

Frank knew a lot about wolves. In the lower U.S. eighty pounds was considered big. But considering the tracks I'd seen, the feeling I had, what I was after was one damn big wolf.

"Just do it, Frank."

"All right."

"Also several portable tree stands. The kind deer hunters use. Black. Metal."

I'd never gone deer hunting myself and neither had Simon, but we'd studied the best techniques. There aren't too many animals on earth more easily spooked than a deer. Those who stalked them knew what they were doing, and they always had the best gadgets.

"Should I send everything to the Ruelle Mansion again?" Frank asked.

"That would be great."

A momentary silence came over the line; then Frank blurted, "Have you seen him?"

I'd done a lot more than see Adam, but that wasn't Frank's business, either.

"Why?"

"I did some asking around. You'd do best to stay out of his way if you can. He's a dangerous man."

"Dangerous how?"

"He was trained to kill in the army."

"Isn't that what the army does?"

"Not like this. He's some überwarrior. I couldn't even buy information on what it was that he did."

Oh, no, the government wouldn't sell info on their top-secret soldiers; what *was* the world coming to?

"I'll be fine," I said.

"Stay away from him."

I doubted that I could. It might be just sex, but it was great sex, and I wasn't giving that up.

As Frank said good-bye, I considered the unknown man who had died in the swamp—the one who'd been strangled with someone's bare hands. Then I thought of Adam's hands, and I wondered: Would he strangle me one night?

I shook off the question. What possible reason could Adam Ruelle have for killing me? What reason could he have for killing anyone?

The mystery man had possessed an illegal rifle with silver bullets. He'd obviously been hunting a werewolf. So why had he been killed by a man? A loup-garou had so many better weapons at its disposal than fingers.

I opened one of Cassandra's books and then another. A few minutes later I found what I was looking for:

A werewolf can only remain a wolf under the light of the moon. Once the sun breaks the horizon, a lycanthrope becomes human. The beast has no choice.

The information in the book gave me a scenario. Wolf becomes man under the morning sun, and he has nothing with which to defend himself except—

"Hands."

Such thoughts made me uneasy. Because if it followed that the stranger had been murdered by someone capable of doing the deed with his bare hands, and the only someone around here of that nature was Adam, didn't it follow that Adam might be a werewolf?

"Well, you thought he was a vampire, what the hell?"

I had a headache.

I decided to go to town, beg a shower, some coffee—or tea, ack—and any food that Cassandra had. Considering my previous ineptitude at making friends, I should feel uncomfortable inviting myself over. But I knew Cassandra would welcome me gladly, as I'd welcome her. Chasing zombies, being confronted by werewolves, and nearly dying in a cemetery made fast friends. Which was probably why I had so few.

I reached New Orleans in record time and practically ran into the voodoo shop. Lazarus slithered down the center aisle and stuck his tongue out at me.

"Hey!" I shouted. "You wanna corral the reptile?"

The snake hissed.

"Well, you are."

"Insults will only get you in trouble." Cassandra scooped up Lazarus and popped him back in the cage.

I'd expected her to have a spectacular black eye after Mrs. Beasly's attack, but I could only discern a faint tinge of blue beneath an impressive makeup job. I suppose having a shiner would not be good for business.

"Why is being called a reptile an insult?" I asked.

"He thinks he's a *loa*."

"I know I'm not going to want to hear the answer, but what's a *loa*?"

She turned from the cage with a soft smile. "You know that vodoun is a religion."

"Vodoun?"

"That's what practitioners prefer to call voodoo."

"Oops." I lifted one shoulder. "Sorry."

"No biggie. The word means spirit or deity in the language of what's now Nigeria. The gods of vodoun are called *loas*."

I glanced uneasily at Lazarus. "He thinks he's a god?"

"As much as he can think."

Which I happened to believe wasn't much, but he was her snake.

"What brings you here so bright and early?" Cassandra asked.

"Desperation."

Her eyes went shrewd. "We're dealing with vampires?"

I opened my mouth, shut it again. So much had happened since I'd left here the last time.

"I meant I was desperate for a shower."

"Oh, sure. Help yourself." She held up a hand as I moved toward the back of the shop. "First, tell me what you found."

Since the reward was hot water and soap, I did.

"You think we were dealing with werewolves, not zombies or vampires?" she asked.

"Was that knife silver?"

"Of course."

I tilted my head. *Of course?* "Aren't those a little rare?"

"Not in my world," she said. "I've learned it never hurts to pack the very best."

Considering what happened at the cemetery, I had to agree.

"You think Ruelle's one of them?" she asked.

"I can't decide."

"What do you know about his background?"

"I never told you what I learned from Mrs. Beasly?"

"Before she rose from the dead, then exploded?"

I gave Cassandra a long look.

"Stupid question. Go on."

"The Ruelle women haven't birthed a girl in over a hundred years."

"OK. Big whoop."

"Adam's dad and his grandfather killed themselves."

"That's a bigger whoop." She frowned. "I don't like it."

"I doubt they liked it much, either."

"The Ruelles could be the cursed family of legend. They've been in New Orleans for centuries. I bet they had slaves at one time."

"If they're werewolves, how can they kill themselves?"

"Yeah, how can they?"

"I mean, aren't they immortal?"

"Immortal doesn't mean what it used to." I gave her another look, and she explained. "Vampires can be killed by sunlight, stake through the heart. Werewolves by silver. That's not immortal. Not really."

"I see your point."

"How did the Ruelles die?"

"Blew their brains out."

"With silver?"

"They didn't get that specific in the newspaper accounts."

"I suppose not. We might be able to get our hands on the autopsy reports." She went silent for several seconds. "Mrs. Beasly told you this stuff and the next thing we know she's climbing out of the family crypt drooling and snarling."

"Pretty much."

"I think we should talk to the Favreau family."

"I think you're right."

23

A quick trip to the Internet revealed that Arianna Beasly's in-laws owned a home in the Garden District, while her family, the Favreaus, still lived in the French Quarter. The calendar might read century twenty-one, but in New Orleans the old ways prevailed.

The original Favreaus had come to Louisiana before the area's purchase was a gleam in Thomas Jefferson's eye. Back then, the upper-crust French resided in the Quarter; eventually the Spanish did, too. However, when the Americans showed up, they were shunned miserably. Kind of like what happens in France today.

Being Americans, they'd taken their filthy money and built the American Quarter, which began in the business district and stretched into what is now known as the Garden District.

Americans—gotta love 'em. Bigger is always better, and if we can't buy what we want, we'll just build what we want and call it superior to the original.

Mrs. Beasly would be considered a Creole, a descendant of Europeans born in the colonies. That and the family residence in the high tax bracket of the Quarter explained the crypt at St. Louis Cemetery Number One.

No doubt the Beaslys owned a crypt in the more modern Lafayette Cemetery Number One, which bordered the Garden District. Perhaps Arianna had chosen to be buried with her side of the family. Not uncommon. Around here, where you were buried was almost as big of a deal as where you were born.

At any rate, Cassandra and I rang the bell at a gorgeous nineteenth-century home on Burgundy Street. The door was opened by a tiny, wizened old lady sporting a ferocious scowl.

"We do not have ghosts, good day."

She began to slam the door, but I blurted, "We came to talk about Mrs. Beasly."

The woman hesitated, blinking through thick bifocals. Considering the murky state of her gray eyes, her cataracts were the problem, not her prescription.

"You're friends of Arianna's?"

"Yes," Cassandra answered before I could say, *Not really.*

Cassandra shot me a silencing glare as the elderly woman invited us inside.

"I'm sorry I was rude, but there are stories about this house, and all those damnable ghost walk tours stop outside and stare at us. Some rude people even ring the doorbell and ask to see the room where it happened."

"Where what happened?" I asked.

"The murder, of course."

"Of course," Cassandra said.

The woman tottered to her chair, and Cassandra took the opportunity to whisper, "There's always a murder or a ghost around here. That's not what we came for."

True. If we got started on the ghost stories in the French Quarter, we'd never get to the werewolves.

"You seem awfully young to know my Arianna." She motioned for us to take seats nearby.

"She was your . . ." I hesitated.

This woman resembled Mrs. Beasly around the eyes and mouth, but was she a sister, an aunt, a mother? Once people hit ancient I was no good at determining their generation.

"Granddaughter. I'm Marie Favreau."

"Ma'am." I nodded respectfully, earning a small smile. "Mrs. Beasly and I met at the library. I was sorry to hear about her . . . accident."

Mrs. Favreau's lips lost the smile and pressed together as if she wanted to keep the words inside. But she couldn't. "That was no accident."

Cassandra and I exchanged glances.

"How so?" Cassandra asked.

Mrs. Favreau looked around, then beckoned us closer. "We wouldn't have buried her so quickly, without benefit of a church service, if we were only talking about a dog."

"What *are* we talking about?" I asked.

She made an odd motion with her arthritic fingers— half sign of the cross, kind of an FU. I wasn't sure what to do.

"Protection against evil," Cassandra murmured.

Mrs. Favreau considered her with a contemplative expression. "You know the old ways."

"Oh yeah."

"Then you know why we stuffed her mouth with monkshood and drew a pentagram on her chest," Mrs. Favreau continued.

"Monkshood?" I asked.

"Wolfsbane," Cassandra translated.

That made sense. I guess.

Of course I hadn't seen anything in Mrs. Beasly's mouth but teeth and hadn't gotten a gander at her chest. Considering she was ashes, I'd have to take Granny's word for it.

"Loup-garou," Mrs. Favreau whispered, and made the sign of the FU again.

Now we were getting somewhere.

"The bitten must be encased in cement and properly prepared or they'll rise and walk as a wolf," she continued.

"I'm afraid she rose anyway," Cassandra said gently.

I wondered how long we'd had before Mrs. Beasly turned into a wolf. Now we'd never know.

Mrs. Favreau went white. "She'll come for me. She'll know I'm the one who had her buried that way."

"Relax," I said. "She's dead for good this time. Shot with silver, we think."

The woman slouched in her chair, shaking fingers pressed to her mouth. "Thank you."

"Wasn't us."

"That doesn't matter as long as she's truly dead. She wasn't Arianna anymore."

Remembering Mrs. Beasly's sharp teeth and propensity for drooling, I had to agree.

"What do you know of the loup-garou?" I asked.

"Only the legend."

"You've never seen a werewolf?"

She closed her eyes, took a breath, then opened them again. "We take care to bury certain bodies in certain ways so the dead don't walk."

"What ways?"

"If a person is killed by an animal, monkshood and a pentagram."

"Any animal?" I pressed. "Not just canine?"

She stared at me over the tops of her glasses, and despite the murky cataracts, I could swear she saw right through me.

"The wolf creates the werewolf. Other animals create other monsters."

Other monsters? Terrific.

"One problem at a time," Cassandra murmured.

I must have been hyperventilating.

"What else?" I asked.

"If there is suspicion of vampirism, garlic and a cross. Salt for zombies. If you think their spirit may walk, bury the dead with Apache tears."

I glanced at Cassandra for clarification again. I wasn't disappointed.

"Obsidian," she said.

Mrs. Favreau sniffed. "Better safe than sorry."

"Do the methods usually work?"

What I really wanted to know: Was there something special about Arianna Beasly that had made her rise despite the precautions? Or did all the bitten do so, but no one ever knew?

"I never had occasion to try the practice until now."

"What about your friends?" Cassandra asked.

"An acquaintance of mine was forced to bury her husband with garlic and a sixteenth-century crucifix made in Provence."

"And that worked?" I leaned forward in my chair. "Her husband stayed dead?"

"I assume so."

"Could I speak with her?"

"She fell off her balcony a few days later. Broke her neck."

Uh-oh.

"Anyone else?"

"A dear friend's child was bitten by a rat." Mrs. Favreau frowned. "My friend had a heart attack not long after."

Another nasty pattern. I had a sneaking suspicion that those who'd been the recipients of the "precautions" visited the ones who'd imposed them as soon as they became undead. Lucky for Mrs. Favreau her granddaughter had exploded in a burning ball of fire. *Lucky for us all,* I was thinking.

Note to self—leave off the monkshood, garlic, salt, obsidian, and pentagrams. They didn't work anyway. Silver, on the other hand, might be useful.

"Mother." Another tiny white-haired woman stood in the doorway. She bustled in, casting Cassandra and me a curious glance. "Isn't it time for your nap?"

"I'll be napping forever soon enough," Mrs. Favreau grumbled. "I was just visiting with some friends of Arianna's."

The newcomer's face fell. "My little girl."

Though I knew Arianna Beasly had a mother, everyone did, it hadn't occurred to me I'd meet her today. Although why it hadn't, since I was speaking with Arianna's grandmother, I wasn't quite sure.

To have three generations alive at the same time is achievement enough. To have them alive at this age was pretty darned amazing. Of course they weren't all alive anymore.

"We're sorry for your loss," I said, feeling keenly how useless those words were.

"Thank you," she said, though she didn't look grateful. She looked a little pissed. "Now I have to get Mother some lunch and a nap. She isn't as young as she used to be."

I wanted to ask how old she was, how old they both were, but I didn't dare. Such questions would be considered rude even above the Mason-Dixon Line. Down here, I just might find myself drawn and quartered.

"Don't worry, Anne." The older woman patted the younger on the hand. "Arianna is at peace." She tottered toward the door, stopping in the entryway. "Someone shot her with silver. She went kaboom."

Silence settled over us as Mrs. Favreau disappeared down the hall. Uncertain of what to expect, I cast a cautious glance toward the other woman.

"My mother-in-law's a little—" She twirled one finger around her ear in the universal hand signal for nuts.

"Really?" Cassandra murmured.

"She was telling you the werewolf story, right?"

I stilled. "That's not true?"

Anne gave a short bark of laughter. "You believed her?"

Cassandra made a staying motion with her hand when I would have spoken. "We shouldn't have?"

"This might be New Orleans, but that doesn't mean we're all lunatics. My daughter was not bitten by a werewolf."

"OK," Cassandra said. "Then why did you bury her so fast?"

Anne's laughter died and something flickered in her eyes before she turned and headed for the front door. We had little choice but to follow. I guess our welcome had run out.

To my surprise, as we filed onto the porch she answered the question. "We buried Arianna so quickly because my mother-in-law insisted. She was hysterical. It was easier to do as she wanted."

The door closed behind us. Cassandra and I stood in the brutal afternoon sun until someone said, "Psst."

Marie Favreau beckoned from the corner of the house.

"I did see a werewolf once," she whispered as we joined her. "I was a child. My papa took me to Mardi Gras. We were coming home and down an alleyway I saw a man and his dog. My papa said the man had drunk too much wine, so he was resting, with his good friend Mr. Dog to watch over him."

She passed a frail, shaking hand over her eyes, as if she were seeing it all again. "Then Mr. Dog began to eat the man's face. I screamed and the animal glanced up. He was not a dog."

"A wolf."

"Yes. But that's not why I screamed and screamed as my papa scooped me into his arms and ran with me all the way home."

"Mother!" Anne's voice came from the rear of the house. "Where are you?"

"I have to go," she said.

"Wait." I reached out, and she tilted her head expectantly. "Why did you scream?"

"The eyes."

A chill went over me, which was downright amazing considering the blistering heat of the sun. "I don't understand."

"I think you do." She glanced over her shoulder, then back. "Though the form may be that of a wolf, a werewolf always retains its human eyes."

24

I saw again the wolf at the window—the wolf that had possessed Adam's eyes.

"Diana?" Cassandra grabbed my forearm as Marie scurried away to intercept her daughter-in-law, and squeezed hard.

"I'm OK."

I wasn't. Not really. I wanted to sit down, maybe lie down, or stand up, maybe throw up. What I did was drag Cassandra away from the Favreaus' and back to her place. Luckily, it wasn't a long trip.

Once inside the cool, shadowed interior, I sat at her kitchen table and put my head between my knees.

"Don't faint on me," she snapped.

"I do *not* faint."

"You're doing a damn good imitation." She sat, too. "The wolf at the window?"

Slowly I lifted my head and nodded.

I'd told her my dream, that I'd seen a wolf with human eyes, but I hadn't mentioned whose eyes they were. From the expression on her face, she already knew.

"When you saw the wolf, where was Adam?"

"In bed with me." I took a deep breath, let it out slowly. "Must have been a dream after all."

"Or a premonition."

"I don't have premonitions."

Cassandra went silent. Still a little woozy, I was having a hard time assimilating the information, having no luck at all interpreting it.

"You dreamed of a wolf with human eyes before we knew that werewolves have them." She glanced in my direction. "Human eyes, I mean."

"Probably just a coincidence."

"A coincidence is running into someone right after you thought about them. What you described to me is *not* a coincidence."

"What is it then?"

"No clue."

"Damn, you're helpful."

She didn't rise to the bait. Why I was baiting her, I wasn't sure. Right now, she was the only friend I had, the only person I trusted. I tried to make amends by making excuses.

"Maybe I read something about werewolves in the past and my subconscious remembered. I read a lot of bizzaro stuff."

"Could be."

"My husband never mentioned it, though."

Cassandra cast me a sharp glance. "He saw one?"

"So he said."

Out on the moors, D-baby. A man became a wolf and then ran beneath the full moon.

"I'm thinking he didn't get close enough to see the eyes." Until that last night anyway.

"There's one thing that bugs me," Cassandra murmured.

Thrilled to leave the memory of Simon and his death behind, I jumped on the comment. "Just one?"

She didn't bother to acknowledge my attempt at levity. "Why is it a wolf?"

"Huh?"

"Or maybe I should ask, *how* is it a wolf?"

"Cassandra, what are you talking about?"

"Marie Favreau said wolves make wolves."

"If we can believe her. If she isn't crazy."

"Do you think she is?"

"If she is, I am." I rubbed my forehead. "I don't feel crazy."

"Crazy people never do."

"Har-har. Could we get back to the topic at hand, which I'm still not clear on?"

"If it takes a wolf to make a wolf, where did the first wolf come from?"

"Is that a riddle?"

Cassandra ignored me again. She was getting very good at it. "No wolves in Louisiana. That's what got you here in the first place."

"There were wolves once. Red wolves."

"Is this a red wolf?"

I shook my head. "Too big, too black, too timber wolfy."

"Which brings us back to the curse."

"According to you," I murmured, "man became beast with no biting involved."

"But *why* a wolf? Why not an alligator, or a snake, or a leopard for that matter?"

Yeah, why?

I had a bad feeling. Without asking permission, I headed

for Cassandra's office, started clicking away on her computer before she even got there.

"What are you thinking, Diana?" she asked.

"Names have power," I muttered.

Seconds later I saw how much.

" 'Ruelle,' " I read. " 'French for "famous wolf." ' "

Cassandra drew in a quick, sharp breath.

"That's why the curse created a wolf."

"We don't know for sure—" she began.

"Maybe not." I stood and started for the door. "But I plan to find out."

No wonder he'd said there wasn't a loup-garou. No wonder he'd volunteered to be my guide. No wonder he'd distracted me with the sex of a lifetime.

What better way to make sure I never found what I'd come to find? If I was looking forward, I wasn't seeing what was right under me—had been right under me more than a few times.

"Wait," Cassandra called. "You need to take a weapon."

"I don't suppose you have any silver bullets handy."

"No, but—" She hurried into the shop, murmuring to Lazarus when he hissed. As I stepped through the beads hanging in the doorway, she slapped her knife into my palm. "Silver, through and through."

The idea of shoving a knife into Adam—

"I can't."

"Believe me, Diana, if he grows fangs and a tail, you can."

"What if he doesn't?" I glanced at the window. "It's daytime."

"Touch him with the thing. See if he smokes."

"Terrific," I muttered. "He's going to think I'm insane."

"Good. If this is insane, then he isn't the loup-garou."

And we had a whole new set of problems. Because if Adam wasn't, who was?

Cassandra bit her lip. "Maybe I should go, too."

"So he can kill both of us?"

"He isn't going to kill you."

"No?"

"If he wanted you dead, you'd be dead already."

"Great."

"You could take Detective Sullivan along. He wants to talk to Ruelle anyway."

I considered the notion, then put it away. "Adam isn't going to tell me the truth if I bring a cop. Besides, he hasn't hurt me. He might hurt Sullivan."

"You have to let me know you're all right. Tell me what happened, what he said."

"OK."

"By—" She glanced at her watch. "Seven o'clock."

"In the morning?"

"Tonight!"

"No. Morning."

If I was wrong about Adam, I might have to make it up to him. Considering the accusation, that could take a while.

25

Deciding to confront Adam Ruelle and actually finding him were two different things. He wasn't conveniently waiting for me in the living room of my rented abode. Of course, as previously noted, it *was* daytime.

I headed into the swamp, reversing the map he'd once drawn to lead me from shack to mansion. He wasn't there, either. Where did he go when the sun shone?

I was tempted to use his shower. Never had gotten to check out Cassandra's. But the idea of Adam arriving while I was naked and streaming wet stopped me, despite the grimy-grainy feeling of my skin and hair. How could I confront him with any sort of bravado fresh from a shower?

I couldn't. So I wandered around his three-room shack, knife in hand, as I searched for clues. They weren't any more available than he was.

Food, soap, clothes—the essentials—but there wasn't a single scrap of the paraphernalia of daily life. No books. No papers. No bills, no checks, no MasterCard. If he lived here, where was his stuff?

The more I looked around, the more annoyed I became. There had to be something that would mark this as Adam Ruelle's place.

Though I knew it was wrong, I went through everything. Every drawer, every shelf, every closet, even the medicine cabinet. I found nothing out of the ordinary. Not even a stray doggie biscuit or a bill from the local veterinarian.

I lost track of time, or maybe the sun faded more quickly in the swamp, because when I pulled my head from under the sink, dusk had descended.

Outside, a long, low howl began in the distance. Just one. But one was enough to make me want to run all the way home.

To Boston.

"Wuss," I muttered. "You promised Simon you'd prove him right, but the first time you actually have a chance to discover something out of this world, you want to run home to Mommy."

As if Katherine O'Malley would ever answer to such a crass monicker as Mommy. I'd been instructed to call her Kate the instant I'd grown a half an inch taller than her. Being me, I'd continued to refer to her as Ma whenever the opportunity arose.

I crept to the front window and peered at the steadily falling night. The cypress trees blotted out the last of the sun. The sky was both bright blue and bloodred—stunning and scary in one. Just like Adam.

My fingers curled around the knife. Staring at it, I frowned. I couldn't kill him. I needed him alive. Which might be tough.

"Maybe I should—"

"What?"

My head went up. He was already inside the room. Fully clothed in loose dark pants, boots, and a black T-shirt, so at least I didn't have to deal with the mind-numbing sight of too much bare, bronzed skin.

What I'd been going to say was *wait for the cage and the tranquilizer gun*. Glad I hadn't mentioned those out loud.

"Go," I finished on a whisper.

His lips turned up just a little. "Stay instead, *cher.*"

He was so damn gorgeous, he couldn't be human.

I slid the hand that held the knife behind my thigh as he crossed the room. I let him get close, put his arm around my waist, press that great body and beautiful mouth against mine. We even did the tongue tango for several seconds. Hey, if I had to kill him, I should at least make sure he died happy. I yanked off his shirt.

Then, while he was nuzzling my neck and stroking my breasts, growing hard against my stomach, making me almost forget one little problem, I brought the knife up fast.

I couldn't stab him. I didn't have it in me. Instead, I pressed the silver against his skin.

He shoved me away with a hiss, and my heart seemed to stop. I stared at his arm, expecting smoke, finding none.

Hell, I was going to have to try again. I tightened my grip, and he kicked my hand. I didn't even see it coming. The knife flew. He grabbed my wrist and twisted it behind my back.

"What de hell?" he growled. "You crazy?"

"I—"

He tugged a little tighter, and agony shot through my shoulder.

"Are you the loup-garou?" I blurted.

He released me so fast, I fell to my knees, peering at him through the tangle of my hair. He stared back with no expression whatsoever.

"I am not," he said.

"I'm supposed to take your word for it?"

"You asked. I answered."

"The knife was silver. You flinched."

"It was a knife, Diana. You think I'd let you stick me and see if I exploded?"

My eyes narrowed. "How did you know silver makes a werewolf explode?"

He swore in French, then stalked to where the knife had fallen, picked it up, and pressed the blade against his bare chest.

Nothing happened.

With a practiced movement, he flipped the thing into the air, caught the sharp end, and offered me the handle. Climbing to my feet, I took the weapon but set it on a table.

"Everyone knows silver and werewolves do not mix," he said.

"Everyone?"

"Everyone around here."

I fidgeted, uncertain what to do or say next.

"You have more questions. Ask."

"Is your family cursed?"

He shrugged. "Some say we are."

"Was your ancestor cursed to run as a wolf under the crescent moon?"

Adam's blue eyes, the eyes of the wolf in my dream, my premonition, my harsh parting from reality, met mine.

"No," he answered.

I tried to determine if he was telling me the truth, but I couldn't. I might have shared more with this man than I'd shared with any other except my husband, but I didn't know him. I couldn't trust him.

"*Ruelle* means famous wolf," I blurted.

"Just like *Diana* means moon goddess." He tilted his head, and his hair slid across one eye. "Maybe I should wonder about you and de silver, hmm?"

He picked up the knife, and a flicker of fear raced through me. Why in hell had I put the thing down?

"Come here." He beckoned with the blade.

I shook my head and backed away.

"Never run, *cher*. Wolves like to chase."

"This isn't funny, Adam."

He wasn't laughing. Neither was I. But we were both breathing pretty hard. A lot of eye contact. Stalk. Retreat.

My shoulders hit the wall. His lips lifted just a little.

I wasn't sure if I was scared spitless or aroused beyond redemption. Maybe both.

He stepped in close, crowding me with his body, bumping me with his erection. I couldn't move. Did I want to?

For an instant I struggled, but that only made us fit together even better. I was more rubbing than fighting against him. When I stilled, so did he.

"Don't," I whispered.

His gaze on my breasts, which strained against the tank top I'd worn to offset the heat, he lifted his eyes to mine as he lowered the knife to the neck of the shirt.

With one deft movement, he split the material. The cotton fell away, hanging uselessly from my shoulders as damp air trickled across my chest. My nipples puckered inside my plain white bra.

"Don't what?" he murmured, pressing the cool silver blade to my heated skin.

"Stop."

"Is it don't?" He lifted the knife, careful not to nick me, and caught the tip in the wisp of material holding the two A cups together. "Or is it stop?"

He was very good with the weapon. He'd no doubt had secret commando training, though I doubted he'd ever used a knife in quite this way. Then again, maybe he had. Maybe he did this all the time, with all the girls.

I gave a mental wince at the thought of other women, which was foolish. This was about sex, not love, and that was how we both wanted it.

I stared into his face, and I saw nothing but a man who desired me as much as I desired him. My suspicions proved groundless, my accusations now seemed foolish.

"Don't stop," I said.

He flicked the knife and my bra snapped open. If I'd had any breasts to speak of, they'd have whapped him in the chest. As it was, they slid along his bare skin, the sensation better than an ice-cream cone in the middle of July. Both relief and desire, sweetness and sin.

I wrapped my fingers in his hair tight enough to make him grunt as I tugged his mouth to mine.

And the knife clattered to the floor.

26

I expected the usual slam bam without even a "thank you, ma'am," sex that bordered on rough, a rocketing orgasm. Instead he slowed things down, and I was lost.

"Come." He took my hand; he pulled me across the floor.

I followed obediently, drunk on the taste of his mouth, the scent of his skin. I figured we were headed for the couch and that was fine with me, yet when I hesitated halfway across the room, he turned, shaking his head.

"Not tonight. Tonight we do this right."

We hadn't been doing it right? Could have fooled me.

His bed was made, which gave me a start. He didn't seem the kind of guy who bothered. Then again, from the military corners and the tight white sheets, maybe he couldn't help himself.

Just like I couldn't help myself. Certainly I'd proved he wasn't an evil soulless beast or the walking undead. But even if he had been, could I have resisted him? I wasn't sure.

He climbed onto the bed, never letting go of my hand. Did he think I'd run if he released me? I wouldn't get far.

Even as a man, he could catch me. Especially since I'd let him.

The ripple of muscle across his abdomen was accented by the line of his pants. Not a centimeter of excess flesh lapped over the waistband. Reaching out, I traced my thumb along a ridge, and his skin fluttered beneath my touch.

I wanted to taste him, feel life against my lips, push aside the button, the zipper, and lay claim to what was beneath. I wanted to make amends for doubting him, if not for the knife.

What guy wouldn't appreciate a blow job apology?

His slacks were worn soft from years of use. The single button popped free with very little encouragement.

He watched me through slitted, lazy eyes, though the hardened length of his body revealed a coiled tension, the tangle of his hair hinted at a certain wildness.

The rumble of his zipper as I tugged it down seemed to fill the room, electrify the air. He continued to watch me without a word or a movement, except to lift his hips just enough so I could slide the pants down. No underwear lay beneath, only skin.

I wanted to learn every line and every curve. Since he didn't appear to be going anywhere, I indulged myself.

A light dusting of hair covered his legs, just enough to make them manly, not enough to nudge them toward beast. I trailed my fingernails through the curls, up the inside of his thighs, and he quivered. How far could I go before he lost control?

My hands roved higher, thumbs skating over the curve where his leg became his hip. He arched, begging me to touch him. I couldn't deny a need I felt so deeply myself.

I lowered my head, and my hair spilled over his chest, hiding me from view as I hovered, my breath brushing his pelvis, making him think, *Yes, maybe, now,* before I pressed my mouth to his belly, let my tongue circle his navel, then trace a moist path downward.

My breasts cradled his erection. His pulse beat in time with mine. He slid through my cleavage, such that it was, simulating the intimate act. I lowered my head and licked him just once.

His body leaped in response. Eyes closed, he moved against me, and I lost myself watching his face. The man enjoyed sex. With him, I enjoyed it, too.

Not that I hadn't before, but when love is involved the act is more about mind than body, heart than hands, lips, and tongue. There was something to be said about sex for the sake of sex.

My nipples tightened, hardening as they brushed his upper thighs. The rhythmic strokes sent a bolt of heat through me. I wanted to lift my body over his, take him deep within. I wanted to ride him until we were both mindless and begging.

But not yet.

I inched downward and he let me go, hands sliding over my shoulders, up my neck, across my face. His fingers tangled in my hair as I took him in my mouth. He caressed my scalp with languid strokes, guiding, encouraging, urging me on.

He lasted a good long while. His control was downright impressive. It became a battle of wills; who would surrender first, him or me? I didn't plan to lose. I wouldn't.

My tongue did things I'd only imagined. I used my teeth where I'd never used them before. Still he didn't come, didn't speak, didn't move anything but his fingers through my hair.

I grasped him at the hilt, ran my thumb down his length, followed with my tongue, scraped him with my teeth, and his hand finally tightened.

His face was set, his eyes brighter, lighter than I remembered. As I held his gaze, I licked him, once, twice, three times, swirling softly, then taking him all and suckling hard.

He swelled and grew, so close to erupting. Frantic, I rode him with my mouth, drawing him to the back of my throat, then nearly setting him free.

"No," he murmured, the rumble of his voice making my lips tingle, my ears buzz. "Please."

I lifted my head and he groaned. I blew on the chilly dampness left by my tongue, and his eyes fluttered closed.

"Please what?"

I closed my teeth over his tip, scored the skin just a little. His eyes shot open. I expected something gruff, perhaps crude. But had anything ever been as I expected with him?

"Take me inside, *cher.* I want to feel your body all around me."

I frowned at the request, too personal, too revealing. I was tempted to finish him off despite any protest. He was too close; a few more strokes, and he'd be able to do nothing but come.

Though oral sex could be more intimate than anything else, right now it wasn't. There was a distance between us, a distance I wanted to keep. Why was he trying to breach it?

His hand still tangled in my hair, his thumb stroked my cheek. My eyes burned, and my chest ached. This was *so* not a good idea.

In spite of that, I was captured by his gaze, compelled by his voice, murmuring words in French that I didn't understand.

I did as he wanted, because I wanted it, too, surrounding him, taking him in. We moved together as if we'd done this a thousand times. The advance, the retreat, so new and yet so familiar, first filling me up, then nearly leaving me alone. The latter made me clutch him tight, hold him close, grasp him in the depths of myself, and consider never letting him go.

"Look at me," he ordered.

I didn't want to. If I didn't see his face, he wasn't a man, or a beast, he was a ride, albeit a damn good one.

Disgusted with my thoughts, I again did as he asked, meeting his gaze, seeing myself. Who was that woman? Could she be me?

"You don't think of him when I'm inside you."

I said nothing, not even when he arched his back and touched me more deeply than ever before.

"Say it," he whispered. "Say it, or I won't make you come."

Even if I could have spoken, I didn't know what he wanted. He stopped moving—a little too late.

The release began so small, so far away and yet so large, so near, I wasn't sure if the spasms were him at first or me. Didn't matter, because both of us were rocking together, coming apart.

I collapsed on his chest; he ran his hand up my back. The world returned, and he was still inside me. I was draped all over him. Uncertain, almost childlike, he began to play with the fleur-de-lis chain at my waist.

"What did you want me to say?" I asked.

"My name. That's all."

I lifted my head, shifted my body, but kept our legs tangled together. "Why?"

"You said 'Simon' de last time you were in my bed."

I flinched at the sound of my husband's name while my body still tingled from another man. I didn't want to talk about Simon. Not now, not ever, and definitely not here and not with him.

"I was asleep," I snapped. "It isn't as if I called you Simon while you were doing me."

This time *he* flinched, and I got worried. Was he expecting more than I could ever give? He didn't seem the type. Then again, what type was he?

"I'm sorry, Adam." I rolled onto my back so we were no longer touching. "I wouldn't like it if you said another woman's name, either. Even though . . ."

I paused, uncertain what to say.

"Even though there's nothing between us but this?" he finished.

I turned my head; our noses nearly brushed. "Yes."

For just an instant I wondered if it could be more. If I could love another man the way I'd loved Simon. If I could love this man.

"I wish I could love you," he whispered.

Was he reading my thoughts? Mirroring them? And speaking of mirrors . . .

"You don't have any," I blurted.

Confusion flickered over his face. "Love?"

"Mirrors."

The confusion fled, replaced by wariness, just before the stoic mask returned. He'd shut me out as if he had something to hide.

"I don't like mirrors, *cher.*"

"Because . . . ?"

He sat up, presented me with his back. "What you want me to say? That I can't see my reflection? Or that I don't want to?"

I sat up, too, but turned toward him. Something was going on here; I just couldn't figure out what.

"There are things I've done," he said softly. "Things you couldn't imagine."

Was he talking about the army? Or something else?

"*What* did you do?"

He stood, muscles rippling in his back, his legs, his arms. "More than I can ever say."

"I meant, what was your job in the army? Detective Sullivan couldn't access your file."

"My life then is dead. I'm here now, and I'll never be free."

He spun around, putting his hands on the bed, leaning over me, crowding into my space. "I'm not de man for you."

"I know."

"I can't love you."

"I can't love *you*."

"Don't ask me to."

"I didn't." My voice was clipped, my back tense to the point of aching.

"Just so we're clear."

"Crystal."

His lips twitched. "What you so mad about, *cher*? I'm just gettin' things out in de open. No hard feelings later that way."

"Fine with me," I said, but my back was stiffer than a scrub brush bristle.

He sank onto the bed, rubbed a big hand over my shoulders.

"Shh," he whispered, pulling me into his arms. "We both want de same thing. While you're here, we'll be together. When you go, we won't be."

"OK."

"Because you *will* go."

"Yes."

Especially since he hadn't asked me to stay.

27

Déesse de la lune.

The words whispered through my mind. I'd heard
them before. Now I heard them in Adam's voice.

I fought the heavy veil of sleep, tried to surface, to see.
Who was speaking? What had they said and why?

Bursting awake as if coming from the depths of a
rolling ocean and into a silent night, I found myself alone.
I glanced toward the window, but nothing was there.

"A dream," I murmured.

I was so sick of dreams.

The room was dark; the moon had disappeared and the
sun hadn't yet arisen. A secret, lonely hour, which wasn't
night or day or even dawn.

The front door closed. Before I even knew what I was
doing, I jumped out of bed and pulled on my clothes. Or
what was left of them. My tank top was shredded, so I
helped myself to one of Adam's, but my breasts tumbled
out the armholes, since he'd shredded my bra while he
was at it.

What had been incredibly sexy last night was merely an annoyance now. I mumbled curses as I found a T-shirt that might have been white once but was now kind of gray, and tugged it over my head.

A quick glance out the window revealed Adam slipping through the shadows and into the tall grass.

This was his place. Where was he going?

Time to find out. I raced through the house and out the front door.

Did I actually believe I'd be able to follow him through the swamp without his knowing I was there? He'd lived here all his life, and while I'd spent a lot of time in some very odd places, I wasn't exactly the invisible woman. Nevertheless, I had to try.

Head down, he barely looked where he was going as he meandered through the weeds and the standing water. Was he thinking of me? Or the us that could never be? What about the us that might be? Did I dare tell him I wanted to try for more, or would that scare him off for good?

Considering I'd never woken in the daylight with him by my side, no matter what we'd shared in the night, scaring him off wasn't hard. Why worry about it now?

Dawn broke, spilling muted sunshine across the land. There was a chill to the morning, but soon the heat would rise. Ahead tires roared across pavement; a horn tooted. I glanced around, uncertain where I was.

Adam climbed an embankment, then crossed a highway I didn't recognize. On the opposite side lay a trailer park.

Frowning, I crept forward, catching sight of him just as he opened the door on one of the mobile homes and disappeared.

What the hell? Was this where he spent his days? Not in a coffin or a grave or a lair but a trailer park? I hadn't seen that coming.

I left the cool shadows of the swamp, slipping and sliding up the embankment, then waiting for a semi truck to pass before I scooted across the two-lane highway.

Expecting the trailer park to be run-down, kind of slummy, I was surprised to find neat plots of grass and flowers planted around the bases of most of the mobile homes. Each was well kept, clean, even shiny.

Tricycles, Big Wheels, Flintstone cars, resided in nearly every driveway. Where Adam had disappeared, they had one of each.

My eyes narrowed. Who lived here? I had a very bad feeling I wasn't going to like the answer.

Tempted to bang on the door, I refrained. Just past six in the morning, I didn't want to be rude. So I slunk around the side and peeked in the window. I didn't mind being criminal.

Cartoons spilled across the TV screen. A little boy of perhaps four or five stared avidly at the square yellow blob with a face, legs, and hands that appeared to be dancing under the sea.

I craned my neck. A young African-American woman stood in the kitchen, pouring cereal into a bowl. Her hair had been left natural, forming a short, tight, attractive Afro around her pretty face. She couldn't have been more than eighteen, maybe twenty.

I returned my attention to the child—dark hair long and shaggy, his skin kissed by the sun. I couldn't see his eyes. He could be hers.

Hers and—

The young woman's head came up as Adam appeared, his hair slicked back from his face, a towel around his neck. Chest bare, he now wore jeans instead of slacks.

"Daddy!" the child screeched, and left the cartoons behind to launch himself into Adam's arms.

I didn't realize I'd stopped breathing until black dots shimmied in front of my eyes. I sucked in air, let it out again. I should sit down, put my head between my legs, or maybe just pound it against the cement. But I couldn't tear my gaze from Adam and his son.

The child clung to Adam like a monkey, arms tight around his neck, legs clutching his waist, and Adam rubbed his cheek against the boy's hair. The love on his face caused a tiny sob to escape.

Adam looked up and I ducked so fast, I got dizzy again. I crouched below the window, breathing as shallowly as I dared, listening for the creak of a door, but nothing happened.

So I sat on the ground, dangled my head between my knees. I should get out of here. Someone, if not Adam or the little woman, was going to discover me dallying in the patch of grass beneath their living room window and wonder what kind of psycho they were dealing with.

A snort of laughter erupted. He'd been angry when he thought I was married and screwing him. What was his excuse?

"Maybe they aren't married," I muttered.

Which was no excuse.

He'd lied to me somewhere along the line. Although I hadn't asked if he was involved, nevertheless, wasn't it good form to mention it? He definitely should have mentioned the child.

Of course Adam had made certain I was leaving, made clear he didn't love me and never would. He probably figured I'd be gone long before it mattered that he had a son and a live-in woman. Maybe she didn't care if he played around. But I did.

A thought niggled at the edge of my mind. If I could just get my brain to function past the sight of that little boy's smile and the sound of his voice shouting, "Daddy!"

But I couldn't. From the way I was hyperventilating and clutching my chest, you'd think I'd just caught the love of my life in bed with another woman.

I cursed, forced myself to my feet, and took a deep breath. I'd head back to the mansion, gather my things, and move in with Cassandra. Then I'd hire another guide, find the freaking loup-garou, put a leash around its neck, and deliver the beast to Frank. All without ever seeing Adam Ruelle again.

I turned and ran right into him.

He glanced from me to the window and back again. Neither one of us spoke.

I lifted my chin and tried to walk away. He side-stepped, putting himself directly in front of me.

"What are you doin' here?" he asked.

"Get bent."

"You followed me."

"Duh," I muttered, which was *so* constructive but the best I could think of right now.

"You shouldn't have."

I was tempted to say "duh" again but managed to stop myself. Instead I said nothing.

He grabbed my arm and dragged me away from the mobile home, glancing over his shoulder as if afraid someone might see. I struggled against his hold, for all the good it did.

"You have to go."

"Damn straight."

"I'll come to de mansion tonight. I'll explain."

"Don't bother." I pulled free.

"You don't understand, *cher.*"

"Do not call me *cher*!" I shouted, and to my horror, my voice broke.

He reached for me, and I stepped back so fast I tripped over my own feet. My eyes burned. I was going to cry, and I couldn't let him see. I just couldn't.

"Diana," he murmured. "It's not what you think."

"Not your son?"

His lips tightened and he didn't answer.

"That's what I thought."

And suddenly I recalled his incredible lie.

"You said . . ." I stared at him wide-eyed. "You said you couldn't have children."

My fingers itched to touch my stomach, where even now his child might be growing. Why on earth had I ever trusted this man?

"I can't." He rubbed his hand through his hair. "Not anymore."

"And I should believe you?"

"Why would I want to get you pregnant? I don't even want—" He broke off.

I could fill in the end of that sentence. He didn't even want me. Not forever. Not in any way that mattered.

I'd deluded myself into thinking I was the type of woman who could have sex without strings, but I wasn't. The instant I'd had sex, the strings were there. They might be invisible, but that didn't make them any less real.

I must have made a movement toward the road, as if I might take off, as if I had a prayer in hell of outrunning him, and his hand snaked out, his fingers encircling my wrist.

"You weren't supposed to see," he said.

"No shit."

"Diana." He sighed. "What am I going to do with you?"

"Not much. Not anymore."

His lips thinned again. He was angry. *Well, join de club,* my mind mocked.

I was the injured party here. So why was he making me feel as if I'd done something wrong?

"Who is she?" I whispered.

The child I could forgive, but a wife . . . never.

Adam's eyes met mine, startled, a little confused, as if he had no idea who I was talking about, and I snapped. My free hand balled into a fist and I swung at his head.

He ducked, quicker than spit, and I nearly fell when I missed him. My other arm twisted sharply, painfully, when he didn't let go of my wrist, and I almost went to my knees. Would have, if he hadn't grabbed me and hauled me against him.

Despite everything, my body recognized his. We still fit together so right. How could everything have gone so wrong?

"Daddy?"

Oh, yeah. That.

Adam tensed. To his credit he didn't shove me away. He released me slowly, almost gently, and stepped back, turning and putting himself between me and his son, as if he could hide one from the other.

"What are you doin' out here?" Adam asked.

The child didn't answer, instead leaning to the side so he could see me. I was struck with the urge to cover my face, as if that would make me invisible.

He grinned, exposing an adorable gap in his front teeth. If that hadn't made my heart clutch, the sight of his bright blue eyes would have.

"I'm Luc," he said. "Luc Ruelle."

He didn't have the Cajun twang of his father, but the South still lived in Luc's voice.

"Go inside," Adam ordered.

The kid ignored him. I had to admire that. Adam wasn't exactly ignorable.

"You gonna be my mom?"

I choked.

"Luc," Adam growled.

"Uh-oh." Luc's gaze shifted to his father, then back to me. "Now I'm in trouble."

He didn't appear worried, and instead of leaving, he advanced. Adam stepped between us again, and I was tempted to shove him out of the way. Honestly, did he think I was going to gobble up the child like a . . . a goblin?

"My real mama died. I got sitters. Lots of 'em." He glanced at Adam. "Sadie says she's quittin'."

Adam groaned as Luc gave a long-suffering sigh. "I know, another one bites the dust."

I laughed and Luc smiled again, even as Adam shot me a glare. How could he remain so sour with such a sweet, funny child to enjoy? And why was he treating Luc like a curse and not a blessing?

My head tilted. Curse? Could Luc be . . . ?

Nah.

"Get back inside," Adam repeated. "I have to take—" he broke off and scowled at me again—"her home."

"Who is her?" Luc asked, undaunted. "What's your name?"

"Diana."

"*Déesse de la lune*."

All urge to laugh fled. I heard again the whisper in the swamp, Adam's murmur in my mind, Luc's voice in the sun.

"What does that mean?"

Luc glanced at Adam, concern wrinkling his forehead. "She don't know French?"

"Not everyone does."

The child peered at me as if I'd just farted in church. Not to know French—what a cretin!

"Goddess of the moon," he chirped. "Diana."

"Oh," I said lamely.

Interesting that a child knew all about the power of names.

"Daddy likes the moon."

My gaze went to Adam, who stared at me with no expression. "Does he?"

"Especially the smiley moon," Luc continued. "Whenever there's one of those in the sky, he's gone all night."

28

"Luc!" The sitter burst out the front door, pausing when she saw the three of us nearby. "I'm sorry, Mr. Adam, he slipped away again."

Hurrying forward, she scooped Luc into her arms. "You're like an eel, boy."

"Bye," Luc said as she turned and carried him back to the trailer. The child cast curious glances at me the entire way.

"You don't belong here," Adam said.

His words hurt, but I was determined not to show it. "I know."

"I'll take you home."

"To Boston?"

"Would you go?"

"No."

"There isn't a loup-garou, Diana. You're wasting your time. If you stay, someone's going to get hurt."

"People are dying. What's killing them, Adam? You?"

"What if I was?"

I blinked. "I—uh—what?"

"What if I was killing them?"

"You said there wasn't a wolf."

"Exactly. So it must be a person."

"But . . . the police found proof of an animal killing people."

"Then it's an animal, which means it isn't me."

"Unless you're the loup-garou."

"I'm not a wolf."

"Yet you disappear under every crescent moon."

"I don't disappear. I stay at my shack."

"Why?"

"Things happen under that moon." He took a deep breath. "I mean things *have* happened. To me, in de army. I try not to remember, but—"

He let the breath out and his shoulders slumped. I wanted to touch his hair, hold his hand, but I knew he wouldn't let me.

"Luc was wrong," he said. "I don't like de crescent moon; I despise it."

"What happened?"

Instead of answering, he took my arm and half-led, half-dragged me to the ancient Chevy parked in the driveway. The thing appeared to be at least forty years old. A little restoration would do wonders, just like the mansion. Right now the car was a mess—rusted, blotchy, no true color to speak of. Adam opened the passenger door and I balked.

"Get in," he said through gritted teeth, "or I will make you."

I glanced at the trailer. Luc waved from the window. I got in the car, wincing when a busted spring thumped me in the ass. The seat was badly torn, as if an animal had clawed it apart.

The car was so old, it didn't have air-conditioning. In a near-synchronized movement, we rolled down the windows. The morning was already hot enough that the wind felt good in my hair.

"I'm not gonna tell you what happened," Adam murmured. "I can't."

The "can't" stopped me. I understood that special ops were a secret.

"What happened to your wife?"

His fingers tightened on the wheel. "She's gone."

"How?"

I imagined terrible things—things that had put the shadows in his eyes. Was this why he couldn't love me? Death was something I understood.

"Packed up her stuff, cleaned out our bank accounts, and ran. The bitch."

I gaped. "What? She's dead."

"I hope so."

"Luc said his mother was dead."

"She is to me. To him, too." His gaze shifted to mine, then back to the road. "She isn't coming back, if that's what you're worried about."

"I'm worried about your sanity. Why would you tell your child his mother is dead when she—?"

"Took off. Abandoned him. Left when he was not much more than a year old and never came back. She didn't want him. She hates him almost as much as she hates—"

His mouth snapped closed over the last word. But I could figure it out. His wife hated him. I doubted he'd tell me why.

"You didn't see her again?"

"Nope."

"Didn't hear from her?"

"Zip."

"So you're still married."

"Not in my mind."

"Terrific," I muttered.

"If I don't know where she is, how can I send her the divorce papers?"

He had a point. Still—

"It was never a real marriage," he insisted.

"You got a license?"

"Yeah."

"Then it was real."

"I never loved her. She never loved me. We got married because . . ." He shrugged and I understood.

"You couldn't keep it in your pants. What a shock."

Silence settled over the interior of the car. But I was unable to remain quiet for long. "Why did you tell me you couldn't have children?"

"I can't. Not anymore. After Luc I—" He fell silent, as if he could no longer find the words.

I had no such trouble. "You were in an accident? Caught the mumps? What?"

"I had a vasectomy."

My mouth fell open. I seemed to have that problem a lot lately. "Why?"

"I don't make de same mistake twice."

"But— What if you met someone? Wanted more children?"

"I won't."

My chest hurt, as if someone were pounding on it with a lead pipe, trying to break my heart.

"You can't know that," I managed.

"I will never marry again. Never have another child. It's de way things are."

I never planned to marry again, either, knew with utter certainty I'd never love anyone the way I'd loved Simon. I hadn't wanted a baby with him; I definitely didn't want one with anyone else. So why did Adam's words bother me so much?

Because I smelled a lie in there somewhere; I just wasn't sure where. Perhaps it was the lie of omission. He had another life, a family I didn't even know about. And if he'd lied about that, he'd probably lied about something else.

"Why didn't you tell me about Luc?"

"My life in de swamp is different from my life with my son."

I stiffened. "And I'm part of your life in the swamp? How flattering."

"Diana, you don't understand—"

"I think I do. You don't want your precious son being contaminated by the trampy woman you're screwing."

His jaw tightened. "That isn't what I said."

"You don't have to." I crossed my arms and stared out the window.

"I'll do anything to keep Luc from being hurt."

I shot him a glare. "You think I'd hurt him?"

"Not on purpose. But—" He lifted his hand from the steering wheel, then lowered it. "He wants a mother. I can't give him one."

"You could."

"No," he said with cold finality. "You plan on stayin', *cher*? You want a ready-made family? A little cabin in de swamp? Drive a car pool? Make bag lunches? Soccer games and Little League?"

When I hesitated, he nodded. "That's what I thought. So I keep him away. Why get his hopes up? He's gonna have a hard enough life as it is."

"Why is his life going to be hard?"

"That's just de way life is."

"You know the future?"

"Sometimes I think I do."

I stared at him as he stared out the windshield. "You say the strangest things."

"I don't want you to tell anyone about him."

I spread my hands wide. "Who would I tell?"

"No one knows he's my son. I want to keep it that way. People around here, they think I'm nuts."

"I wonder why," I said dryly.

He ignored me. "Luc should have as normal of a life as possible."

"Why wouldn't he?"

"My life isn't normal."

"It could be."

"No. I have responsibilities. Things I have to do—"

A thought broke through my confusion. "Are you still in the army? Some super secret agent crap?"

"No," he said shortly.

"What, exactly, do you do?"

He didn't bother to answer, which only made me more suspicious. But his next words hurt so much, I forgot all about that.

"I don't want you to see Luc again."

"Fine," I snapped.

I didn't plan on seeing Adam again, either. Just because I didn't want children didn't mean I was going to take kindly to being told I wasn't allowed near one. Adam was making me feel bad, and I already felt bad enough.

He turned off the main road and slowed at the sight of a car parked in front of the mansion. Cassandra sat on the porch. As we pulled up she stood, hand raised to shield her eyes from the bright morning sunlight.

I glanced at my watch. Seven forty-five. Damn, I'd told her I'd call by 7:00 A.M. and let her know I was okay. I was surprised Detective Sullivan wasn't here, too.

"Who is that?" Adam murmured.

"Cassandra."

"She don't look like a voodoo priestess."

"Exactly what does a voodoo priestess look like?"

"Hell if I know."

Cassandra's face flooded with relief when she saw me. Her gaze went to Adam, and her eyebrows shot up. I'm sure he had that effect on all the women.

I climbed out of the car. "Sorry. I forgot to call."

"I can see why."

I turned to introduce Adam, and he drove away. I was left gaping at the taillights of his Chevy. Sure, I'd planned to blow him off, but he hadn't even given me the chance.

"Antisocial much?" Cassandra murmured.

"You have no idea."

"What happened last night?"

"He isn't the loup-garou," I blurted.

Her only reaction was a slight lifting of her dark eyebrows. "How do you know?"

"I touched him with your knife, and he didn't explode."

"Not into flames anyway."

"What's that supposed to mean?"

She smirked. "You had sex."

"See that in your crystal ball?"

"Didn't have to. I can tell by the way you watched him go."

"Hell," I muttered.

"Isn't it? So where were you?"

I opened my mouth to tell her, then remembered Adam's admonition about Luc. Not that I'd promised anything. Not that I owed Adam anything. Not that Cassandra was any type of threat.

Then again I had no idea whom I could trust and whom I couldn't. I'd thought Adam and I had something—if not love, well, at least lust and extreme like.

Discovering he had a son, that he was, technically, married, had shaken my confidence. Go figure. Having him say he didn't want me near his child hurt. But I wasn't going to make myself feel any better by telling Cassandra. I don't think anything would make me feel better.

"Diana?" Cassandra pressed. "Where were you?"

"His place."

"In the swamp."

I nodded. We *had* been, most of the time.

I remembered something else about Luc—he wasn't supposed to exist. I'd found no record of his birth at all. Had I missed it? Had it been lost, stolen, misplaced? I was so confused.

The sound of vehicles turning off the main highway made both Cassandra and I glance up. A delivery truck and an unmarked police car rattled down the driveway.

"Sullivan," Cassandra murmured. She didn't sound pleased.

"Ms. Malone." He nodded at me, then Cassandra. *"Priestess."*

He put a sarcastic twist on the title and Cassandra's eyes narrowed.

"You better watch it or she'll turn you into a toad," I said.

"Wish I could," Cassandra murmured.

Sullivan didn't appear worried. "I'd be happy to call you Miss, Mrs., or Ms. if I knew your last name."

"You mean you haven't been able to uncover that information with your superior detecting skills?" Cassandra asked.

"I've been a little busy."

"What *is* your last name?" I asked.

"I don't need one. 'Priestess Cassandra' sets me apart. It isn't as if there are two in town."

I tilted my head. She didn't want to tell me. How interesting. I never would have thought Cassandra had something to hide. Maybe everyone did.

"Which one of you is Malone?" the deliveryman asked.

"Me." I took the clipboard he offered and signed next to my name.

The stuff from Frank had arrived. Thank goodness. In less than a week the crescent moon would rise and now I'd be ready.

"What's that?" Sullivan asked as the delivery guy unloaded a cart with a long, thin box atop two shorter fatter ones.

"Cage, tree stands, tranquilizer gun."

"You got a permit for that?"

I stopped in the middle of opening the box on the top. "I was told the gun laws in Louisiana are . . . lenient."

Sullivan scowled. "You got that right. But trapping an animal and transporting it across state lines is a different matter."

Hell. I hadn't thought of that.

Luckily Frank had. On top of the dart gun lay documents, all made out and stamped nice and legal, signed by the governor and giving me the right to take pretty much anything anywhere I wanted to. Frank might be an annoying pain, but he was an organized, think-ahead, rich annoying pain with a lot of connections.

I handed the papers to Sullivan. Frustration washed over his face. He handed them back to me with a scowl. "Did you ever tell Adam Ruelle I wanted to talk to him?"

"We already had this conversation."

"He still hasn't contacted me."

I shrugged. Adam wasn't going to call the detective. Not in this lifetime.

"Why did you call me if it wasn't about Ruelle?" he demanded.

I'd forgotten about the call I'd placed, the message I'd left, but I remembered the question I'd had.

"Did you ever identify the man who was strangled in the swamp?"

"No."

"Isn't that strange?" Cassandra murmured. "Shouldn't someone be searching for him?"

"Eventually. Maybe." Sullivan shrugged. "You'd be surprised how many John Does there are in the world. Especially around here. Speaking of which, we never found Charlie Wagner's body."

I tried very hard not to look at Cassandra. Probably as hard as she was trying not to look at me. The detective glanced back and forth between us. His eyes narrowed.

Before he could ask us questions we wouldn't answer, I asked one of my own. "The St. Tammany police thought there was a rabies problem in the swamp."

"There's something. My boss called in a specialist."

"What kind of specialist?"

"There's been a problem in several states with a new strain of rabies."

"Really?" Cassandra murmured. "Funny we didn't hear about it."

"They try to keep information of that nature quiet. People panic."

"Can't imagine why," I said.

"Guy should be here in a couple days. He'll do his thing, and then we can concentrate on our other problems."

"Which are?"

"Who strangled a stranger and who's stealing dead bodies."

He squinted at Cassandra as he said the latter. She just rolled her eyes and turned away.

"Maybe you should wait to do your trapping until our rabies expert is finished," he said.

"What if my wolf is the one with the rabies problem?"

And I kind of thought he was—if you considered *rabies* was a euphemism for the curse of the crescent moon.

"Then you'd definitely better back off. You don't want rabies, Ms. Malone. Even with the new medicines, it isn't pretty."

Hey, I didn't want to be baying at the moon, either. I wasn't going to take any chances.

"You'll wait until I give the go-ahead before you move forward with . . . ?" Sullivan made a vague motion toward the cage and the dart gun.

"Of course."

"Great. I'll be in touch."

The detective climbed into his car and rumbled down the drive toward the highway.

Cassandra cleared her throat. When I glanced at her, she lifted a dark brow. "You really plan to wait?"

"Hell, no."

29

Cassandra left after I assured her I wasn't going to set a trap in the swamp. What would be the point? There wasn't a crescent moon tonight.

However, I did want to scout the area and figure out the best location for the cage when the time was right. I should be safe in the sunshine, at least from a loup-garou. If there were rabid wild dogs, coyotes, or even a real wolf, I might be in trouble.

Except I didn't believe that. Not anymore.

I loaded the tranquilizer gun before I took a walk. I also had the pistol Adam had given me, but the thing made me nervous. What if I shot someone accidentally? Heck, what if I shot them on purpose?

As jumpy as I was, that could easily happen. There'd been enough death in the Honey Island Swamp. I preferred not to cause more. The tranquilizer gun would only put someone to sleep for a few hours instead of permanently.

I was so close to proving what Simon had always known. Werewolves existed right under our very noses.

How they managed to do so and not be found was a mystery. One I wanted to unravel.

I understood now what had obsessed my husband. My guilt at not supporting him while he was alive returned, but I refused to let depression take hold. I could atone for my lack of foresight if I proved his theory. If I found a loup-garou and presented the beast to the world, Simon's reputation would be saved. No one would ever dare speak his name and laugh again.

I hadn't realized in what direction I was walking until I reached the top of a small rise and saw Adam's shack in the narrow valley below.

"Guess I don't need the map anymore," I muttered.

I was *not* going in there. I was not talking to him again; I was definitely not going to get close enough for him to seduce me.

I made a derisive sound. "As if."

I wasn't going to jump into bed with a man who didn't think I was fit to share airspace with his son.

"Asshole."

There. I felt better now.

So why didn't I leave? I stood on the ridge and stared at the shack, watching a shadow moving beyond the window. I remembered what we'd shared there.

I glanced at the yard. And there. Not to mention several other places.

My sigh was pathetic. I stiffened my spine and forced myself to turn away.

It wasn't as if I'd loved him. I'd wanted him. I'd had him. We were done.

Then why did I feel as if I'd buried my best friend?

Because you did. You just forgot about him while you were boning a stranger.

"Nice," I murmured. "With a conscience like that, who needs enemies?"

Still, my conscience was right. I'd let myself be distracted by bulging biceps, rippling abs, and an excellent dick.

Which just might be an oxymoron.

While I was having this conversation with myself I'd kept walking and managed to get all turned around. The swamp was tricky; a section could appear similar or very different depending on the time of day, the direction of the sun, the slant of the shadows.

I nearly slipped into a tributary that was far too wide to cross without an airboat, even without the alligators bobbing in the center. One splashed at the edge of the water and slunk onto the bank. I patted my pocket, relieved to find the gris-gris still there.

Pulling the bag free, I rolled it in my hand, as much for courage as magic. My heart rate returned to normal when the gator did an about-face and slid noiselessly into the water. That was so weird.

Backtracking to a familiar path, I glanced at the sky, then took off down the trail double time. The sun was fading fast.

I heard a rustle, then the thud of pursuit—something that possessed more feet than two.

I would not glance over my shoulder. How many times has the idiot heroine in a horror movie tried to catch a glimpse of what's chasing her? Then she trips over her feet, falls to her knees, and we've got snarling and screaming and blood. Basically, she's too stupid to live, so she's dead.

Not me. I heard the pitter-patter of multiple feet, and I ran. I'd thought I was within shouting distance of the mansion, not that there was anyone to shout to, but I was wrong.

Minutes later I still hadn't burst out of the tall grass and into the overgrown yard. I wished like hell I hadn't run. I'd have been better off facing the predator than making myself the prey. Although I had a feeling I'd *been* the prey since that fire iris had made an appearance on my bed.

A body hit me between the shoulder blades and I fell. *Hard.* My hands took the brunt of the fall, but still my forehead banged into the ground, and I saw stars. Whatever had knocked me down ran right over my back and kept going.

Definitely not a person—a little too quadrapedal.

I lifted my head as the tip of a tail disappeared into the foliage. With a groan I rolled onto my back and stared at the night sky. Three-quarters of the way up, a full moon shone. How could the loup-garou be out now?

It couldn't. Or at least not according to legend. However, according to legend, and Mrs. Favreau, wolves made wolves. Which explained the howls I'd heard in the night.

I thought about Charlie, Mrs. Beasly, the other missing persons, and the missing bodies.

There might not be wolves in New Orleans, but if there were werewolves, there were probably a lot of them.

I dragged myself to my feet, sore and scraped but thrilled to be alive. My dart gun had flown into the weeds when I'd fallen, and I bent stiffly to pick it up.

The only person who'd been of any use in this mystery was Marie Favreau. Well, Arianna Beasly had been helpful, too, but she was dead.

Twice.

If I ever got back to the mansion, I'd call Mrs. Favreau and ask if she knew anything else worth knowing.

I continued down the path, skittering into a semi-run when the howl of a wolf from the east was answered by another from the west. Then a whole chorus began, making the hair on my arms stand up almost as high as that on the back of my neck.

When the howls died away, I could have sworn I heard the grass swishing in my direction, from several locations.

I tried not to run, but it was hard. I wanted to be at the mansion, inside, right now. Why hadn't I stayed there in the first place?

After what seemed hours, I caught a glimpse of the Ruelle place between the dripping branches of the cypress trees. I hesitated at the edge of the swamp, concerned any number of beasts could be waiting for me once I left the cover of the greenery.

More howls commenced, much farther away, and I stepped into the yard. Nothing attacked me.

I popped the trunk of the car and retrieved Adam's pistol; then I went into the house and shut the door, not bothering with the lock, since all the windows were broken anyway.

There was no way I was sleeping here tonight, but first things first. I called information and moments later the phone was picked up in the French Quarter. "Hello?"

I recognized Anne's voice and considered hanging up, but that would be childish. "Is Marie there?"

Silence came over the line. I didn't like the sound of that silence.

"Who is this?"

"Diana Malone. I visited the other day."

"She's dead," Anne said flatly.

My fingers tightened on the phone. "How?"

"She was old. Heart attack."

I frowned. "Didn't Arianna have a heart attack?"

"This wasn't the same."

"No? How was it different?"

"Mother wasn't attacked. She just . . . died."

"Where?"

I didn't much care for the way people were dropping like flies not long after I talked with them.

"In the garden. She likes to sit outside and watch the stars."

And the moon, too, I'd bet.

"There weren't any bite marks?"

"She's gone." Anne made a disgusted sound. "Can't she rest in peace?"

"I hope so. Did you happen to stuff her mouth with wolfsbane and draw a pentagram on her chest? Maybe shoot her with silver, just to be sure?"

I started when Anne slammed down the phone hard enough to damage my eardrum. I couldn't say I blamed her.

Marie's death disturbed me. The old woman's heart might have given out. Then again, she could have been confronted by a werewolf and gotten a little help.

The way people were dying around here, they'd be dubbing me Typhoid Diana soon. I was tempted to call Cassandra, make sure she had no plans to stand outside and stare at the moon. Ask if she owned any silver jewelry. Tell her to put some on and save a piece for me.

Maybe I'd just tell her in person.

I began to gather my things, but a soft footfall on the porch made me lift the pistol. The door slid open, creaking loudly. I had an instant to think, *Wolves can't open doors,* before a figure darted inside.

A figure too small to be a man and too human to be a wolf.

30

Luc Ruelle blinked at the gun. I gasped and shifted the weapon away. This was why I didn't like to use them. More often than not, the wrong person got shot.

"Guns are dangerous," he said solemnly.

"Damn straight."

"Curse word."

My lips tightened. "Sorry."

He shrugged. "Heard it before."

I bet he had.

"Just not from a lady."

He still hadn't, but I wasn't going to point that out.

"What are you doing here?" I craned my neck. "Did your dad bring you?"

I heard the hope in my voice and wanted to curse again. If Adam had brought Luc, then maybe he'd changed his mind about me seeing the boy. And if Adam had changed his mind about that, then—

What?

He'd buy me an engagement ring, fix up the mansion, we'd move in and start playing Ozzie and Harriet?

Doubtful.

At any rate, I needed a reference a little more up-to-date. Was there an example of a happily married couple on TV these days? For the life of me, I couldn't think of one.

"My dad doesn't know I'm here."

"Uh-oh," I said before I could stop myself.

Luc shrugged and drew his toe across the floor in an "aw shucks" gesture. Only then did I realize he was barefoot. On closer examination, his shirt was inside out and his shorts weren't zipped.

"Were you in a big hurry to leave?" I asked.

"Huh?" He stared at me with innocent Adam-eyes.

"Your . . . um—" I waved vaguely. "Barn door."

He glanced down, then presented me with his back. "I forgot to X-Y-Z."

The sound of the zipper being zipped punctuated his words.

"What's X-Y-Z?"

"Examine your zipper. Duh."

As I said, I knew nothing about kids, particularly male ones, having never been one myself. I felt pretty "duh" all around.

"I should call your dad," I said.

"No phone."

"No phone?"

He shrugged. "Don't need one."

Everyone needs a phone. Don't they?

Luc wandered around the mansion, glancing at my stuff, peering into corners, then staring upstairs.

He saw me watching him and shrugged. "Never been here."

I frowned. This was the family home—despite its disarray. Why hadn't Adam brought him?

I hate that place. I wish it would rot, but de damn thing never will.

Oh, yeah.

"I cut through the swamp," Luc said. "Wasn't far."

"Do you walk around the swamp a lot?"

"Uh-huh."

I wasn't sure that was such a good idea. He was so little, the things out there so big. Or at least they'd seemed big while chasing me.

"Did you see anything . . . strange?" I asked.

"No."

Well, that was informative.

"Did you see *anything*?"

"Trees, gators, water, snakes. Critters."

"What kind of critters?"

He shrugged. "I didn't really *see* any. Just heard 'em scratchin' around."

"Maybe you shouldn't go in the swamp for a while."

His face creased into a mulish expression that resembled a dried-apple doll. "I've been playing in the swamp since I could walk."

"And your dad doesn't care?"

"He says I need to know how to survive there. Someday I might have to."

What a bizarre thing to say to a child.

The two of us stared at each other. I smiled a trifle uneasily. What was I going to do with him until Adam showed up?

He *would* show up. Wouldn't he?

I'd wait a half an hour; then I'd take Luc back myself and head into town as I'd planned.

"Are you . . . hungry?"

"Always."

I smiled. "I've got crackers."

He made a face. "That's not food."

"Cookies?"

"OK."

I dug out the package, handed it over.

"How many can I have?" he asked.

"Go nuts."

Which was probably the wrong thing to say to a kid, but he wasn't my kid, and Adam had made it clear he never would be. If Luc went home on a sugar high, well, that was no more than the man deserved. What kind of father allowed a child to roam the swamp?

What did I know about it? Maybe down here, or anywhere for that matter, a four-year-old was plenty old to swamp-wander.

I eyed Luc's size, then thought of his speech, his behavior. Maybe he was older than four. Regardless, he wasn't twenty-four. Which is how old I thought he should be before he went into the swamp alone again.

"How old are you?" I asked.

"How old are you?"

"It isn't polite to ask a woman her age."

"How come? Don't you know?"

God, he was cute.

"I'm thirty."

"That's old."

"Is not."

"You're older than my dad."

Well, wasn't that special?

"How much older?"

"A year."

In my opinion, that didn't count.

"OK, your turn."

I took a cookie myself, earning a scowl of reproof from Luc. Did he plan to eat them all? From the way he was wolfing them down—stupid question.

"I'm seven."

"Really?"

"I'm little, but I'm quick. And smart."

"I bet you are."

"My mom was little. And Dad said he didn't grow until he was twelve. Then he grew five inches in one year."

"That must've hurt."

"Hurt?" His eyes went wide and his lip trembled.

Hell. I had no idea how to talk to kids.

"I meant *helped*. That must have helped. With . . . basketball."

From his expression he didn't buy the excuse. He *was* quick.

"Dad didn't play basketball."

"No? What did he play?"

"Nothin'." His lip stuck out. "He says life isn't a game, it's a responsibility."

"Well, yippee."

Luc grinned. "Yeah."

That gap in his teeth just did me in.

"Shouldn't you be in school?" I asked.

"Dad teaches me."

Huh. Mobile residence. Multiple babysitters. Homeschooling. But why?

Another question for Adam, if he ever spoke to me again.

"You wanna play cards?" Luc asked.

"I don't have any cards."

He reached into the pocket of his shorts and pulled out a deck.

"Just one game," I allowed. "What do you play?"

"Hold 'em."

I put my hand out to take the cards, and he stared at my palm, confused.

"You don't want me to hold them?" I asked.

"I meant Texas hold 'em."

"Like on TV?"

"That's where I learned it."

He started shuffling with card-shark precision, which was both adorable and scary. Also sad. The child had to learn games from TV?

"How often do you see your father?"

"Every day."

"Then why the babysitters?"

"They stay all night."

"Where's your dad?"

He shrugged. "Workin', I guess."

"Working at what?"

"Dunno."

Stranger and stranger. I'd slept with the man, shared intimacies untold, yet I didn't know what he did for a living. But, to be fair, neither did his son.

Luc beat me at hold 'em. Badly. Several times.

I forgot about "just one game." I forgot about leaving in a half an hour. An hour later we were still playing; I was still losing.

"I think that's enough." I tossed in another hand of junk.

"That's what they all say when I win."

I contemplated his tangled hair, his gappy teeth, his familiar eyes. "Why did you come here, Luc?"

He pocketed the cards and crawled into my lap. I was so surprised, I let him.

"Dad likes you." He shifted his butt, snuggled his head

under my chin, and put his arms around my waist. "I can tell."

"I don't think he does."

I left out *not enough* and *not anymore*.

"He's never mumbled a girl's name in his sleep before. That's gotta mean somethin'."

I knew what it meant, and I wasn't going to tell Luc.

"I thought he worked all night," I said, wondering how Luc could have heard Adam mumbling in his sleep.

"Then he sleeps most of the day. That's when I watch hold 'em."

What was Adam up to all night that made him sleep when the sun shone? I had a feeling I didn't want to know.

While we'd been talking, my arms had automatically circled the child. My cheek rested on his hair. His body was warm, both bony and soft. His hair smelled like summertime in the rain.

"If Dad likes you," he murmured, his voice slurred with sleep, "I like you."

I didn't say anything until his breathing evened out and he went slack. I wasn't going to be taking Luc home anytime soon. He might be little, but he was probably too big for me to carry. Besides, I didn't want to wake him.

I stretched out on the bedroll, letting his body tumble onto the cover next to me. When he mumbled and shifted, I stroked his hair and whispered, "I like you, too."

He fell back to sleep, his hand resting in mine.

I found myself fascinated by that tiny, soft hand. He had a scrape on one knuckle, a scab on the palm; his fingernails were encrusted in dirt. Had he been digging with them? I suspected that might be something little boys did, but I wasn't sure.

Luc looked so much like Adam. From the blue eyes, to the dark hair, to the skin that turned bronze beneath the sun. Was there anything of Luc's mother in him at all?

I'd never had a maternal yearning in my life. Never heard the biological clock ticking. Never went gaga over babies. I didn't drool over sunsuits and tiny shoes. So why did holding Luc Ruelle's hand make my stomach flutter?

A movement at the corner of my vision made me glance up. I wasn't surprised to find Adam watching me from the window.

From his expression, Luc was wrong. His father didn't like me very much at all.

31

Adam came into the house as I sat up, careful not to disturb the sleeping child. Without a word, Adam bent and lifted Luc into his arms. Equally silent he walked out of the house. I expected he'd walked out of my life forever.

What was it about the Ruelles that made me feel things I never had before and never expected to again? What was it about a silent man and a chatty boy that made a foolish, lonely cryptozoologist long for a life she'd never wanted?

This wasn't me. To ache for a child. To contemplate loving again with the same depth I'd once loved before. To consider a future so far gone from the one I'd planned as to be unfathomable.

I had to be under a spell.

The thought gave me pause. Was I behaving so oddly, thinking so strangely, longing so deeply because of . . . magic? The very idea should make me laugh, but after what I'd seen since coming to the Crescent City, laughing was the furthest thing from my mind.

There was only one person I trusted here, and conveniently that person knew magic. I grabbed my bag and my keys and drove to town.

Bourbon Street was hopping. I heard the music, saw the lights, from several blocks away. I was tempted to take a detour and soothe my problems with a zombie. But I figured the way things were going, I'd actually run into a zombie.

Cassandra opened the door before I even knocked.

"How did you know I was here?"

She lifted a brow. "I peeked through the window."

"Oh."

"Lock the door. You need a drink."

Right again. Sometimes I thought she was more than a little psychic.

Within minutes I sat across from her at the kitchen table, sipping from a glass of something complete with a tiny umbrella.

I took a big swig. "Fruity."

Probably had twelve types of alcohol. Just what I needed. I took another glug. "What do you know about love potions? Maybe a charm or a spell?"

Cassandra took a ladylike sip and set down her glass. "More than you, I suspect. Why?"

I wasn't sure. Adam had insisted he couldn't love me, didn't want me to love him. What good would a love spell do?

But Luc was another matter. The child wanted a mother. If I fell hopelessly in love with him, wouldn't I take the job?

I couldn't bring myself to tell Cassandra about the boy. Adam didn't want anyone to know. And while I trusted Cassandra with my life—had on several occasions already—it wasn't right for me to trust her with Luc's. He wasn't mine to give.

"You're talking about Adam," she murmured. "You love him?"

"I something him," I muttered. "I don't like it."

"Just because you don't want to love the man doesn't mean you've been put under a spell. In truth, if you had been, you'd be thrilled about it. That's part of the magic."

I took a huge slurp, and the end of the paper umbrella went up my nose. Sneezing, I tossed it aside.

"You better slow down," Cassandra said. "You're going to be smashed."

"OK."

I'd been right about the twelve kinds of alcohol. Right now, every one of them zipped through my bloodstream, both relaxing and revving me. My cheeks felt on fire.

"I love my husband."

"Shouldn't you say *loved*?"

"I don't know how to stop," I whispered. "He still feels alive to me." I touched my chest. "Right here."

"Maybe that's why you saw him in your dream. In your heart he's still alive. You need to let him go."

"No."

The idea of letting Simon go, of giving up, giving in, going on, was too much for me. Maybe that was why I had come up with the notion that my feelings for Adam had been induced by voodoo. They couldn't be real, because if they were, I didn't love Simon anymore. And if my love for him died, then so did he.

I know, I know, he already had. But when was love ever rational?

I took another swig of courage before blurting what I'd

been wondering since I'd seen Simon at the window. "Could you raise him?"

I stared at my fingers, clutched together in my lap. Cassandra took a quick, sharp breath and held it. Afraid she'd pass out if she didn't breathe, afraid I'd panic if she didn't speak, or maybe if she did, I glanced up, then right back down again. The sorrow, the pity, in her eyes made me want to crawl under the table and stay there.

"I'm not that powerful," she said softly. "Not yet."

Something in her voice made me tense—hope and fear at war. "But you might be soon?"

"Someday, perhaps. But even if I was, I couldn't raise Simon."

"Why not?"

"How long has he been gone?"

"Four years."

She reached across the table and took my hand. "He wouldn't be the same, Diana."

"I don't care."

"You would care. Dead is dead; there's no going back."

"There is—you said so yourself. There *are* zombies. They're real."

"But they aren't alive. They aren't the same people. They aren't even *people*. You want to rip Simon out of the afterlife, reanimate his disintegrating body, have him look at you with hollow, lifeless eyes? Wonder why he's here? Ask who you are?"

"He'd know me."

"Maybe."

"I miss him."

"I know."

She squeezed my hand, and I met her gaze once more. "Simon didn't have to die. I could have saved him."

Cassandra stared at me for several seconds. "So that's what this is about? Guilt?"

Now that I'd started talking, I couldn't seem to stop. "I didn't believe him when he said he'd found a werewolf. Again. I was so sick of his wild-goose chases. We went here; we went there. He saw something and every single time, when I got there, there was nothing. Everyone thought he was crazy."

I took a deep breath and admitted my secret shame: "I started to think so, too. Then that last night, I lost my temper, shouted at him, and we fought. He stormed out alone. The next thing I knew, he was dead."

"I missed the part where your going with him could have saved him."

I shot her a glare. "I'd have saved him."

How I wasn't sure, but I'd have tried. And if I'd failed, I'd be dead, too. Sometimes—hell, most times until I came here—I wished that I was.

"He's gone now," she said, "and you need to move on. Quit sabotaging your chance at a new life by clinging to the old one."

"I have to find the loup-garou. Prove that Simon wasn't crazy. Clear his name."

"All right. *Then* maybe you can move on."

I considered her words, which were an echo of my own earlier thoughts. Maybe I could. Except— "How do I know if what I feel is real?"

Cassandra sighed. "You really believe Ruelle put a hex on you to make you love him? I thought it was all sex, all the time."

"Not all the time," I muttered, though she did have a point.

"There might be a way to discover the truth."

"How?"

"A ceremony."

"Voodoo?"

She lifted a brow and didn't bother to answer.

"What do I have to do?"

"Come to the temple. We'll ask the *loas* if you're under a love spell."

"That works?"

"So far, whatever I've asked, they've answered."

I frowned. She was starting to scare me.

"If they say you're not being influenced by magic, will you quit fighting the feeling and tell the man you care?"

I wasn't sure. Adam had said he couldn't love me, that I shouldn't ask him to.

"Diana?" Cassandra pressed.

"Let's just do whatever voodoo that you do, and then we'll see."

"Promise you'll give him a chance."

"What difference does it make to you?"

She put her hands on her hips. "I'm not going to waste a perfectly good voodoo ceremony on someone who's too stubborn to reap the benefits."

"OK. Fine. Let's get it over with."

"Take a breath. Slow down. The temple is peaceful. You might enjoy your time there."

Instead of heading out the back door, Cassandra returned to the shop and picked up a wooden bowl. She proceeded to add items from her shelves, then turned toward the snake cage.

"Whoa," I said, my voice a bit slurred from the alcohol. "No snake."

"We need him for the ceremony."

"I hate snakes."

"Consider him Danballah."

"I know I'm going to be sorry I asked, but what's Danballah?"

"The Great Serpent. Father of the *loas*."

I recalled her earlier explanation. "A god."

"More of a spirit. In vodoun there was an original supreme being known as the Gran Met. When he finished his work and returned to the other worlds, he left the *loas* behind to help the people."

I'd been raised Catholic, though I hadn't practiced since I'd left my parents' house. Nevertheless, all this talk about gods made me twitchy. "You don't really believe this, do you?"

Her sigh was aggrieved. "You can't ask me to perform a voodoo ceremony for truth, then wonder if I believe."

I very nearly pointed out that I hadn't asked her to do anything, but she was on a roll, so I let her go.

"If I don't believe, then what in hell am I doing here? For that matter, what are you?"

"All right. You believe."

"Gotta believe in something," Cassandra muttered, and shoved the bowl into my arms.

I didn't see it coming and bobbled the thing, nearly dropping it. "Hey!"

She shot me a glare. "You wanna hold the snake?"

"Nope." I waved my hand. "Carry on."

She pulled Lazarus out of the cage, murmuring softly. He took one look at me and hissed. The feeling was mutual.

"Think of the *loas* like saints." Cassandra led the way from the shop, through her living area, and out the back door. "They're a kind of bridge to the supreme being."

"I can see why the Catholic Church was so snarky about the whole voodoo thing. A snake spirit is a far cry from a saint."

"Didn't Saint Patrick charm the snakes out of Ireland?"

"Watch it when you talk about Saint Patrick and Ireland," I muttered.

Cassandra spared me a smile. "When the slaves arrived they were baptized Catholic right off the boat, and their religion was outlawed, so they secretly combined the two and got—"

"Vodoun."

"Bingo."

Behind Cassandra's shop lay a partially enclosed courtyard filled with plants, flowers, and a fountain. The ground was hard-packed earth—no grass, no stones, no pavement. A door had been set in one wall; Cassandra opened it.

"No lock?" I asked.

"On a temple?" She flicked the light. "Besides, most people are too scared to come in here *with* me. They certainly wouldn't come without me."

"Terrific," I said, and followed.

I stopped just inside the door. The room was so full of stuff, I didn't know what to stare at first. Cassandra placed Lazarus in a cardboard box near a flat stone covered with candles and smaller, more colorful flat stones. She proceeded to light the wicks, and I continued to stare.

Surrounding the stone were flowers, pebbles, tiny flags, and charms. The walls were decorated with brightly colored symbols: a cross, a heart, a snake, a box of some sort.

Long, thin.

"Is that a coffin?" I asked.

"Mmm," Cassandra said. "The drawings are *veves*. They act as magnets, to draw the *loas* to the earth. The coffin is the symbol of Baron Samedi. He is Saturday, the day of death."

"I'd think you would want to avoid that one instead of magnetically sucking him into your personal space."

"We've been over this." She gave me a look that I recalled from my third-grade teacher—extreme annoyance from a very patient woman. "Death is powerful, and it isn't necessarily a bad thing."

"Then why does everyone try so hard to escape it?"

"It's human nature to fear what we don't understand. I try to see death as a beginning."

"Of what?"

"Who knows?" She finished the candles and joined me. "A new plane, a different world, an adventure."

She could be right, but I'd rather wait as long as possible to find out.

"The cross is for Legba," she continued, "god of the sun and the way of all spiritual communication."

I could see why that would be handy.

"The heart is Erzulie." Cassandra met my gaze. "Goddess of the moon."

A warm wind seemed to brush my skin. I'd have thought I was imagining it, except the candles fluttered.

"She likes you," Cassandra whispered.

"Will that help?"

"Won't hurt."

"What about the snake?"

I glanced at the python on the wall, whose bright green eyes seemed to shine.

"Danballah."

The snake god. Spirit. Saint. Whatever. I should have known.

"Now what?" I asked.

"The ceremony brings the *loas* to earth; then we ask for guidance."

"How, exactly, do they come to earth?"

Her gaze slid from mine. "They inhabit another living being."

For a second my brain refused to accept the information my ears had heard. But only for a second.

"Possession? Are you nuts? That's dangerous!"

"Which is why I don't take the ceremony lightly. It's also why people are scared to come here. Word gets around."

"If you think I'm going to let some snake spirit possess me, you are off your rocker."

"I doubt Danballah would be interested in you. I was thinking more along the lines of—"

She traced a finger through the heart, her touch smudging whatever had been used to draw the symbol on the wall.

"*Déesse de la lune,*" she said.

The candles fluttered again in a nonexistent wind. As I gazed into their wavering flame I murmured, "That just might work."

32

I tore my gaze from the flames. "You've done this before, right?"

"A few times."

"Anyone spend the rest of their days mumbling and drooling? Any former customers sitting in a corner of the insane asylum doing this?" I took my index finger and wagged it back and forth across my bottom lip, making the crazy noise from childhood.

"Not yet," she said.

"Great."

"I'm not saying it isn't dangerous, and maybe we shouldn't do it."

I considered her warning, but I wanted to know the truth. I was tired of being confused.

"When the *loas* come I want to ask more than if I'm under the influence of a love spell. I want to know if there's a loup-garou and, if so, where can I find it?"

She smiled. "You don't exactly ask questions."

"What, then?"

"You'll be her—or she'll be you. As one."

My skin went a little prickly, a little cool, and I shivered. "What if . . ."

"What?"

"What if she doesn't want to leave and I'm stuck with voices in my head forever?"

I wondered momentarily if that was what was wrong with schizophrenics, then shook off the notion. Not every person who heard voices could have been the recipient of a voodoo-*loa* ceremony. Or at least I didn't think so.

"Relax, Diana. Erzulie is a goddess. As much as we enjoy our time on earth and fight not to leave it, to her this place sucks."

She probably had a point.

"Ready?"

I took a deep breath. Was I?

"Yes."

Cassandra knelt next to the flat stone, which resembled an altar, picked up the clay bowl, and started to mash the ingredients together with a pestle.

"What should I do?" I asked.

"Sit. Relax. Open your mind."

Easy for her to say. My mind had been closed for most of my life—especially to stuff like this. But I sat on the floor and continued to breathe deeply. Hyperventilating would probably scare away the *loas*.

Cassandra spread the concoction on the altar; then she spread some on my forehead. I cringed, but she didn't stop. Instead she began to chant in another language. Luckily, the stuff was pink and smelled like flowers. If it had been blood, I was out of there.

She picked up a rattle that appeared to be encircled with bones—I didn't want to know whose—then shook it. Lazarus hissed, and she scooped him up as she passed his box.

In front of the *veves* she stopped and tapped the heart with the rattle. "I ask you, Legba, to open the door for the spirits."

The wind returned, swirling through the closed room, skimming the candles, lifting my hair. Something pushed at my forehead, something I couldn't see. I closed my eyes.

Instead of black, there was a wash of silver, like the full moon shining on a still lake. I actually heard the lap of the water, smelled it, too, could almost feel the cool, gentle drift on my skin.

Let me know the truth, I thought, and opened my eyes.

The candles went out. Every last one of them.

Open your mind.

"Cassandra?"

"I'm here."

"Did you say something?"

"I said, 'I'm here.'"

"Before that."

"Wasn't me. You heard Erzulie. Listen to what she says. Hold on; I'll light the candles."

I wasn't sure how to open my mind. I wasn't the touchy-feely type.

A cool finger brushed my forehead. *Open.*

I closed my eyes again and imagined a door. Reaching out, I turned the knob and pushed it open. On the other side a woman waited.

She was tall, voluptuous, with mahogany skin and the best Afro I'd ever seen. I expected her eyes to be dark, too. Instead they glowed silver. Her body was covered in a loose white robe that looked really comfortable, as did her sandals.

She beckoned, and I stepped into a midnight garden. "Where am I?"

"Physically, still in the temple, but your mind has joined with mine."

Her voice was as lovely as she was, smooth, calm, the voice of a woman who knew her own strength, her own place, all the answers.

The garden was filled with flowers in colors I'd never imagined. The moonlight caused them to appear as if they'd been painted with rain. But the air was warm, comfortably moist, like the last day of summer before autumn descends.

"Are you Erzulie?" I asked.

"What is it you wish to know?"

Was that an answer? For her, probably.

"Am I under the influence of a love spell?"

"Perhaps."

"Is there a loup-garou?"

"What do you think?"

I frowned. This was not going well. "All I want is the truth."

"And the truth you will have."

She led me down a rock-strewn path. Not the usual gravel but a hardscrabble gray rock that reminded me of the moon. As we walked, her robe changed colors, reflecting every shade of the moon—white, silver, blue, gold, even red.

"Where can I get one of those?" I asked.

Erzulie's lips curved as she pointed to one flower amid a hundred others, the bright red petals unmuted by the night.

A fire iris.

"Take a piece," she murmured, "and the truth will come to you."

"I thought the fire iris was bad luck. That they attracted animals."

She turned her cool, silver eyes in my direction. "The truth comes with some risk."

I guess everything worth having did.

As I tore a tiny petal from the fire iris, the now-familiar scent of cinnamon in flames tickled my nose.

"Which truth are we talking about?" I asked, and turned.

The garden was empty except for me.

I blinked, and I was back in the temple. The candles were lit. Cassandra stared at me as if transfixed.

"Which truth?" she whispered.

I opened my hand. In the center of my palm lay a bright red petal. Then I opened my mouth and two voices came out—mine and Erzulie's.

"All of them."

33

"What happened?" Cassandra asked. "Are you OK?"

I wasn't sure. I'd been here, but not here. Myself, yet not myself. The sensation should have been frightening; instead it had been . . .

"Comforting." My voice was my own again. I no longer felt . . . full.

"What was comforting?" Cassandra asked.

"Erzulie. She's like . . ." Again I groped for a word to describe her.

"A mother."

I tilted my head. "If you say so."

My mother was nothing like Erzulie.

Cassandra frowned, but she refrained from exploring that avenue, thank goodness. Bending, she untwined Lazarus from her ankle, then dumped him into his box.

"Tell me everything," she ordered, so I did.

When I was finished, Cassandra bit her lip, and her forehead crinkled. I began to get uneasy.

"What?" I asked.

"You went further than anyone else ever has. Most only hear the voice of the *loa,* become a little scrambled. You traveled to Ife."

"I didn't go anywhere. Did I?"

"Not physically."

"I just traveled to Ife in my head." I paused. "What's Ife?"

"There's a town called Ife in Nigeria, but the one you went to is a legendary place, the mecca of vodoun, where the revelations of the *loas* came to the first faithful."

"Terrific," I muttered. "And what about this?"

I showed her the petal of the fire iris that I'd picked in a place I hadn't actually gone.

"I can't believe you brought a piece back."

"What does it mean that I did?"

"Not sure."

"Wow. You're as helpful as she was."

Cassandra ignored me. I wished I could do that whenever someone was annoying. Instead, I always felt compelled to sarcasm them to death—or at least until they went away.

"Keep the petal nearby," Cassandra said. "Any questions you have should soon be answered."

"Just like that? *Poof.* I know the truth?"

"Got me."

I narrowed my eyes. "What happened in the past when you performed this ceremony?"

"The *loas* came, inhabited someone else, and answered their questions."

"Truthfully?"

"*Loas* don't lie."

"Then why didn't she answer me?"

"Maybe you had too many questions. Maybe she didn't know the answers. Maybe you could only discover the truth by seeing it yourself."

"Maybe this is all bullshit."

Cassandra tilted her head, and I had to admit, if the previous hour had been bullshit, it was extremely convincing bullshit.

"Never mind." I tightened my fingers around the petal. "I'll just wait for the answers. Should be along anytime now."

"You believe?" she asked.

I considered the question, remembered what had happened, where I'd been, how I'd felt.

"Yeah." How could I not?

"I need to do some research," Cassandra said. "Make some calls. Find out why you traveled to Ife. How you could have brought something out."

A thought occurred to me. "Isn't there both good and bad voodoo?"

"They're mirror images. Can't have one without the other."

"So Erzulie might have been bad."

"No. The *loas* are all about truth. It's the maker of the magic who brings about good or bad. We call the evildoers 'ones who serve the *loas* with both hands.'"

"You used both hands."

"It's an expression. Don't you trust me?"

She appeared so crestfallen, I wanted to reassure her, but I didn't want to lie, either. "I've never dealt with voodoo, Cassandra. For all I know you could have been calling Satan himself. He could be running around New Orleans having a grand old time."

"He already is," she said dryly.

"Ha-ha."

"You spoke to the *loa,* Diana, which means the good or the evil intent came from you. Are you evil?"

I thought about it. "Sometimes."

"That just makes you human. When you asked for help, direction, truth, did you ask so you could use the result to hurt someone else?"

"No."

"Then go in peace."

I glanced at my watch and my eyes widened. "It's almost morning."

"Time flies," Cassandra said. "Let me put that petal into something before you ruin or lose it."

She rustled through the mess on one of the shelves and came up with an empty gris-gris bag.

"Do you have those lying around all over the place?" I asked.

She didn't bother to answer, just held open the bag.

I hesitated. "Will it work in there?"

"Of course."

I guess I had to take her word for it.

I should leave. I wanted to discover if the petal would reveal the truth, but— "How will I know what's true?"

"You just will."

"That is *so* not helpful."

"It's like love—you'll just know."

"I'll know the love I'm afraid is contrived is real because I'll just know. That makes no sense."

"What does?" As usual, she ignored my scowl. "If you find a charm, destroying it should break the spell."

"What does a charm look like?"

"Could be a gris-gris, or maybe a fetish."

"Which is?"

"A small figure—wood, bone, maybe stone, even cloth—fashioned into the shape of a person. Many cultures use totems for luck, for curses or charms—both good and evil."

"All right," I said. "Find something weird, destroy it, and the magic is gone." Although how I would destroy stone, I had no idea.

"Or you could just leave it be."

I glanced up. "What?"

"Is being in love with him so bad?"

"I need the truth, Cassandra. That's just the way I am."

She nodded as if she'd known I'd say that. Hell, she probably had. "If Erzulie said the truth would be revealed, it will. I'm not sure how, or why, or when, but have faith."

"Faith has never been my strong suit," I muttered, and left.

If I'd had faith in Simon none of this would have been necessary. But if I hadn't had it then, in him, how could I have it now in someone I barely knew and in something I didn't trust?

Got me.

Never one to put off what I could do today, I drove past Adam's trailer, but his car wasn't there. I even walked out to the shack, but it was empty.

So I spent my time setting up a trap in the clearing where Charlie had died. Scene of the crime and all that. Besides, I didn't have a better idea.

I also had my doubts the snare would work. If a werewolf had human eyes, it might have a human brain, and then the beast would know better than to creep into the cage and let the door close behind it.

However, I planned to be sitting in a tree with my loaded tranquilizer gun. If I had to, I'd shoot the thing, then shove it inside myself. There was more than one way to skin a cat. Although I'd never actually figured out a second way.

I spent several days tramping through the swamp in the heat, went to town a few times for supplies. Then I endured as many nights with very little sleep, lying alone on the floor, listening to weird noises and faraway howls that should be coyotes but weren't. I hadn't seen Adam, and I'd kind of stopped looking for him.

I'd been all gung ho for the truth, but the more time passed, the more time I had to think about things, the more afraid I became. What if he'd misled me about something important? Something I wouldn't be able to forgive.

What if Luc had cast a spell over me, and what I felt for both of them was a lie? I didn't want it to be a lie. Caring for Adam and his son was the first thing that had felt right in a long, long time.

I considered Cassandra's suggestion that I just let everything be. It wasn't a bad suggestion.

However, what if there wasn't a spell? What if I truly loved Adam and he didn't love me?

I considered all the questions that had no answers as I took a sponge bath in the tributary in front of the mansion. I never had managed to rent another hotel room.

I fell asleep eating a sandwich on my sleeping bag. I must have been near meltdown, because I didn't wake up until sometime after sunset and only then because I sensed I wasn't alone.

My heart kicked up a notch, but before I could fully panic, a silhouette appeared in the window. I'd know that shape anywhere.

"Adam."

He didn't answer, just crossed the room and lowered himself onto the sleeping bag.

Hell, let's be honest, he lowered himself onto *me*.

The only thing adorning his upper body was his bracelet. I liked him best that way. His khakis were soft, his body already hard. Despite the clothes, we fit together just right. Pressure, friction, heat. What more could a girl ask for?

Truth.

In that moment, I understood that I couldn't go on without knowing it. Where was that petal?

I kept one hand on his shoulder while the other crept around like Thing from *The Addams Family.* I was distracted by Adam's lips crushing mine, his tongue sweeping into my mouth. I wore loose shorts and his fingers skimmed my thigh, drifted higher, slipped beneath. His thumb stroked in a rhythm to match his tongue, and I forgot about the gris-gris bag.

After my makeshift bath, the high temperature had made me opt for a thin light green camisole. I hadn't even considered a bra. So when his lips closed around my nipple, the moist heat encircled me as if there weren't anything between us but air. Not long after, there wasn't.

He hadn't spoken, had barely looked at me, and I needed him to, so I touched his face.

His eyes met mine at the very first thrust. My free hand clenched as did my body, and my fingers brushed the gris-gris.

I gathered the small bag into my palm, and a breeze swirled through the room. Scented with cinnamon, it whispered indecipherable words but left behind a feeling of certainty.

Whatever else might be a lie, this was the truth.

34

My eyes snapped open. How long had I been asleep?

I lay on my sleeping bag, alone—nothing new there. What *was* new was the crescent moon centered in the window, a bright silver slash against an indigo sky.

"Showtime," I muttered.

I'd rather Adam were with me, wouldn't mind having him around while I spent the rest of the night in a tree with my dart gun. But he hadn't offered and I hadn't asked.

In fact, neither one of us had said a word. He'd behaved as if he were drawn to me even though it was wrong, stupid, destructive. He'd behaved like a man who couldn't help himself, and that wasn't love.

But it was something.

I dug out some jeans and a dark T-shirt. As an afterthought I tucked both gris-gris in my pocket. Alligators I didn't need, and one never could tell when the truth might come in handy.

The dart gun was loaded, but I put some extra darts into my backpack, along with a bottle of water and some cookies. I could be out there all night. Last, I opened the cooler I'd bought in town yesterday and withdrew a long white paper-wrapped package from the ice.

The trek to the clearing was uneventful. Though it would be too much to hope for that the loup-garou was poised to step into my trap, nevertheless, I approached quietly, just in case. However, when I pushed through the tall grass, the only thing I saw was an empty cage.

Not that it was easy to see it, if I do say so myself. I'd positioned the apparatus, large enough to hold ten grown men, beneath a particularly weepy-looking cypress tree. After I rearranged the moss and the ground cover, the metal was almost impossible to distinguish by the simple light of a crescent moon.

I tossed the contents of my white paper package inside. "Fresh steak ought to entice you."

Wolves preferred live prey, but they weren't against a free meal when they could find one. Me, I couldn't stomach tying up a live creature to await a bloody death. Prime rib would have to do.

Over the past few days I'd not only readied the cage, the darts, the gun, I'd also readied a second perfect cypress nearby: tall, with acres of moss. I'd placed a portable tree stand about twenty feet off the ground.

I tied my rifle to the rope I'd strung over a branch. Using the heavy-duty nails I'd pounded into the tree, I climbed to the flat metal stand.

After allowing my gaze to wander over the area, I hoisted my gun upward by way of the rope pulley, secured the safety strap around my waist—more fatal hunting accidents occur when hunters tumble out of their trees because they fall asleep, have a heart attack, or are just plain stupid than when they are actually shot—and settled in to wait.

The sounds of the swamp surrounded me. I'd thought the place loud when I was inside the mansion? I hadn't met loud yet.

Birds, insects, alligators, nutrias—out there some-where I could have sworn I heard a pig squeal. A farm an-imal gone wild? Or were there wild boars in the depths? I probably shouldn't have been wandering around as much as I had been without a gun.

My gaze was caught by shifting swamp grass beneath an ebbing moon. Not the wind. Something was coming.

Slowly I raised the gun. I don't know what I expected, but when the wolf stepped from the swamp into the clear-ing, lifting his nose and sniffing, I had to bite my lip to keep from making a sound.

His fur shone in the sliver of moonlight, glinting black, then blue, then black again. I'd been right to gauge the dosage for an Alaskan timber wolf. This thing might even be larger than that.

The animal paid no attention to the steak. Instead he trotted around and around the open area as if he knew something was there but couldn't find it.

I wasn't surprised; I didn't even consider it magic to have the wolf from my dream materialize. I'd seen a black tail. I knew what a wolf looked like. Put one and one together and I got two, even in my sleep.

But how was I supposed to determine if this was a real wolf or a werewolf?

Mrs. Favreau's words came back to me: *Though the form may be that of a wolf, a werewolf always retains its human eyes.*

I squinted against the night, against the distance, as the wolf circled away from me again, but I couldn't see his eyes, let alone determine if they were human.

Suddenly he stopped, stiffened, and stared right at me. I hadn't made a movement, not a sound. What had caused him to sense I was there? Wolves did not peer into trees for their prey.

I lifted the gun to my shoulder. He didn't care. He charged across the clearing as if he planned to climb up the trunk, snarling as if he would tear me apart once he got there.

Why wasn't he afraid of the rifle? He couldn't know that I didn't have silver bullets. Right now that seemed like a big mistake.

I forced myself to remain steady. To be patient. To aim. I didn't think a wolf could clamber this high, but I wasn't taking any chances.

Right before I squeezed the trigger, I saw his eyes, and I had no qualms about shooting. I couldn't determine a color, but I did see the whites.

Real wolves didn't have any.

The dart struck him in the chest. He yelped, leaped. My heart did, too. The thing had a damn nice vertical extension. Too nice. If he hadn't been shot, he might have cleared the lowest branch of my tree, about a yard below my feet. Not that he could have done much damage hanging there, but the ability startled me. What else could he do?

The wolf fell to the earth, staggered, toppled, and went still. The silence following so much sound seemed deafening.

I needed to drag the beast into the cage, then call Frank. Lucky for me, the animal had dropped over right in front of the enclosure. I wasn't sure how far I'd be able to move deadweight that approximated my own.

Once on the ground, I wasted no time. Though I didn't want to, I leaned my weapon against the tree. I couldn't do much with one hand.

The grass was damp, so when I tugged on his rear legs, the beast slid. After much grunting and groaning, I had him in the cage.

Straightening, I allowed myself to smile. I'd done it.

Like a dog dreaming of a rabbit, the wolf's legs twitched, and my smile froze. He lay between me and the door.

"Idiot," I muttered, and leaped over his inert body, skidding on the grass and falling on my ass.

Stunned, I didn't immediately move. Until I heard a low, rumbling growl.

I rolled onto my feet in a single movement, which was pretty darned athletic if I do say so myself. Terror will do that to a woman.

I dived for the open door as the wolf slowly sat up, shaking his head as if he were coming out of deep water. The dart hadn't worked very well.

Of course it had been fashioned for a 120-pound animal. This one weighed quite a bit more than that. I guess I should count myself lucky he'd fallen over at all.

The door clanged and I turned the key, then yanked it out of the lock and backpedaled as quickly as I could. Slipping again, I fell to my knees. Could I be any more of a klutz?

I'd specifically requested a lock and key on the cage. A wolf couldn't undo a catch, but a person could. And if this animal was what I thought it was, he'd have opposable thumbs by morning, if not before.

A body slammed into the bars. Snarling and slavering commenced.

Still on my hands and knees, I looked up and my whole world shifted.

The wolf was *exactly* like the one in my dream. Huge and black, he also possessed the eyes of Adam Ruelle.

35

"Oh, my God. Oh, my God."

I couldn't stop muttering, couldn't stop staring. How could this be? I'd touched Adam with silver. He hadn't minded.

The thing in the cage appeared mad, throwing his body against the metal, trying to chew a way out. Blood marred the white spittle dripping from his snout. Maybe the wolf was rabid after all.

"That's not a wolf," I whispered.

Absently I shoved the key into my pocket, and my fingertips brushed the gris-gris. The animal howled as if in pain and began to change.

The transformation was something from a horror film; at first my mind refused to accept what my eyes couldn't help but see.

The sleek, dark fur receded, becoming shorter and shorter as if it were being sucked through the skin. Paws became feet at the ends of legs and hands at the ends of arms. The claws evaporated the same way the fur had.

The neck twisted; the spine lengthened; the animal moaned. Going from quadrapedal to bipedal couldn't feel good.

His snout shortened, dividing into nose and mouth as the canine teeth shrank. The tail disappeared with a thick, wet *thunk*. The eyes remained the same.

Inside the cage stood a naked Adam Ruelle.

He didn't appear upset to be revealed a monster. Didn't seem to care he was in his altogether for the world to see. In fact, he seemed to like it, or maybe, if the size of his erection was any indication, he liked me.

What he didn't like was the cage. He slammed both hands against the bars and growled, "Let me out."

I shook my head. I couldn't speak.

"Goddammit, bitch, set me free!"

I blinked. That didn't sound like Adam. Of course, what did I know? I'd believed him when he said he wasn't the loup-garou.

He tilted his head to stare at the crescent moon. "How did you do it?"

"D-do what?"

"Make me shift."

His voice was heated, his gaze anything but. Staring into his eyes, I was reminded of Lazarus—cold-blooded and empty of emotion. This man would kill without flinching and forget about it before the blood dried on the ground.

The Adam I knew wasn't exactly warm and fuzzy, but he wasn't evil. Or maybe I'd just been too busy getting my brains screwed out to notice.

My hand ached from clutching the gris-gris. I glanced down, opened my fingers, and understood. I'd been unable to see the truth until magic cleared my eyes.

"I run as a wolf under de crescent moon. I have no choice."

I lifted my gaze. "The curse."

"Oui. But I become a man when I choose, or when de sun comes." He swept a hand down his body. "This was not my choice."

I folded my fingers around the gris-gris. I *had* asked for the truth.

"Why you lock me up like this?" he whispered. "You know I'd come to you in de night. I like to hear you scream when I fuck you. You didn't have to put me in a cage."

I winced at his language and the thought. I'd been sleeping with a monster. I'd believed myself in love with him, had begun to imagine a life together.

I was a fool.

"Let me go, and I'll do you right here."

He took himself in his hand and pumped, then moaned a little. The sound was more of a growl and marched along my skin like biting red ants.

"I've been imagining such things, Diana. You, me, this way and that. Have you ever wanted to mate with a beast?"

My eyes widened. I couldn't speak. Adam seemed like a completely different man. Was he possessed by Satan under the crescent moon?

Apparently.

"I'll shift again. It'll be doggie style like you've never had before. And if you make me howl, I won't even kill you tonight."

I took a step back and he smiled. Were his teeth growing longer along with his—?

I yanked my gaze away, but not before he saw my unease and smirked.

"With de flower I marked you as mine."

How could that be? Adam had taken the fire irises away from me, thrown them into the swamp, told me not to pick them again.

Was he schizophrenic? That would make a certain kind of sense.

I'd read all of Simon's research into lycanthropy. Many psychiatrists and other physicians believed the historical reports of werewolves stemmed from the behavior of the insane. Back then mental illness was labeled possession.

I stared at Adam, locked in a cage. I could understand the theory.

"I watched you whenever I could. De others knew you were mine to keep or kill."

I guess I hadn't been crazy when I'd heard more than one wolf in the swamp, seen slinky shadows in town. History often repeated itself, and one of its great lessons is that evil loves to beget evil.

"I wanted to be inside you that first night," he continued, "but de crescent moon called. I had to make do with a few touches."

No wonder I'd had such an erotic dream at the hotel on Bourbon Street. My skin went clammy at that memory and several others.

"Set me free. I'll get out sooner or later. But if it's later, you'll pay. I will do things you never imagined. I will keep you alive forever. You will beg to die, Diana, and I will never let you go."

I wasn't stupid. If I let him out now, obsession or no, he'd kill me.

I rubbed my thumb over the outline of the key in my pocket. If I had my way, he would never see freedom again.

"I have to get back to de boy," he whispered. "He expects me come morning."

Black dots danced in front of my eyes. *Luc.* How could I have forgotten?

I couldn't connect the man who'd so tenderly held his son, who had refused to allow me near him lest the boy be hurt when I left, to the one who spoke so calmly of both killing and fucking me.

Definitely possessed by Satan.

Without another word, I walked away. Adam's voice followed me down the trail: "What de hell? You think you can leave me here?"

"Just did," I muttered.

"I will kill you!"

"Redundant."

"I will tear out your guts and strangle you with them. I will drink your blood; I will bathe in it."

"Original."

And pretty scary. Nevertheless, I had to get to Luc and take him away.

I ran all the way back to the mansion, grabbed my stuff, and tossed everything into the trunk except the dart gun, Cassandra's knife, and my cell phone. Those I placed on the front seat. I stared at Adam's pistol for a second, then realized he wouldn't have helped me out by loading it with silver, and left the thing in the trunk. Around my waist I secured a fanny pack with my money and travel documents.

As I climbed behind the wheel, a howl rose toward the descending moon. Uneasy, I glanced at the swaying swamp. That had sounded close.

I floored the accelerator, spewing grass and dirt until I fishtailed onto the highway. Then I used one hand to dial

Frank. Since it was the middle of the night, I wasn't surprised when his machine answered.

"Your loup-garou is confined in a cage in the swamp about a mile east of the Ruelle Mansion," I said. "If you have a problem finding him, call Detective Conner Sullivan and have him take you to the place where Charlie died." I hung up and muttered, "The first time."

I didn't consider where I was going, what I was doing, or how I would hide from Adam for the next fifty years. I focused all my attention on getting to Luc and getting him gone.

The moon was nearly down; the sun would soon be up. I parked in front of Adam's trailer. I'd walked halfway to the door before I went back and grabbed the knife.

"Better safe than sorry," I murmured, and tucked the weapon into the pack at my waist.

I decided to make that my mantra.

A few seconds later, hand poised to knock, mind occupied constructing a stupendous lie for Sadie, the babysitter, I hesitated, then tried the doorknob.

The door swung inward without a sound.

After glancing over one shoulder, then the other, I scampered inside. I'd been bent on doing anything it took to get to the child and then kidnap him, but strolling into a house uninvited made me uncomfortable.

I crept down the hall. In the first room, Sadie slept on the bed. I pulled the door shut and moved on to the room illuminated by a night-light. A gaggle of boy toys—a football, a bat, a deck of cards that appeared to have been the victim of fifty-two pickup—were strewn across the floor, as well as several dirty T-shirts and a dozen smelly socks.

Luc lay on top of the covers, arms and legs flung apart with wild abandon. I let out the breath I'd been holding in a rush and Luc's eyes snapped open. He must have been a real treat to get down for a nap as a baby.

I put my finger to my lips, and he grinned as I hurried across the floor to kneel at his side. Before I could speak, he flung his arms around my neck and hugged me. What I wouldn't give to be able to trust like that. After this, I probably never would.

"We're going on a trip," I whispered. "Do you have a suitcase?"

"You and me and Daddy?" he whispered back.

"Just you and me."

"Is that OK with Daddy?"

"No," said a familiar voice from the door.

36

Adam leaned against the wall just inside the room. He wore jeans, a sleeveless shirt, tennis shoes. His bracelet gleamed dully in the half-light from the hall.

Now that I thought about it, he hadn't had that bracelet on in the cage. Then again, something like that could fall right off your paw.

"How did you get out?" I demanded.

Confusion flickered over his face. "Out?"

I cast a glance at Luc, who was staring back and forth between us. I needed to get Adam away from the boy, especially since I might have to kill him.

"Let's discuss this outside."

"Fine." He gave Luc a stern glare. "Stay here."

Adam headed for the front of the house, and I followed, fingers surreptitiously unzipping the compartment that held the silver knife.

Outside, the night was completely dark. The moon was gone; the sun wasn't yet up. I pulled out the weapon, tightening my fingers around the hilt. "I'm taking Luc."

Adam faced me, saw the knife, and laughed. "Didn't we do this already? I'm not a werewolf."

He was so different from the man I'd left in the swamp. Sure he looked and sounded the same, but the snakelike coldness had left his gaze and the nasty smirk no longer twisted his mouth. When he spoke he didn't say evil, hurtful things. At least not yet.

"I saw you change," I said.

Something flickered in his eyes. "When?"

He didn't deny it, and even while I'd seen the truth, believed it, too, somewhere inside I must have been hoping for a miracle. "You don't remember?"

"Just tell me when and where."

"About an hour ago. Where Charlie died. I left you in a cage."

He cursed.

"How did you get out?" I repeated.

He ignored my question, clenching and unclenching his fists in great agitation.

"Adam! I'm not going to let you hurt Luc."

Fury spread across his face, and quick as a forked tongue, his hand shot out and grabbed the knife by the blade, taking it away with an ease and quickness that was mind-boggling. He flipped the weapon end over end and it stuck in a fence that separated the trailer park from a used-car lot.

I fought the urge to run. "I'm not leaving without him."

"You aren't leaving *with* him, either. He's *my* son."

"You lied to me."

"I lie all the time, *cher.* Anymore I wonder if I even know what's a lie and what isn't."

"You said you weren't the loup-garou!"

He sighed. "I'm not."

"And I should believe an admitted pathological liar?"

"Believe what you want."

I had a thought. Maybe the loup-garou wasn't harmed by silver. Maybe all the tests I'd run on Adam had been a waste of time. Hell, maybe he could slip through bars, or at the least bend them with his superhuman strength.

Adam started for the trailer.

"Where are you going?"

"To tell Sadie I'll be back in an hour. I have to go into the swamp."

"What? Why?"

He ignored me, disappearing inside for a few moments before coming out again, then grabbing me by the arm. "You're going with me."

I tried to pull away. "I don't think so."

He could easily strangle the life out of me and toss me into the swamp as alligator bait. I was starting to think he'd done it before.

His grip tightened. "I leave you here and you disappear with Luc. I don't have time to search for you. I can't leave New Orleans until the new moon comes."

I was so surprised he'd admitted that, I allowed him to shove me into the passenger seat of my car, where I promptly got a dart gun up the ass. I moved the paraphernalia out of the way as he skirted the front fender, then got behind the wheel.

His gaze flicked over the gun. "So that's how you did it."

I didn't bother to answer.

He picked up the weapon, checked the ammo, found it empty, and tossed the thing into the backseat.

"Why are we going into the swamp?" I asked.

"I have something to do."

"I don't suppose I can convince you not to."

"No."

"Frank Tallient will wonder what happened to me. When he gets here—"

"He's coming?" Adam's voice deepened, and the glare he shot my way was downright cold. This was the man I'd left in the cage. "What did you do?"

I swallowed and forced myself to answer. "I told Frank where he could find the loup-garou."

Adam cursed. "When was that?"

"Less than an hour ago."

Some of his tension eased. "We'll be there before him."

"He'll raise a stink if he can't find me. You can't leave Luc alone."

"What are you talking about?"

"If you kill me, you'll fry."

The death penalty was alive and well in Louisiana, though I didn't know for certain if they actually fried people anymore, or how often.

"You think I'm going to kill you, *cher*?"

"You've killed before."

"I've risked more than I've ever risked in my life to protect you," Adam said softly.

"I don't understand."

"You will."

We remained silent for the rest of the drive to the mansion, as well as the hike into the swamp.

The sun was up. The day was going to be another scorcher. Nevertheless, I couldn't stop shivering.

Adam was insane, if not a werewolf. He was going to kill me and probably everyone I'd spoken to about him. Cassandra, Detective Sullivan, Frank. Had he killed Mrs. Favreau?

He'd most likely killed Charlie, the mystery stranger,

and Mrs. Beasly. Such carnage was beyond my comprehension.

But what really made me ill was the idea of leaving Luc in Adam's care. What would happen to the child with a monster for a father?

I stepped into the clearing first, stopping so abruptly, Adam nearly ran me over from behind.

The cage was still there; the lock was still locked.

And Adam was still inside.

37

Dizziness washed over me and I swayed. "What—? Who—? How—?"

Adam rushed to the enclosure, saw the lock, and turned. "The key."

I was having trouble breathing, so I sat down and put my head between my legs. After a few minutes, the black dots receded.

When I glanced up, two men, so alike in appearance and yet so different, stared back. Now that they stood together, how could I have thought they were the same? One look into their eyes and I saw the difference. The Adam in the cage was evil; the one who'd brought me here was not.

"Twins?" I asked.

They shook their heads, and their hair swirled around their shoulders.

"My great-great . . . well, several-greats-grandfather." The Adam outside the cage jerked a thumb toward the one inside. "Henri Ruelle."

The naked man bowed.

"The picture," I murmured.

Henri smirked. I hated that smirk.

"Obviously taken before you became a loup-garou." Considering my trouble photographing them.

"Obviously," Henri returned.

"Why would you leave it on the wall where anyone could see?"

"I only wanted *you* to see."

"Grandpère likes to confuse people."

He'd confused me all right.

I returned my attention to Adam. "You said your family wasn't cursed."

"No. I said, 'Some say we are.' "

"I specifically asked if you'd been cursed to run as a wolf beneath the crescent moon."

"*I'm* not."

"You look so much alike." I stared at Adam. "Couldn't you at least cut your hair? Make some distinction?"

"The better to protect me, my dear," Henri said.

I glanced at him, then back at Adam. "You protect it?"

"Hey!" Henri protested.

"There will always be a loup-garou of Ruelle blood. If Grandpère dies, the next Ruelle male becomes the beast."

"You."

He nodded. "Then Luc."

So many things were starting to make sense.

"Your father and grandfather?"

"They couldn't bear knowing what they might become."

"Pussies," Henri spat.

"Who did you piss off?" I demanded.

"I didn't know she was a voodoo queen. She was—" Henri shrugged. "A slave. I wanted her; I took her."

"You raped her?"

"No." Confusion flickered over his face. "She was *mine.* I never understood what she was so angry about."

I rubbed between my eyes. "Why didn't she just turn him into a bug and squash him?"

"Too easy," Adam murmured.

"Dismemberment would have been too easy."

"She called on the moon goddess to make me a beast."

I lifted my head. "What?"

"Queen of heavens, mother of creatures, lady of de wild, patron goddess of de outlaw werewolf, the instant I heard your name, *déesse de la lune,* I knew you were here for me."

I glanced at Adam, who shrugged. "He's been obsessed with you from de beginning, but he couldn't figure out if you were here to help or hurt him."

"Diana is a huntress," Henri continued. "You rule all dark forests; you command de moon. Queen of witches, daughter of Satan."

"I think you've got the wrong Diana."

"I'm cursed by a woman who calls on a moon goddess, then you show up? How can that be a coincidence?"

"It's a hundred and fifty years later!" I shouted.

"Time means nothing to me."

I suppose after the first century, that's true.

"Listen," I said. "My name is just a name. It was my grandmother's, and you can bet your everlasting life she wasn't a moon goddess."

"Did you come here to make me stronger, to be at my side until we ruled the world?" Henri asked.

Did this guy *listen*? "I don't think so."

"Then you came to cure me, and you have to die."

"Huh?"

"The one thing Grandpère fears is being cured. He likes what he is. He doesn't want to go back to the way he was."

"In life I was at de mercy of forces I could not change—weather, government, stock market, death. Now everyone is at de mercy of me. Like this, I'll never be hungry or poor again."

I looked at Adam. "I thought you were poor now."

"I want none of his money."

Couldn't say I blamed him.

"I can understand cursing Henri," I said, "but why the entire line?"

"Curses are funny that way," Adam said. "They tend to hang around for more than a generation."

"You're certain killing him will curse you?"

"I can't kill him and find out!" Adam shoved a hand through his hair. "I've spoken with voodoo experts; they all say de same thing. A curse like this is on every Ruelle born until de curse is lifted. And that I don't know how to do. No one does."

"So what, exactly, is the curse?"

"He is an evil, soulless thing. A selfish prick who cares only for himself."

"Wasn't he that already?"

"I didn't know him before," Adam shrugged, "but most likely."

"I'm right here," Henri muttered.

"Under de crescent moon he runs as a wolf," Adam continued as if Henri hadn't spoken. "He murders de innocent and creates more werewolves."

"Like Charlie."

"Yes."

"He told me he *has* to change under the crescent moon."

"He does. Many more nights of being a beast that way."

"A blessing, not a curse, if you ask me," Henri said. "I like to kill."

"We didn't ask you," I snapped. God, he was annoying. Something occurred to me. "I saw Charlie under a half-moon."

"Charlie was a werewolf; Grandpère is a loup-garou."

"My head hurts."

Adam's mouth tightened. "Grandpère wasn't bitten; he was cursed. Those he bites rise and run as wolves within twenty-four hours—day, night, doesn't matter. After that, only de full moon compels them to shift. Under any other, it is their choice."

Which made as much sense as anything else around here.

"What about him?" I jerked my thumb toward the cage. "When the moon isn't a crescent?"

"He's a man—or as much of a man as he can claim to be."

"Sounds like *less* of a curse."

"The longer he's in human form, de more violent he becomes when de wolf is upon him."

I scowled at Henri, who shrugged and examined his fingernails. I considered all that I knew and all I did not.

"When did you find out about the curse?" I asked.

"Luc's first birthday." His face softened. "Family tradition. By then you're in love with de boy. You'd do anything to protect him."

"I couldn't find a record of Luc's birth," I said.

Adam cast Henri a suspicious glance, and Henri shrugged. "Less people know of us, de better."

"Once your father told you the truth," I continued, "he killed himself?"

Sadness flickered over Adam's face as he nodded. "I was old enough to watch over Grandpère, and by then I'd had Special Forces training. Didn't know I'd need it for this."

"Your father left you alone to raise your son, protect that thing, *and* find a cure? He couldn't stick around to help?"

"Knowing what was to come preyed on his mind, drove him over de edge."

I got the feeling Adam was talking as much about himself as his dad.

"When I was a boy he would be gone certain nights and come home beat to hell. He was a gentle man, a scholar. He didn't know how to fight; he had no idea how to counteract evil and violence."

Henri snorted but refrained from comment for a change.

"Your mother?"

"She left the instant she knew the truth."

I tilted my head, and Adam looked away, refusing to meet my eyes. No wonder he'd been so worried I'd leave him and Luc behind. Every other woman in his life had.

"My father asked me to enlist," he continued. "I'd always been fascinated with weapons, interested in military history; I believed he wanted me to be happy. Later I understood he wanted me trained to do de family dirty work better than he had been."

"You plan on taking the easy way out when Luc's old enough to protect that monster?"

"I'd let de curse fall to me before I'd leave him to suffer."

"You'll like it," Henri whispered. "You'll see. The power is exhilarating. With one stroke you can kill or impart life everlasting."

"Unless someone has a silver bullet," Adam snapped.

"So few do."

"Wait a minute," I said. "Doesn't everyone he kills rise again?"

"No, thank God, or we'd be overrun. If he kills but doesn't drink their blood or eat their flesh, they become a werewolf. If he partakes of de kill, they're just dead."

"I do so love when they beg for their life," Henri murmured. "I usually give it to them."

"Shut up, old man," Adam said.

The incongruity of calling someone who didn't appear a day over thirty "old man" made me giggle. Hysteria was obviously not far behind.

I swallowed the inappropriate laughter and tried to focus. "Why are there no Ruelle girls?"

"What?" Adam blinked at the sudden change in subject.

"No girls born for over a century. I checked."

"De curse. Grandpère's voodoo queen wanted only men to suffer. I don't think she cared too much for them."

"I can't imagine why."

Henri grabbed the bars and rattled his cage. "Let me out!"

"Not so fast," Adam said. "You will leave her alone."

Henri's gaze flicked to me. "What if she tries to kill me? Will you protect me then, Petit-fils? Will you trust her with your soul? What about de boy's?"

"If she meant to kill you, Grandpère, I'd be dead. She thought I was you."

Henri frowned. I didn't think he was the brightest star in the sky. Or should I say the fullest moon on the calendar?

"True," he agreed. "She'd have slipped a silver knife between your ribs while you were doing her. That's always de best time."

"You two seem to have me confused with someone else," I murmured. "A psychopathic serial killer perhaps?"

"But if she doesn't want to kill me—"

"I didn't at first, but now that I've met you I've changed my mind."

"Diana—" Adam began, but Henri interrupted: "What *do* you want?"

"To prove a werewolf exists and show it to the world."

"That isn't going to happen." Henri glanced at Adam. "Right?"

Adam sighed. "Right." He let his head fall forward, and his hair sifted over his face.

I stood, resisting the urge to shove it back.

He lifted his gaze. "I need de key."

"He wants to kill me, or maybe screw me—"

"How about both?" Henri whispered.

"Why you think I said I'd be your guide?" Adam demanded. "I wasn't going to let him hurt you. I still won't."

Sadness filtered through me. Adam hadn't hung around because of my charms—no kidding—but because he'd wanted to make certain Henri didn't tear out my throat or worse. And what better way to get close than to pretend he wanted to sleep with me and then do so?

I'd been right: This wasn't love. It wasn't even lust, just duty.

Voices floated on the still morning air, startling us all.

"Frank," I muttered. How had he gotten here so fast?

"Hurry up," Henri snapped.

"I have to let him go, Diana." Adam's gaze captured mine. "If they don't kill him here, they'll dissect him somewhere else. If he dies and I'm possessed, there'll be no one to care for Luc."

"You think Henri should be free to kill people?"

"I do my best to contain him. And I spend de nights he can't shift eliminating those he's made."

My eyes widened. "You shot Charlie."

Adam nodded.

There was a shout, much closer, and Adam held out his hand. "Please."

I looked into his eyes, saw the shadows and the pain. I also saw his fear, his need, and his son.

I gave him the key.

38

Henri barreled out of the cage and started toward me. Adam hauled back and decked him on the chin. He staggered.

"I won't kill you." Adam jerked his head toward the tall grass. "But they will. Get lost."

Henri glared at me, a promise in his eyes, but he went, gliding into the swamp and disappearing.

"I'll take care of you. I swear."

I wanted Adam's words to mean something, but they were only words he'd say to anyone who'd helped him protect his son. He owed me, and while I should tell him to stuff his help, I'd looked into Henri's eyes and I didn't ever want to run into him again alone.

"Diana?" Adam took one step toward me, hand outstretched.

"Don't move, asshole."

Adam froze. So did I.

Big, muscle-bound men with bandoliers of bullets strung across their impressive chests spilled into the clearing. Each of them had a rifle in his hands, a pistol on his hip, and a knife strapped to his thigh.

Another man walked into the clearing carrying Frank Tallient. Frank's legs hung uselessly over his helper's arm, revealing why he'd sent me to find the loup-garou instead of coming himself.

Frank was placed atop a rotted stump at the edge of the clearing. He pointed a handgun at Adam's head.

"How did you get here so fast?" I blurted.

"I knew you'd find him this time, Diana." Frank never took his eyes or his gun off of Adam. "I came to New Orleans yesterday so I'd be close by when your call came."

"He-he got away," I blurted.

Frank made a tsking sound. "He's right here. Henri, it's been a long time."

"No—" I began.

Adam shot me a silencing glare, and I zipped my lip. Then he returned his attention to Frank. "Do we know each other?"

Fury washed over Frank's face. "I suppose it's nothing for you to wipe out an entire family and leave a man crippled."

"Where was this?" Adam asked.

"You really don't remember?"

Adam shrugged.

"Iron Mountain." At Adam's blank expression Frank continued, "Upper Michigan."

I inched closer to Adam with the vague idea that maybe Frank wouldn't shoot him if there was a chance of hitting me. With my shoulder pressed to Adam's, I felt him jerk at the words.

Michigan? When had Henri gone there? And if he'd traveled that far, where else had he been? How many others had he killed? How many werewolves had he made?

"*When* was this?" Adam's voice was a bit hoarse.

Frank didn't seem to notice. "Seven years, one month, three days, and five hours ago, you son of a bitch."

Seven years meant Henri had left Louisiana *before* Adam had taken over his protection. That was irrelevant to Frank. His family was dead and he meant to have his vengeance.

I stepped forward and Adam yanked me back. "No."

One glance at his face and I understood. Adam was going to let Frank riddle him with silver bullets on the off chance the man didn't know a werewolf would explode. Then Frank would leave, believing his vengeance complete.

"Protect Luc," Adam whispered. "Find a way."

My eyes widened. He was putting his son in my care? I didn't like this plan. However, I didn't have a better one, except— "He isn't Henri."

"Diana . . ."

I ignored Adam's plea. Henri had lived this long; he'd no doubt live a lot longer. He was probably halfway to Acapulco by now. Frank hadn't been able to find him without me, and I wasn't going to oblige him by locating Henri a second time.

"The one who killed your family and hurt you is out there." I pointed to the swamp. "This is *Adam*. His great—a bunch of times—grandson."

"Bullshit," Frank said conversationally. "I saw Henri maliciously murder everyone I loved. Then he left me alive to remember and mourn."

"He was a wolf; how do you know it was Henri?"

Frank's eyes glazed over with the memory. "I'd taken my family to our cabin. We were having dinner in town and Henri was at the bar. He and I struck up a conversation. He was an interesting, intelligent man. I even considered fixing him up with my daughter." He shuddered. "You should have seen what he did to her."

No, I shouldn't.

"He leaped right through our picture window. I tried to stop him, and he knocked me down the steps. Something snapped in my back, and I couldn't move my legs. I had to watch him kill them all. I'll never forget his eyes. I see them every night in my sleep."

"The curse makes all the Ruelle men look alike," I blurted.

I wasn't certain that was true, but the explanation made sense, especially when combined with the lack of females born into the family since the voodoo queen had done her thing.

"This is Adam," I insisted, "not Henri."

"I don't believe you." Frank sighted down the barrel of his gun.

I threw myself in front of Adam as the weapon fired. I expected pain; instead all I felt was Adam's arms close around me.

"He missed," I breathed in wonder.

Adam glanced at his bicep, where blood dripped from a two-inch gash. "Not exactly."

"Get out of the way, Diana," Frank ordered. "I don't want to, but I *will* kill you."

"I'm not moving," I said.

Adam's hands tightened on my shoulders. I smiled, thinking the movement was affection, then gasped when he tossed me aside to land with a thud out of the line of fire.

"Adam!" I shouted, scrambling up, tensing in expectation of a gunshot, but there wasn't one.

Detective Sullivan stood behind Frank, pressing his sidearm to the base of Frank's skull. "Drop it," he said. "And your friends, too."

Frank complied, as did his goons.

"You don't understand—" Frank began.

"I understand plenty," Sullivan snapped, the hula dancer on his tie undulating with the force of his anger. "You're under arrest. You tried to kill that man, and you threatened that woman."

"But he's a werewolf."

Sullivan blinked, then glanced at me. I shrugged and made the crazy sign by rolling my index finger next to my ear.

"He asked me to find a wolf in the swamp." I looked at Adam, who was letting the blood drip down his arm and into the ground, making no attempt to stanch the flow. "I didn't realize he was nuts and meant werewolf."

"This is the guy you work for?" Sullivan asked.

"Not anymore," Frank muttered.

Sullivan put away his weapon as the clearing filled with cops who began to cuff the minions and collect the evidence.

"Do you know who I am?" Frank asked. "I'll have your job for this."

Sullivan made a motion and two cops carried a struggling, cursing Frank Tallient away.

I hurried across the short space separating me from Adam, tearing a strip off my shirt as I went. He must have been feeling pretty woozy, because he let me bind his arm without arguing.

"Why did you come here?" I asked Sullivan.

"Some guy wanted to know where Charlie died. Since that's an open case, I got suspicious. I came to your place and saw them head into the swamp. That much guns and ammo, couldn't be good. So I called for backup and here we are."

"I appreciate de help." Adam offered his nonbloody hand.

"I've been wanting to talk to you for a while." Sullivan took it and they shook.

"Talk."

"You know anything about the man strangled on your property?"

"No."

"Ever seen any animals behaving oddly? Maybe rabid?"

"No."

Sullivan's gaze slid to mine. "A regular fountain, isn't he?"

"You have no idea."

"The rabies expert has arrived. He was supposed to meet me at the mansion—" Sullivan glanced at his watch. "Damn. Thirty minutes ago. I need to get over there."

He disappeared pretty quickly for such a big guy. Within moments, everyone else had followed, and Adam and I were alone.

"There's something I've been meaning to do," Adam murmured.

"Now?"

His lips quirked before he reached out and yanked the gold chain from around my waist, then tossed it into the weeds.

"Hey!"

He lifted his hand and another spilled out—interlinking silver fleurs-de-lis. "I'd put it on for you, but—" He shrugged, then winced when the movement tugged his wounded bicep.

I took the gift and looped it around my belly, unreasonably touched. I had to admit, silver flattered my skin much better than gold. "Thanks."

"Anytime." Adam shifted his gaze from my stomach to the trail. "Sulllivan's expert will be Henri bait."

"You don't think Henri is long gone?"

Adam snorted. "Even if he left, he'll be back. This place is as much a part of him as his fur."

"I'll have to tell the expert there's no wolf, no rabies. Considering my credentials, maybe he'll believe me and go away."

Adam nodded but continued to stare into the swamp with a frown. I followed his gaze to a nearby cypress tree where a tall, gaunt, ancient man watched us from the shadows.

"Hello," I called. "Are you lost?"

He approached slowly, his gait more measured than pained. Despite the heat, he was dressed in black, which only made him appear more skeletal.

I figured his age at eighty-plus. His hair might once have been blond but had faded to a dusky white. His blue eyes had faded, too, but they still shone with a fervor that made me want to snap a salute.

"Diana Malone?"

The accent was German—less pronounced than if he still lived in the motherland but thick enough to reveal he'd been born there.

"Yes?"

"I am Edward Mandenauer. I was called by Detective Sullivan about a rabies problem." His gaze flicked to Adam. "Would he be you?"

Adam merely shook his head.

"This is Adam Ruelle." I spared Adam a "don't be rude" glare. "He owns this land. Detective Sullivan returned to the mansion to meet you."

"Ah, I must have missed him. His men directed me here." Mandenauer strode to the cage, inspected the lock, the moss, the bars, then lifted a yellowed brow in my direction. "You have caught nothing?"

I met his gaze squarely. "No."

He presented us with his back, then looked into the nearest cypress, where my tree stand remained.

"Hmmm," was all he said—until he turned with a pistol in his hand. "Where are the werewolves?"

39

"Werewolves?" I laughed. "You've been watching too many B movies."

Mandenauer's face didn't change. He didn't find me funny. Imagine that? "You lie to everyone else, but you cannot lie to me. I have hunted these beasts for longer than you have both been alive. Unless . . ."

He considered us. "Unless one or both of you are possessed by the demon werewolf." His gaze lowered to Adam's bloody arm. "I don't suppose you were shot with silver."

"As a matter of fact—" I began, and Adam elbowed me in the ribs. "Hey!"

"Who de hell are you, mister?" Adam demanded.

"I will be happy to tell you as soon as you prove you aren't evil."

"And how are we supposed to do that?" I asked.

"Well, in the good old days, I would just shoot you and see if you exploded. But as everyone has been telling me, that causes too many questions. I hate questions. So I have come up with another way."

He reached into his pocket and pulled out a huge silver crucifix, throwing it at me before I knew what he was up to. I had no choice but to catch the thing or let it hit me in the nose.

"No smoke," Mandenauer said. "You live."

My silver fleur-de-lis chain had disappeared down my shorts. I tugged it free. "I could have shown you this."

"Oh well." He shrugged and glanced at Adam. "Are you wearing one?"

Adam snorted.

The old man lifted a brow in my direction. "If you please?"

"I've already done this test," I said.

"Humor me."

I pressed the cross to Adam's nonbloody bicep, then lifted a brow in Mandenauer's direction. "No smoke, no flame, no explosion. Happy?"

The old man lowered his gun. "Ecstatic. Now where is the beast?"

"What beast?" I asked.

"You have a cage in the swamp. You have been hunting from a tree. You understand about the silver. If I didn't know better, I'd say you were one of mine."

"Your what?"

"*Jäger-Suchers.*"

"My German is a little rusty."

"Hunter-searchers," Adam said.

Mandenauer's gaze narrowed. "You know of us?"

"I know a little German. My guess is you hunt things no one else believes in."

"Ja."

"You'll find nothing here."

"I know better. Even without the physical evidence, the

newspaper reports of disappearances and deaths, the rabies concern, there's what I know about her."

"Me?" I squeaked.

"Diana Malone, obsessed since her husband's untimely death with finding evidence of a paranormal creature and clearing his name. For the past four years you have traversed the globe searching. But at last I think you have found one. My question is, why are you not calling the national media?"

I tightened my lips and kept quiet.

"Could it be because you're in love with the thing?" His gaze turned to Adam. "Lycanthropes are accomplished at the physical. They will do anything, say anything, to keep themselves alive."

"Are you hinting that I've allowed myself to be seduced to the dark side?"

"It has happened before," Mandenauer muttered.

"I just showed you that silver doesn't affect him."

"Perhaps the beast in the swamp is a different kind of beast from the one I am used to. Perhaps whatever hunts beneath the crescent moon in the Crescent City has grown strong enough to survive the usual methods."

He lifted his gun, and I stepped in front of Adam again. "No. I mean, yes. But . . . hell. Adam, I think we should tell him."

"There's nothing to tell."

"I sent a man down here a few weeks ago," Mandenauer continued as if we'd said nothing. "He saw wolves where they did not belong, led by a black wolf with all too human blue eyes. Then my man disappeared. Now I learn he was strangled not far from here. Do you know anything about that?"

I started to sweat—actually I'd been sweating all along, it was *hot,* but the sweat trickling down my back turned cold.

Although Adam hadn't told me so, I was pretty sure he'd been responsible for the strangulation. What would Mandenauer do if he discovered Adam had killed one of his operatives to protect the evil, murdering loup-garou? Edward Mandenauer might appear too old to do much of anything, but in his eyes I recognized a steely resolve, a lack of compassion reminiscent of the beasts he hunted, and that made me nervous. Because even my grandpa could fire a gun. Maybe Adam was right and we should keep quiet.

"I can cure lycanthropy," Mandenauer murmured.

Adam's sharply indrawn breath was drowned out by my blurted, "You can?"

"Not me, but there is someone I would call."

I turned to Adam, hope making me babble. "This could be the break you've been looking for."

"Or a trap." He lowered his voice. "He said he's a hunter. All he knows is how to kill."

True. Why should we trust someone who'd walked out of the swamp? He could be anyone. I stilled. Or anything.

"You were in the army, Ruelle," Mandenauer continued. "Elite Special Forces. A team known as Company Z—last resort. You were assassins."

"How do you know that?" Adam demanded. "No one is supposed to know that."

"I have worked for the government most of my life," Mandenauer said. "Even now, though I am in complete charge of my unit, I receive my funding from them." He pulled a cell phone off his belt and tossed it to Adam. "You must have a contact, a friend, still in the employ of Uncle Sam. Call him."

"If you are who you say you are, no one will tell me anything."

"They will if I say so. Call your friend; have him access my file, then type in *A-I-R-A-M* when asked for security clearance. After he relates the information, you can decide if you want to tell me the truth. But remember, I will either kill or cure whatever I find here. It is your choice which it will be."

Adam's gaze met mine and I shrugged. What could it hurt?

He followed the instructions, then listened as his contact recited the information in Mandenauer's file. Adam disconnected, appearing a little shell-shocked.

"He is who he says he is," Adam confirmed. "He runs some Special Forces monster-hunting unit."

"You mean werewolf-hunting?"

"According to my contact, there are a lot more than werewolves out there."

I caught my breath. "Simon was right all along."

"And often quite helpful to us," Mandenauer murmured. "We monitored his Internet and library usage, his book purchases—"

My eyes narrowed. The Patriot Act could be a real pain in the ass. Although this seemed to be slightly beyond the realm of the rightly paranoid Homeland Security Force. Just what kind of power did Mandenauer wield?

"Your husband was very good at weeding the truth from the lies," he continued. "Often we followed him, and on more than one occasion we eliminated what he found."

"Those times he said he'd discovered something, but when he took me to see it, it wasn't there?"

The times I'd wondered about his sanity.

"We killed the beasts before they killed someone else."

"What about the night he died?"

I'd always wondered what had really happened. Not that it made any difference. Dead was dead.

Or was it?

Simon had died from a fall. His body had been broken, marked, torn. Then, I hadn't thought to check for bite marks. If there'd been one—

I stiffened. The Simon I'd seen at the window of Adam's shack could very well be running around the swamp on four paws. And if Mandenauer actually had a cure—

My heart leaped with hope, even as my gaze went to Adam. What would I do? I loved them both.

I turned to Mandenauer. "Was one of your agents there that night? Did they see what happened to Simon? Is he—?"

"Out there killing people? No. We made certain he would not rise again."

"He was bitten?"

"Yes."

I winced. "But you said you could cure lycanthropy."

"The developments are recent. I am sorry."

"Me, too."

I glanced at Adam. He smiled softly. He understood.

"You couldn't save Simon before he was attacked?" Adam asked. "What kind of army are you?"

"The best that we can be. But sometimes even the best are too late. All the *Jäger-Suchers* can do is continue to fight as we've been fighting since the war."

"War?" I asked.

"World War Two."

Adam and I exchanged glances. The idea that monsters had been multiplying for sixty years was disturbing, to say the least.

"You had better explain what you mean by that," Adam ordered.

The old man collapsed onto the stump where Frank had been. "I was sent to Berlin to find out what Hitler was up to."

"Hitler," Adam muttered.

"I hate that guy," I said.

Mandenauer's lips twitched. He didn't seem like a man who would smile much or laugh ever, but I'd been wrong about the nature of a man before. I took Adam's hand in mine, some of my tension easing when he not only let me, but held on, too.

"The führer ordered Josef Mengele to create a werewolf army."

"Mengele was the one who performed the experiments on the Jews?" I asked.

"And the Gypsies and those lacking in their mental capabilities, and anyone else Hitler did not like."

"Which means he had plenty of test subjects."

"He had no shortage," Mandenauer muttered. "Mengele was given a laboratory in the Black Forest. By the time I discovered this, D-day came and went. Hitler panicked and ordered Mengele to release what he'd created into the world. I was only able to watch as unimaginable atrocities emerged from the trees."

"And the werewolf army?"

"Has been multiplying ever since, as have all the other beasts he created."

"What others?"

Mandenauer didn't answer at first; then he clapped his hands on his knees and rose. "One problem at a time." He fixed Adam with a stare. "I can help you, if you will help me. What is going on in New Orleans that has left so many dead and so many others undead?"

Adam took a deep breath and began to tell Mandenauer the history of his family and the curse. He revealed everything, except that he had a son. The old man listened without interrupting.

Though Edward Mandenauer was spooky, he seemed to know what he was doing, and while his story about the Black Forest was far-fetched, it was also plausible.

I had no problem imagining that Hitler might demand a werewolf army; I found it easy to believe Mengele would concoct monsters. He had, after all, been one of them. And it made perfect sense that those horrors had been released into the world to wreak havoc for the next half-century and beyond.

I'd always known Hitler was far too evil to just die.

"My *grandpère* wasn't made by Mengele," Adam finished. "But by a voodoo queen."

"Not all the monsters came out of the Black Forest," Mandenauer explained. "There are things walking the earth so ancient it is beyond the scope of our minds. Every culture has its myths, legends, and monsters. Each day new beasts are born and others mutate by accident or design." He spread his hands. "Magic, if you will. What worked to kill them once, does not a second time. This is why my *Jäger-Sucher* society is getting larger with each passing year."

"It's a wonder I've never caught wind of you," Adam said.

"We are a secret society."

"Yet you told *me*."

"I am sure you can keep my secret as you have kept your grandfather's for so long. I've sent agents here before. None of them were able to discover anything until this one. And they all disappeared."

"Maybe they got tired of working for you."

The two men held each other's eyes like two alpha wolves over a fresh kill.

"Maybe," the old man conceded.

They both turned away at the same time.

I knew as well as Mandenauer did that Adam had taken out those he'd sent. But the *Jäger-Sucher* didn't seem angry about it. Instead, he appeared intrigued.

"Will you give me a chance to end the curse?" Mandenauer pressed.

Adam rubbed his forehead, his hair swinging forward to cover his face as he considered the request. If the cure didn't work, Mandenauer would most likely kill Henri, then Adam. From the looks of Mandenauer, he'd probably kill Luc and only lose a single night's sleep.

"All right," Adam murmured. "I'll give you one chance at a cure, but I won't let you kill him. I'll kill you first."

"You can try," Mandenauer said, and pulled out his cell phone.

While he gave orders to someone named Elise, Adam beckoned me. "I'm going after Grandpère. I want you to take Luc out of town. In case de miracle cure doesn't work."

"Or in case it's bogus."

He smiled and brushed my hair off my cheek. "Great minds, *cher*."

"All right," I agreed. "But I need to know if the cure is successful; then I can bring Luc home."

Adam lifted his chin in Mandenauer's direction. "He'll know."

"So will you."

"You can't contact me until you're certain de cure has worked, and if it hasn't you need to disappear. If Mandenauer kills Henri, I'll be searching for you, and I won't be me anymore."

I remembered Henri's cold eyes, his vicious words, the blood he'd spilled just for kicks. I didn't want to see Adam like that. I'd do anything to keep his son from seeing it. Still—

"You wouldn't hurt Luc."

Sadness flickered over Adam's face. "Wolves are very good parents, but werewolves could care less about their young. To them a child is just another midnight snack."

I winced.

"Promise me." His voice was urgent; his gaze, intense. "Promise you'll take care of him if I can't."

"Of course."

His eyes gentled. "Thank you."

Mandenauer ended his call. "My assistant is on her way. She has the cure and will meet us at your mansion in—" He glanced at his watch. "Three hours. Is that enough time for you to locate the beast?"

"It'll have to be."

Adam stared into my face. I answered his unspoken question with a faint smile, and he kissed me on the forehead, then disappeared.

Ignoring Mandenauer's curious gaze, I touched the place where Adam's lips had brushed. A good-bye if ever I'd felt one. I guess he wasn't as confident as Herr Mandenauer that the cure would work.

The old man still watched me. "I have to run some errands," I said, and headed for the mansion.

Mandenauer followed. I hoped he didn't plan to stick to me like gum on a shoe until Adam came back. If he did, I'd have to take drastic measures.

My eyes searched the underbrush for a great big branch or maybe a rock.

To distract him, and because I was curious, I kept asking questions. "What is this cure? A serum? A pill?"

"No. Although Elise *has* invented an antidote that can restore the bitten if they are injected before the first change."

"Which would be handy if you were around some when you were attacked."

He shot me a speculative look. "My point exactly. Most people aren't, and they don't realize they've been infected until it's too late."

"Then what do you do?"

"That is where the cure comes in."

"What is it?" Mandenauer didn't answer, and I glanced at him. "A big secret?"

"You shall see," he said cryptically, which only made me more nervous. "Elise has also invented a serum that will fade the bloodlust under the full moon," he continued.

"Did it help with the—" I wasn't sure how to explain the soul-deep evil I'd sensed. "Henri appeared human, but he wasn't. Not really."

Mandenauer nodded. "Lycanthropy is a virus, passed through the saliva when a werewolf bites a human. The virus destroys their humanity, leaving behind pure wickedness. What we call the demon."

I guess I'd been right about possession.

"But Henri wasn't bitten," I said. "Does he have the virus?"

"Did he make others by biting them?"

"Yes."

"Then I assume the curse created the infection. It is impossible to know without testing him."

"If he isn't like the others will the cure work?"

"Also impossible to know."

We reached the mansion. The police had gone. The place was deserted.

"I'll be back as quickly as I can," I lied.

Mandenauer studied me with faded yet sharp blue eyes. "It is good that you leave him. Even if the loup-garou is cured, your lover will never be normal. There are too many memories, too many secrets, too many deaths."

He thought I was hitting the road because I was afraid of what Adam might become, or the problems he might have adjusting to all that he'd done to protect an evil thing.

Fine by me. The old man could believe anything he liked as long as he didn't prevent me from climbing into the car and leaving him behind.

Though I doubted Mandenauer would follow, since he didn't want to miss Henri, I wasn't going to take any chances, so I drove around and around the area before I headed for the mobile home. By the time I got there, noon had come and gone. I knocked on the door, and when no one answered, I tried the knob. Just like the last time, it turned in my hand.

I stepped inside and saw the blood.

40

"Luc!" I shouted, running into the house, skidding across the floor.

I didn't see a body, and I wasn't sure if that was good or bad.

I stopped in the doorway of Luc's room.

Definitely bad.

Henri sat on the bed, holding Luc in his lap, his hand over the child's mouth. From what I could tell, the blood wasn't Luc's, although Henri was a mess.

I guess we were short another babysitter.

Henri smirked. "I figured you'd show up eventually."

My mind grasped for a plan. Would Adam be able to follow his great-grandfather's trail to this place? I had a feeling Henri wasn't that stupid.

"What do you want?" I asked.

He lowered his hand from Luc's mouth but kept his arms locked around the child's body so he couldn't run away. Luc's bright, happy blue eyes were now dull and very sad. What had he seen? How long would it take him to forget?

"This isn't Daddy," Luc whispered.

"I know."

"Who is he?"

For an instant I was surprised Luc didn't know the truth, but Adam *had* said he kept his two lives separate. He must have used a very serious threat in order to keep Henri on a leash, so to speak.

"I'm your grandpa."

I guess the threat was gone or Henri didn't care anymore what Adam did to him. Maybe both.

"My grandpa died."

"I'm a few generations removed, true. But I'm blood of your blood. You'll understand better when you have a child of your own."

Luc's face crinkled in confusion. "Where's Daddy?"

"In de swamp," Henri said. "He has a very bad headache."

My eyes narrowed. "What did you do?"

"Nothing permanent. I need him. But first I'm going to figure out if I need you. Having him around is too goddamn distracting."

"Watch your mouth in front of Luc."

"That's de least of your worries." Henri shoved the child from his lap as if he were a pesky dog. "Go in de bathroom and turn on de shower."

Luc ran to me and I hugged him. Henri had managed to smear blood here and there. Maybe a shower wasn't such a bad idea. At least Luc would be out of harm's way by a few feet.

"He hurt Sadie," Luc whispered. "She cried and cried and I wished she'd stop." He swallowed. "Then she did."

"That's not your fault." I pushed him gently toward the bathroom. "Do what he says, Luc."

"But—" The boy stared at me with worried eyes.

"I'll be fine."

He went, dragging his feet all the way. The door closed and the shower turned on.

"You won't be fine," Henri said.

"I know."

A cunning expression came into his eyes. "I'll let you go if you leave now."

"Me and Luc?"

"No. Either you or de kid dies today."

"Me," I said automatically.

He tilted his head the same way Adam did. The similarity made me nauseous. "Why so hasty? He isn't even yours."

"Doesn't matter."

"I suppose it doesn't, but did you ever wonder why?"

"What?"

I was having a hard time focusing, trying to listen to Luc, to think of a plan, to pray that Adam wasn't dead and was already on the way.

"Ever wonder why you fell so hard and so fast for Adam and his son?"

"Who said I fell? Normal human beings don't sell out others just because they can; they don't sacrifice children to save themselves."

"You're wrong," he said. "Most people aren't exactly human and without exception they pick themselves over strangers, even lovers and children."

"I don't believe you."

"What I can't believe is that you're one of de few to be self-sacrificing. And now I understand why. Ever seen one of these?" He held up a gris-gris.

My hand went to my pocket. Mine were still there. "A few."

"I found this one under de boy's pillow. It's a love charm."

Huh. I had been under a spell, and I no longer cared.

The sound of a match being struck made me jump. Henri held the flame to the bag, and when it went up as if drenched in lighter fluid, he dropped the gris-gris to the floor and stomped on it.

"How you feel now about de boys now?" he asked.

I thought a minute, then couldn't help but smile. "Exactly the same."

Henri frowned. "That's impossible."

"Guess you were wrong about the magic. We got true love."

"Adam doesn't love you," he said. "He's as incapable of it as I am."

He might be right, but I wasn't going to admit that. I shrugged and his face darkened.

"We'll find out soon enough. He'll have to choose, too. You or his son."

A hysterical bubble of laughter spilled from my lips. "You're a moron."

Fury washed over his face. He moved so fast, I didn't even see him coming. His hand at my throat, he slammed me against the wall. I saw stars.

"Watch *your* mouth," he said.

Since I couldn't talk, that wasn't going to be a problem.

"I like to make people choose," he murmured. "I smell their fear, de sweet aroma of despair. I swear it makes me stronger."

He put his nose to my neck, inhaling deeply. "Mmm. Like that."

I toyed with the notion of bringing my knee up, hard, but I had a feeling he wouldn't react like a regular man.

Until Adam, or even Mandenauer, got here, I needed to keep Henri away from Luc.

Henri licked my neck. I fought the gagging reflex. "Tallient, despite his holier-than-thou attitude, chose himself over his family without a quibble."

I frowned. Was that why Frank had become so obsessed? Grief and guilt did funny things to a person's mind. I should know.

"We have time before Adam comes, and I want to discover if screwing a moon goddess will give me any power over de moon."

"We've been over this. I don't have any magic. My name is just a name."

"Then you're dead." He laughed. "But that was my plan anyway. I just want to make sure."

He ground his erection against me; then he yanked off his shirt. He looked so much like Adam, my eyes burned. After this, would I ever be able to be with Adam again without remembering Henri?

I'd be dead soon; the worry was moot. One less thing.

Henri fisted his hand in my shirt and tore it down the middle. His body was so close to mine, he didn't see the fleur-de-lis chain, but he certainly felt it when the silver touched him.

I heard the hiss, smelled flesh burning, even as he howled and spun away.

My gaze lowered to his stomach, where the image of a dozen tiny French crosses had been scalded into his skin. I'd be able to tell them apart after all.

"What de hell?" he shouted. "Where did you get that?"

"Adam."

His eyes narrowed. "Someone will pay." He turned toward the bathroom.

I vaulted after him, grabbed his arm. "No. Come on, let's, uh, do it."

He shook me off as if I weighed no more than a fly, and I stumbled. Before I could regain my balance, he'd opened the bathroom door. A roar of fury made my ears ring.

The bathroom was empty. Luc was gone.

Henri backhanded me. I flew across the room, crumbling in a heap near the bed.

"Where did he go? How did he get out?"

There were no windows in that room. My only thought was a trapdoor somewhere. No wonder the child hadn't fought against going into the bathroom. Clever, clever boy.

I shook my head as Henri advanced, and stopped mid-movement when my ears began to ring again. He'd hit me pretty hard.

He pulled me to my feet by the hair. Damn, that hurt. But not as much as when he wrapped his hands around my throat. I choked, clawed at his fingers, saw black dots. But my life didn't pass before my eyes. Only Adam's face, and then I heard his voice. "Let her go, Grandpère. Now."

The weight on my chest lightened. I could breathe just a little.

"What will you do?" Henri murmured. "I wonder."

I tried to speak, to tell Adam he didn't have to choose, but my voice was gone.

"*He* will do nothing."

Mandenauer's voice. How many people were in this cavalry?

"It would make my day, as they say, to blow you back to hell. Let her go."

I was falling and someone caught me. Before I opened my eyes I knew it was Adam. I recognized the gentleness of his touch, the strength in his arms.

"You OK?"

I nodded, wincing at the pain in my throat. "Luc—"

"He's fine. Used an escape hatch under de sink." Adam shook his head. "Can't trust a beast to follow de rules forever."

He'd always known Henri would come one day.

"Where's Luc?" I asked.

"We ran into him coming up de road." Adam leaned closer and whispered, "He wanted to rescue you with guns blazing, but I convinced him to wait for us next door."

Soothed by the knowledge that Luc was fine, I managed to force back the dizziness. Cassandra waited in the hall with a willowy blonde, who wore hot pink shorts and an electric blue tank top. Talk about bright. I was dizzy again.

Henri sat on the bed, Edward's pistol stuffed in his ear. Why hadn't I thought of that?

"How?" The word dissolved into coughing, so I just pointed at Cassandra.

"I got worried when I didn't hear from you. Came to the mansion just as Adam stumbled in."

"Grandpère was insane with the idea I'd sold him out."

Adam couldn't stop touching me. I sat on the floor, still a little woozy, and he knelt at my side, holding my hand.

"Insaner, you mean?"

"If that's possible. He knocked me out." Adam's mouth tightened. "When I came around, I knew he'd gone after what mattered to me most."

"Luc."

"And you."

I blinked. But now was not the time to examine his sudden change of heart.

"Why is he so obsessed with Diana?" Cassandra asked.

She didn't know about the goddess-of-the-moon part of the curse, so I told her.

"Hmm," she murmured. "That bears looking into."

"I'm not magic," I protested.

Cassandra just shrugged.

"She'll leave," Henri blurted. "They always do. Your wife couldn't take it. The woman had no guts. Or at least she didn't when I was through with her."

I glanced at Adam as shock spread over his face. He hadn't been lying when he'd said she'd left and never come back. He just hadn't known she was dead.

My shirt hung in two pieces, and I tied them together under my breasts, which was the best I could do. With Adam's help, I got to my feet.

"Fix him," I said, voice hoarse.

Henri scowled. "I don't want to be fixed."

"They never do." Mandenauer nodded to the woman.

Henri reared up from the bed, and Adam left me to shove him back down. He hovered over his grandfather nose to nose. The resemblance was downright creepy.

"You like so much de choice, here's yours. Be cured or die."

Henri's top lip curled back. "I choose to die."

He banged his hands against Adam's chest. Adam flew into a nearby wall and slid to the floor. Henri ducked as Edward fired, and the bullet plowed into the bed.

Adam scrambled up, but Henri was already streaking toward the door. The blonde stood in his way. I tensed in expectation of her flying through the air next. Instead, she slammed the palm of one hand against his forehead.

Henri jerked as if in pain. "You're like me."

"Not really," she said, and her eyes closed.

Henri appeared frozen. Adam, Cassandra, and I gathered closer to watch.

"What's she doing?" I asked.

"Magic." Mandenauer didn't appear happy about it.

"Cool," Cassandra said. "What kind?"

"I have no idea. According to a dead old native woman, Elise has been blessed, though I cannot see it."

"She's your werewolf cure?" Adam asked.

"Ja."

"And she's a werewolf."

"Ja."

"But you haven't killed her."

"She is different."

"How?"

"No demon," he said simply.

"That would be handy," Cassandra murmured.

Mandenauer shot her a suspicious glare, but she just smiled.

A thud drew our attention to Henri and Elise. He lay on the floor, twitching. She stared at him, uncertain, one hand fiddling with a tiny white wolf icon she wore around her neck; then slowly she turned up her palm to reveal a tattoo in the shape of a pentagram.

"What's with that?" I asked.

Elise blinked as if she'd forgotten we were there. "I received it in the Land of Souls."

I glanced at Cassandra, who shrugged. "Not a voodoo land."

"Ojibwe," Elise murmured. "Another time, another place, different werewolves."

"I thought a pentagram was protection *against* a werewolf," I said. "Although from what I've heard, it doesn't work."

"According to legend, the points ascendant are benevolent." Elise held up her hand so we could see she was one of the good guys. "Descendant points indicate evil."

She returned her attention to a still-unconscious Henri. "Something's wrong."

"What?" Adam demanded.

"Usually I touch a werewolf and the demon is gone. *Poof,* they're human again."

"Just like that?" I asked.

"Pretty much." She frowned. "I see their soul on the other side of darkness. A faint light that becomes brighter and brighter until it fills my mind and theirs."

"But not this time?"

"I saw his soul, but it wasn't very bright. Kind of hazy and gray."

"He wasn't much of a human to begin with," Adam said. "Getting his soul back isn't going to change that."

"Maybe," Elise said, but she didn't sound convinced.

"Do the cured werewolves remember what they did?" I asked.

"No. The big problem has been trying to explain to them why they've woken up in a different century and enabling them to live in this one."

"That *would* be a problem," I murmured. "What do you do?"

"We have a branch specifically created to deal with those issues," Mandenauer said.

He hadn't really answered my question; however, I didn't care when Henri started to wake up.

His eyes opened. They were different now, no longer evil but haunted.

"Oh, God," he whispered, his voice quavering. "I can hear them screaming."

He slapped his hands over his ears and started to scream himself.

Elise grabbed her medical bag, put on gloves, then used a hypodermic needle on Henri. He went limp again. We stared at the man on the floor. No one spoke for a very long time.

"He has his soul back," Elise murmured.

"How do you know?"

"Only someone with a soul would care about those he's killed. Which is why none of them remember what they've done. I think if they could, they'd go mad." Elise cast a considering glance in my direction as she snapped off the gloves. "Maybe you should touch him."

"Me?" My lip curled.

"This goddess-of-the-moon thing might help."

"I've touched him. Well, he's touched me. Nothing happened except nausea. Names may have power, but I don't."

"His soul is restored. Perhaps your touching him now would be different."

I hesitated, but Adam looked at me with such hope, I sighed. "Fine."

Kneeling, I put my palm against Henri's head as Elise had.

Nothing.

I shut my eyes, opened my mind, got a little creeped out to be so close to him while unable to see, and opened them again.

"Zip," I said.

Elise joined me. "Let's try it together."

She pressed her fingers to Henri's forehead, too. A jolt, like an electric shock, made his body jump. I yanked back, and so did she.

"Hell. I'd forgotten how much that hurts." Elise lifted her gaze to Mandenauer's. "He's still a werewolf."

"How can you know that?" Adam demanded.

"When we touch, skin to skin, we know." She rubbed her brow. "Major ice-cream headache."

Henri appeared unaffected by everything we'd tried. I wondered what she'd doped him with and how long it would last.

Elise dropped her hand. "I don't know what to do. This hasn't happened before."

"You're forgetting Damien," Mandenauer murmured.

"Who de hell is Damien?"

"He was a werewolf," Elise answered, "but he was cursed by an Ozark Mountain magic woman to get his soul back."

"That doesn't sound like a curse to me," I said.

"The lycanthropy stayed. He was cursed to shift, to hunt, to kill, all the while knowing exactly what he was doing but unable to stop."

"OK, I can see where that would suck."

"We need to make a decision," Adam interrupted.

I glanced up and saw what he meant.

The sun was going down.

41

"Stand back." Mandenauer pointed his gun at Henri's head.

"Old man, you try my patience," Elise muttered.

Confusion swept over his face. "What did I do?"

"You can't shoot someone with a soul."

"Since when?"

Her mouth moved as if she was counting to ten. I kind of thought she was. "We've been over this. Put the gun away."

"Never." But he did lower it. "What do you suggest? A mad werewolf, soul or no, is not something I plan to let run free."

"I'm with him," Adam said.

Elise stared at Henri as if he were a brand-new science experiment. "I wish I could cage him until I'm certain what we're up against."

Adam and I exchanged glances.

"I've got a cage," I said.

"I'd forgotten," Mandenauer murmured, and Elise shot him a glare.

"That's not something that should be forgotten."

"I'm ancient." He sniffed. "Sometimes I forget."

"One day you'll forget to shoot the bad guys, and then you'll be dead."

"Perhaps." He didn't appear concerned. "We must hurry and incarcerate Henri before the sun disappears."

A flurry of activity ensued, followed by a frantic trip to the mansion; then we practically dragged Henri through the swamp, and tossed him into the cage.

Not a minute too soon.

I turned the key on the padlock as he came awake with a howl of agony. His body bent; his clothes tore; hair sprouted from every pore. I'd seen him change from wolf to man; now I watched as he went from man to wolf. That had to hurt.

His too human eyes peered at us from behind the bars. When I'd seen them before they'd been full of hate and hunger. Now the hunger was there, but the hate was gone.

He paced back and forth, whining, pawing the ground, then throwing himself against the bars until he bled.

"Give him the serum, Elise," Mandenauer ordered.

She'd already pulled a vial from the pocket of her shorts and snapped gloves onto her hands once more. Another migraine she didn't need.

"What's de matter with him?"

"The hunger is maddening. On the night of the full moon I have to run as wolf. Without this," she held up the vial, "I'd kill. I wouldn't be able to help myself. For him, the same thing must happen under the crescent moon." She shook her head. "One night a month is bad enough."

"Why is he whining?" I resisted the urge to cover my ears, the pathetic noise grating on my nerves like sandpaper.

"Killing sickens him," she whispered, "but he can't resist the desire."

Elise walked to the cage, and Henri slammed against it right in front of her.

"Be careful," I called.

"He can't hurt me. I'm a werewolf already."

In a lightning-fast movement, she reached inside and grabbed Henri's snout. Then she poured the contents of the vial down his throat. When she was through, he actually licked her hand before falling asleep.

"Does Damien still get furry every full moon?" I asked Elise.

"My touch cured him."

"But you can't cure yourself?"

Something flickered in her eyes, and she looked away. "Not yet."

"And Henri? What's his problem?"

"I'm not sure. I'd like to take him back to the lab and figure that out."

"No," Adam said flatly.

"I can fix him," Elise insisted. "I haven't spent much time in the lab since this." She lifted her palm. "Works better than any medicine. But not so long ago, I lived there. I'm sure I can discover what his secret is."

"You can't kill him. If he dies, I'm cursed."

"The curse might be lifted. His soul is restored."

"De only way to know is for him to die. I'm not willing to take that chance."

"He'll be safe with me. You should see the compound we built. Impregnable this time."

"This time?" I asked.

"Last one went boom. But the werewolves survived the blast."

"That really sets my mind at ease," Adam muttered.

Cassandra, who hadn't said a word since we'd gotten

here, moved closer to the cage. "I think I might know why your cure didn't work."

"I'm all ears," Elise said.

"Henri was made a loup-garou through voodoo, not by science or by being bitten." Cassandra stared at each of us in turn. "A voodoo curse can only be removed by voodoo."

My heart kicked against the wall of my chest. "You can fix him? Why didn't you say so?"

"Not me."

"Who?"

"Only the one who placed the curse can take it away."

My shoulders slumped. "She's gotta be long dead."

"Exactly." Cassandra's eyes met mine. "But the dead can rise."

"Zombie."

Elise's eyebrows shot toward her silky blond hair. I was amazed that in her profession she could still be surprised.

"Zombies are dangerous," Mandenauer muttered. "And unpredictable."

"You've seen one?" Cassandra asked.

"Ja."

"You know someone who can raise a zombie?"

"I did." He sniffed.

"That means he killed the guy," Elise said. "Grandfather, sometimes it's better to keep them alive."

"Wait a second." I held up a hand. "He's your grandfather?"

That the head werewolf hunter had a granddaughter who was a werewolf was a little hard to digest.

"Yes," Elise confirmed. "Neither one of us is too happy about it."

I could imagine.

Adam turned to Cassandra. "Tell me about raising de woman who cursed my family. Could you do it?"

"Not me, no. I'd need to find a practitioner powerful enough to perform that kind of magic. I'm not even sure it's possible to raise someone who's been dead that long."

Adam's shoulders slumped. I moved closer and slipped my hand into his.

"Until then, let *me* try," Elise urged.

I understood why Adam didn't want to give anyone power over Henri. In relinquishing his *grandpère,* Adam relinquished control over his own and Luc's destiny. But we'd exhausted our options. Protecting Henri wasn't get- ting us anywhere. We needed the experts' help.

Adam must have thought the same thing, because he squeezed my hand and said, "OK."

The night passed; the sun rose; Henri became a man again. A very crazy man.

Elise was forced to sedate him to get him back to the compound in Montana. She'd been right. The knowledge of all he'd done had sent him over the edge. He did a lot of moaning and muttering. If I hadn't almost been one of his victims, I might have felt sorry for him. As it was, I was glad to see him go.

Cassandra decided to take a trip to Haiti, courtesy of the *Jäger-Sucher* society.

"Mandenauer wants me to discover more about voodoo, zombies, and this goddess-of-the-moon ques- tion. I'm game."

She'd hired a local to run her store and take care of Lazarus when I refused to. Cassandra and I were friends, but I drew the line at snake-sitting.

"I think we've proved I'm not a moon goddess," I said.

"Maybe. Maybe not. It won't hurt to look into things a little more. You want Henri cured, don't you?"

"For all I care, Henri can burn in hell."

"He probably will. But if we can make certain Adam and Luc don't follow him there—"

"I'll do anything," I said.

"That's what I thought. I made a few calls after you traveled to Ife and spoke to Erzulie."

"Do *not* tell me I'm a lost priestess of the voodoo nation. I'm a cryptozoologist from Boston. Period."

Cassandra's shoulders shifted, as if something were crawling down her neck. "I think I sent you to Ife."

"What?"

"I performed the ceremony. The magic came from me." Cassandra appeared sheepish. "I might be more powerful than I thought."

"That's good news, isn't it?"

"Don't tell Mandenauer. He gets weird when people talk about power."

I couldn't imagine why.

"What's next for you?" Cassandra asked.

"I don't know."

She tilted her head. "Love, marriage, mommyhood. I see it in the cards."

"You don't read cards."

She put her hand over mine. "Your future is with them."

"I haven't seen Adam or Luc since Henri went away."

Three days ago. I'd hung around the mansion waiting. Pathetic but true. I'd have to get a job soon, considering Frank hadn't paid me. Since his butt was in jail, courtesy of me, I didn't think he was going to.

Before Mandenauer had left he'd told Detective Sullivan there'd been one rabid wolf in the swamp and he had killed it. Case closed. I had no reason to hang around.

"Adam loves you," Cassandra said.

"I'm not so sure."

"He put his son in your protection. There's no greater love than that."

"Henri found a gris-gris under Luc's pillow."

"Really? I guess that's the love charm you were so worried about." She narrowed her gaze. "You want me to give you one to counteract the magic?"

"He burned it."

She peered into my face. "And you still love them both, don't you?"

"Desperately."

I'd realized sometime over the past few nights I'd slept alone that I'd fallen for Adam before I'd even met Luc. The gris-gris was irrelevant, even if it weren't dust.

"Maybe you need to say good-bye to your first love before you move on to the last one."

At my confused expression, she continued. "Simon. You've never really put him to rest."

"And how do you suggest I do that? Another gris-gris?"

She smiled and squeezed my hand. "Only you can say good-bye to him, Diana."

I wasn't sure how I'd say good-bye to a dead man, but I certainly couldn't do it long-distance.

I packed my things and went to Chicago, where I'd buried Simon four years ago. The place no longer felt like home. I'm not sure it ever had.

The cemetery was peaceful, deserted. No one would see me talking to a headstone.

"You were right, Simon. There's more in this world than anyone could imagine."

I sat on the grave and ran my hand over the grass. "I had to break my vow, and I'm sorry. I couldn't clear your name. I'd only hurt more people. I figured you'd understand."

Absently I pulled out the gris-gris that contained the fire iris petal. A little truth wouldn't be so bad. Where was Simon now? Had he truly come to me in the swamp? Was there any way of getting him back? Did I want to?

When I touched the sack, the tie fell off, and when I peered inside, I discovered the petal had disintegrated into dust. The wind swirled the particles away.

I guess some truths are better left unknown.

"I still miss you," I said. "I probably always will, but I have to say good-bye."

The breeze, warm despite the autumn chill off Lake Michigan, stirred my hair. I wanted to smell Simon's aftershave, hear his voice, feel his love, know that he'd heard me. I closed my eyes and wished for him, but he was as gone as the wind.

When I opened my eyes, Adam was there. Talk about magic.

"You scared me to death, *cher*. I thought you'd left for good."

How had he found me?

"Cassandra," I said as I got to my feet.

He shrugged, then indicated Simon's grave with a tilt of his head. "You were saying good-bye."

"I can't live in the past anymore."

"Me, neither."

Hope lit my heart and probably my face, because he held up his hand. "There's something I have to tell you. Luc and Sadie did a love spell."

"I know."

He started. "You do?"

I nodded.

"I was going to destroy it, but Luc can't find de gris-gris."

"Henri burned it. One of his insane little mind games."

"But . . . I still feel de same way."

"Which is?"

"Crazy mad in love with you."

"Ditto," I said. "And your little boy, too."

Adam gave me a rare smile. "I never thought I'd love anyone but my son."

"I never thought I'd love again."

"I guess we were both wrong." He tugged on my hair. "What you think about fixing up de mansion?"

"I thought you hated the place."

"Kind of grew on me. Lots of good memories there now."

My face heated at some of them.

"I can't promise a certain future."

I lowered my gaze to Simon's headstone. "Who can?"

After several moments of silence, Adam said, "Mandenauer offered us jobs."

"Us?"

He nodded. "We'd be perfect."

"What would we have to do?"

"Same thing we've been doing."

I wiggled my brows. "He's going to pay us for that?"

Adam snorted. "He wants you to chase down rumors of paranormal beasts. He wants me to kill werewolves."

I frowned. "That sounds dangerous."

"I've been doing it for years, *cher*."

"What about Luc? We can't both traipse off, tra-la-la."

His lips curved. "You're thinkin' like a mother already."

I was. When had that happened?

"You sure you want a ready-made family?" he asked.

"I'm sure I want you and Luc."

"There'll be no more children."

"I'll be lucky if I can handle the one we have."

"You'll do fine," he said. "The boy was crazy about you from day one. That's why he did de love spell. Couldn't bear to lose you. I have to say I understand why, but he's still grounded."

I stifled a laugh at the notion of being grounded for performing a voodoo love spell. My life certainly had taken a turn for the strange.

"I figure if we take Mandenauer's offer we can take turns bein' away from home."

"Home," I murmured. "That sounds nice."

Adam reached into his pocket. For an instant I thought he'd brought another belly chain. I still wore the one he'd given me. I planned never to take it off.

"Partners?" he asked, and held out his hand.

In his palm lay a circlet of interlinked silver fleurs-de-lis with a moonstone center. The ring was so beautiful, I ached to put it on. But not yet.

"When you say partners . . . ?"

"I'll understand if you don't want to marry me. Who knows when I might change under de crescent moon?"

"I'd still love you, even then."

He just shook his head.

"The only way I'll do this is if we're married," I insisted. "I adopt Luc. I'll protect him if you can't. Once that's settled, we take the jobs, help save the world. Together, we'll face whatever comes."

He hesitated so long, I feared he'd take back the offer and the ring. At last he slipped the silver circlet onto my finger, sealing the deal without saying a word.

But there was one thing that still bugged me.

"Did you really believe everything that was between us was the result of magic?"

"I still believe that."

My startled gaze flicked to his. "What?"

Reaching out, he touched my cheek. "Don't it feel like magic to you, *cher*?"

I couldn't speak, could only nod, as he took my hand, then led me away from my past and into a bright new future.

Visit **www.panmacmillan.com** to read more about all our books and to buy them. You will also find features, author interviews and news of any author events, and you can sign up for e-newsletters so that you're always first to hear about our new releases.